'My cousin tells[...] a rogue, sir.'

'Your cousin is a wise lady.'

'Are you such a disreputable gentleman?' she asked, looking through her lashes at him.

'Playing the coquette doesn't suit you, Bess,' Harry said abruptly.

'I have no graces as have the ladies from France, you mean?' she retorted.

'You have your own grace, Elizabeth. Simple and innocent, or so I thought last night.'

'You think me just a little country maid.'

'Are you not a maid and also from the country?' he asked gravely. 'All the wine in the cellars at Greenwich will not make you as the other court ladies.'

THE BLACK PEARL

PEARL

Laura Cassidy

*First published in Great Britain 1991
by Mills & Boon Limited*

© Laura Cassidy 1991

*Australian copyright 1991
Philippine copyright 1991
This edition 1991*

ISBN 0 263 77256 X

*Masquerade is a trademark published by
Mills & Boon Limited, Eton House,
18–24 Paradise Road, Richmond, Surrey, TW9 1SR.*

*Set in Times Roman 10 on 10½ pt.
04-9105-82697 C*

Made and printed in Great Britain

CHAPTER ONE

THE bleak January weather of 1536 had worsened during the long journey. Elizabeth de Cheyne clutched her shabby woollen cloak closer around her body and tucked tendrils of wet hair back beneath her rain-soaked hood. She thought with longing of her home far away in the west. The gentle Devon hills, which would now be softly blurred in the falling rain, seemed to call to her as she bumped along in the wooden cart behind the resentful near-toothless old horse. She looked sideways at the sullen old man who was driving her to a place she did not want to go to, to live with people she did not know.

'Is...is it very far now, sir?' she asked him timidly.

'Eh?' The old man hunched his shoulders and flicked the whip over the plodding horse. Throughout the dreary miles he had pretended not to understand her soft voice, which held only a trace of Devonshire, and this had added considerably to her misery. At the numerous inns they had stayed in he had left her almost entirely to fend for herself when, knowing many of the places well, he could have eased her path. All his days he had been a pedlar and had travelled the way to London many times. It was for this reason that Elizabeth's father had engaged him to take his daughter on this her first trip from home.

At the thought of her father Elizabeth's eyes filled with tears again. She dashed them away and as the wind sharpened and chilled her to the bone she said angrily, 'Answer me, sir. I asked you how much further we travel this day.'

The old man paused in his tormenting of the horse and looked at her in astonishment. It was the first time the little country mouse had shown any temper. Under-

neath his surly manner he had developed a grudging admiration for her. She had borne all the discomforts of
a long journey at the worst possible time of year without
complaint. Although he had chosen to ignore her tentative attempts at conversation he had marked the good
nature with which she greeted each new mishap, and his
failure to secure for his young charge a hot meal or a
clean bed after a hard and miserable day's travelling had
invariably been met with a sweet smile and a soft word.
Now she was all of a sudden bright with anger. Well,
after all, she was the daughter of a knight. A poor
raggedy knight to be sure, crippled early in his career
by an unlucky fall in a tournament, but a gentleman for
all that. Well-connected, too. He had married beneath
him, of course: a neighbouring farmer's daughter, a
plump pretty girl with a reputation for sturdy good sense.
They had produced only Elizabeth, always called Bess,
who obviously took after her father's family with her
delicate bones, silver-gilt hair and eyes the colour of blue
skies. She had pretty manners too, despite her humble
home; her father had seen to that. At this moment those
blue eyes sparkled like iced water and he said placatingly, 'We'll see Greenwich before dark, mistress.'

'Oh.'

If possible Bess's spirits sank lower. Despite the miserable days behind them it seemed almost preferable to
go on jolting along the muddy rutted roads than to face
what lay ahead. She thought with resentment of the
casual whim which had been visited on her father's sister
who, suddenly thinking one day of her younger brother,
had resolved to bring her niece to the attention of her
daughter, a lady of the Tudor court.

Since Robert de Cheyne's accident there had been no
contact between him and his older sister Isobel, save his
stiff communication seventeen years ago advising her of
Elizabeth's birth. A handsome silver christening cup
stood in the parlour to mark Isobel's acknowledgement
of this event. Their parents were long dead and Isobel,

after her offers of help at the time of the tragedy had been uncompromisingly rejected, had abandoned him to 'sulk away in the depths of rural Devon', as she had put it to her friends. The truth was that Robert de Cheyne had been an intensely athletic young man, a fine sportsman and a great favourite of the young King Harry. Suddenly bedridden in agony and facing a long convalescence before he could even hope to walk again, his one thought had been to crawl away and hide his shame. Henry and his friends, who were all in the same mould— handsome, daring and somewhat scathing of the less able—had seemed to forget him overnight. Robert de Cheyne rarely spoke of his days at court and as his body gradually healed he had tried to find consolation in settling on a small farm, marrying a young wife and putting as many miles between himself and his humiliation as possible.

Bess was aware of very little of this; she knew her father only as a gentle, kindly man, sometimes withdrawn but usually patient and good-humoured. But she knew of his proud birth and thought that this was what set him apart from the other men she knew—her uncles and the local farmers—and unconsciously she had modelled her speech and behaviour on his. She shared his sense of humour too, rather dry and ironic, as well as his handsome good looks, and she was the light for him in the hard and often tedious life on the farm. She had been very happy for all of her seventeen years. Hard work and long hours were all she had ever known but her mother made sure that her one little chick had the best of the farm produce to eat and Bess had grown up healthy and beautiful.

She thought back now to the events that had brought her on this uncomfortable journey. Eventually even in the sleepy Devon village had come the news that Catherine, the royal and pious wife of their King, had been unceremoniously cast aside for a commoner and, some whispered, a black witch. Bess bit her lip; she knew

nothing of the ways of royalty but she remembered her
father frowning and saying in a stern voice that to so
treat a great and kind lady and a princess in her own
right brought shame to an English gentleman. Her
mother had taken a different view. A man needs sons,
Robert, she had told him briskly, and a king needs an
heir more than most. And Queen Catherine, however
royal, was the mother of only a princess and fast approaching an age when she must be barren. Of course
Joan de Cheyne came from stout farming stock where
a farmer without sons to work his land was in a poor
state. Without the help of her numerous strong nephews
the de Cheynes would not have made a living at all.

Robert de Cheyne's disappointment in not having a
son had been almost forgotten over the years in his delight in his pretty daughter. For Bess was docile and
sweet-natured; practical enough to please her capable
mother but with a good, intelligent mind which reached
out beyond the everyday life of the farm—a quality
which Robert had encouraged, while never being able to
see much future for it. But he had sometimes reflected
that at least a pretty girl could marry well and be raised
to her husband's station in life; a boy had no such
option. And he knew that it would have hurt something
half buried inside him to see a son of his struggling to
wrest a living out of the soil. So when the gracious request for Bess to join her cousin Margaret at court had
come it had pleased both parents, her mother because
the advancement of her daughter was close to her heart,
and her father because he wanted her to learn a little of
the world he had once been part of. She should have her
chance. Isobel's husband John was an intimate friend
of Thomas Boleyn, the Queen's father, and therefore his
family would necessarily receive preference in his
daughter's court. Preparations had begun immediately
to dispatch Bess into the turmoil of Anne Boleyn's enchanted circle. The winters of that time usually made
travel overland impossible, but a mild Christmas and a

fair start to the year had enabled the arrangements to be made all too soon for Bess.

By chance Will Soames the pedlar had been wintering in the west before returning to London with his wagon of tinware and dress materials and sundry items to tempt the farmers' wives in the isolated smallholdings, and Robert had asked him to take Bess with him. Bess did not much like the old man and he was obviously reluctant to take charge of her, but Robert was a good judge of character. The old man was dirty and taciturn, but under his disreputable air he was honest enough and, paid a small sum, would carry out his obligation.

'Mistress.'

Bess was startled out of her bleak reverie by Will's touching her arm. He pointed with the whip. 'Yonder lies Greenwich.'

She peered through the drizzle at the imposing T-shaped stone mass rising out of grey mist. A sense of foreboding allied with a thrill of excitement gripped her as she gazed at the sprawling palace and saw the dark spire of the church within its confines pointing accusingly at the dull sky. The horse, old Grey, sensing that warmth and food were near, forced his old bones to a faster pace and they soon crossed the flooded lawns and clattered into one of the cobbled courtyards which divided the palace apartments.

Bess sat bolt upright, dazed by the noise of what seemed to be hundreds of voices all clamouring at once and by the unfamiliar sights which widened her eyes. Surely all London was here in this place, talking, laughing, on horseback or wagon? She threw back her hood and attempted to tidy her mass of curling hair with trembling hands. Will Soames surveyed the scene without concern. He looked around consideringly until he found a liveried official then reached into his jerkin, withdrew a parchment, and got out of the cart. Shouldering his way through the crowd, he planted himself before the uninterested man and thrust the document under his long nose. It was Isobel's letter inviting her niece to court, and the man perused it slowly.

Bess watched stunned until the horse, made nervous by the crowd, took a few paces forward, rolling his eyes in fright. The half-rotten wooden brake slipped and Bess gripped the plank seat frantically to keep her balance. The rows of tin kettles hanging from the back of the cart set up a clatter, disturbing the animal still more.

'Look to your horse, mistress!' a rough-looking man shouted angrily as he was jostled by the terrified Grey.

Another man, who had been standing near and now observed her distress, leapt gracefully into the cart and, picking up the reins, made soothing noises to the horse as he adjusted the brake. He turned to Bess. 'All's well, mistress.'

She stared at him, her blue eyes large as she noted his dazzling silver-grey costume and bejewelled white hands. He bore her scrutiny with arrogant ease as his black eyes roved over her rain-soaked hair and shabby clothes.

'I thank you, sir,' she murmured.

'There was no danger,' he said lightly. 'This poor beast has no strength left in him to create much damage.'

Bess flushed, feeling sure he scorned her as much as he did poor Grey.

'Harry! Come, leave your serving wench,' shouted one of a group of gallants lounging in the palace doorway. 'Would you keep the Queen waiting?'

Bess drew a quick breath. 'Sir, I am no serving wench. I am the daughter of a knight——'

The man in silver paused in his elegant descent from the cart. 'Indeed?'

'I am Lady Elizabeth de Cheyne of Devon,' she said quietly.

'My compliments, lady.' He swept off his hat and stood bareheaded in the falling rain. 'Sir Henry Latimar at your service.' He took one of her cold hands and raised it to his lips.

At his touch something within her stirred and came to life. 'I am honoured to meet you,' she said with dignity, withdrawing her hand and tucking it back beneath her cloak.

For a moment Harry Latimar studied her intently, then he replaced his gay feathered cap, made a slight bow and disappeared into the throng to join his friends.

Will came back grumbling. 'No one has no knowledge of your coming, mistress. They have sent to the Lady Margaret about you. We must wait.'

Bess drew on her hood once more. The rain splashed spitefully down, large drops bouncing off the shining cobblestones. Grey stood patiently now that the crowd was fast dispersing to escape the downpour. Will slumped beside her, muttering to himself.

After what seemed an age a small boy in a blue and purple tunic came splashing through the puddles. 'You are Lady Elizabeth de Cheyne? Then please come with me. The Lady Margaret awaits you.'

He helped her out of the cart and held her as she slipped on the wet stones, her legs numbed from the long damp drive.

'My man?' she asked, indicating Will.

'He is to stable the animal and go to the servants' quarters for food. Come, lady, before we both drown.'

She followed him after raising her hand in farewell to Will. Her last link with home hunched his shoulders and flicked the reins without glancing at her. She trailed after the page into a side-door and up winding stone stairs. They hurried through a maze of passages until at last he threw open a heavy oak door, drew aside the velvet curtain hanging just within and announced breathlessly, 'The Lady Elizabeth de Cheyne.'

She heard the door thud behind her as she moved slowly forward into the candlelit room. It was a square low-ceilinged chamber with windows ranged along one side fitted with seats, furnished with richly covered chairs and couches and warmed by a vast fire burning in a stone hearth at one end. To the left of the fire through an open arch she could see another chamber containing a massive four-poster bed covered in snowy linen. The cold stone floor beneath her muddy boots was laid with silky patterned rugs in brilliant colours. Bess thought it the most beautiful room she had ever seen.

A woman rose from one of the window-seats and came towards her.

'Elizabeth? Cousin, I welcome you.'

Bess was enveloped in a sweet-smelling embrace. The woman who kissed her so warmly was small and rounded. She shimmered in cream silk and her smooth butter-coloured hair was confined beneath a little three-cornered cap studded with brilliants. She was not beautiful, but her plain face was made so by a wide sweet smile. Involuntarily Bess smiled too.

'How pretty you are,' Margaret exclaimed. 'You have all the de Cheyne beauty, whereas I...' She made a rueful gesture with her soft hands. 'My brothers inherited all the handsome looks, the young popinjays.'

Bess said quietly, 'You are most...elegant, cousin.'

Margaret laughed and drew her guest to the blazing fire, its leaping flames turning the carved stone roses above rose-red.

'And of course elegance is all where beauty is not,' she returned gaily.

She quickly removed Bess's sodden cloak and tutted over her wet dress.

'Off with this little brown hen costume, coz; I have the very gown for you.'

She rummaged in a deep chest and drew out a cloud of lilac silk. 'The very colour for you with all that beautiful hair,' she announced.

Chattering and exclaiming, she encouraged Bess out of her damp clothes and into the fine new ones. Then, seizing a silver-backed brush, she set to work on her cousin's tangled hair, curling it around her fingers and drawing it back into a heavy knot at the back of her head.

'There...' She stood back and admired her work.

Leading Bess to a long mirror mounted in gilded wood, she smiled at the reflection of Bess's amazed face. The lovely gown and skilled hairdressing had performed a miracle on the bedraggled little country girl. Now the glass pictured a fragile creature with a halo of silvery hair framing a pale oval face. The lilac silk deepened her eyes to sapphire and the candlelight played gently over high cheekbones and a delicately moulded chin and neck.

'I am quite——'

'Beautiful? Yes, you are,' Margaret said delightedly. She hugged the girl again. 'We will have the greatest fun together, coz. I have been lonely here. The other ladies are, well...most gracious, of course. But so many have been long in France and have French ways. And I am not in their confidence.'

Meg's pleasure in her cousin was quite sincere. In truth she had not been sure what to expect when her mother had written to say she had commanded her niece to court. Had Bess been a large uncouth farm girl Meg would have welcomed her equally warmly—it was her nature to be kind—but like many plain people she was irresistibly drawn to beauty and she immediately thought how much more...convenient it was to have charge of a girl whose breeding was similar to that of the rest of the court ladies. True, there was that slight West Country burr in the soft voice, but that would fade in time and was not in any case unattractive. Indeed, it added to the unusual quality the girl possessed. She told Bess, 'We will share this chamber. The Duchess of Berkshire, who occupied it previously, is elderly and has now retired to her country estates, and so I requested it for myself. Naturally I enjoyed the company of the other ladies in the main apartments, but 'tis difficult to gain a moment's privacy...'

She broke off and Bess saw her brown eyes alight thoughtfully upon a little prie-dieu holding an open prayer book in a little alcove. She is religious, guessed Bess, envying her her comfort of strong faith.

'What will be my duties, cousin?' she asked.

'Duties? Oh, to be my companion, my friend. I care for the Queen's wardrobe,' she ended on a note of pride.

'The Queen? Queen Anne?'

'Of course. Who else?'

Sensing some restraint in the other girl's manner, Margaret drew her to the window-seat. 'Elizabeth, do they call you Bess? Good, then so shall I... Bess, I know many people regret Queen Catherine's passing and I loved her too, but a wise subject does not question the King's choice. Many say also that the Boleyn star is already falling, but wise men don't speak of that either. At this moment madam is carrying another child. Perhaps this time a boy...'

Meg's voice was no more than a whisper above the crackling of the fire.

'What is she like?' Bess whispered too.

Margaret turned her face to the window, through which Bess could glimpse the dark river winding black as a coil of woman's hair past the palace.

'There are those who say she is hard and ambitious,' Meg said slowly. 'That she schemed and lied and used... evil means to entrap the King. But to me she is like no other woman I have ever known. When she enters a room the candle flames leap higher, and when she has passed by the air is charged as if before a summer thunderstorm. She is like a bright sword that catches the light and draws the eye. You know it is sharp and dangerous, but you long to handle it——' She stopped abruptly and turned again to Bess. 'I am chattering too much, and I know you must be faint from hunger.'

She went quickly to the fireplace and jerked a thick plaited cord impatiently. A page appeared almost at once and she gave the order for food and mulled wine, sternly telling the boy that it 'must be hot for my lady cousin'.

Bess stared out of the window at the descending night. The rain had ceased, and the clouds had rolled away to reveal a full moon bright as a coin hanging over the quiet river. She sensed that Margaret regretted her words about Anne Boleyn, but they had endeared her to Bess. She liked people who saw behind the arrangement of skin and bones of a person's face and were curious enough to try to identify the personality beneath. Yesterday she would perhaps have been puzzled by Margaret's description of the Queen. But today she understood it. Today she had met Harry Latimar and knew that some men and women lit up the world just by being in it. Her heart beat faster, as she remembered his brilliant glance on her face, the touch of his lips on her fingers. She thought, If he could see me in this dress... Impulsively, she said, 'Margaret, do you know a gentleman named Harry—Henry Latimar?'

Margaret's sweet mouth became pinched. 'I do. But I shall not live to regret it as some ladies do. But cousin— surely you cannot know Lord Harry?'

'We met upon my arrival,' Bess murmured. 'He helped me when my horse became unruly. I thought him most... courteous.'

Margaret sat beside her again. 'As he undoubtedly is,' she said, noting her cousin's flushed face. 'Discourtesy is not one of Harry Latimar's many faults.'

'What are these faults?' Bess raised her eyes to her cousin's face.

'Harry Latimar is a rake and a spendthrift, a gambler and a rogue,' Margaret said firmly. 'There is not a lady at court who has not fallen under his spell and been as swiftly disillusioned by him. His gambling is legendary for its recklessness—he has won and lost fortunes on the fall of a card—and——' she sniffed '—his tailor's bill is as long as my arm and never paid.'

'He seems to have little to recommend him,' said Bess gravely.

Margaret laughed. 'Of course he is handsome and amusing and brave and the best dancer at court—but, dear coz, he is not someone a little girl like you should think of. He is of the Queen's intimate circle, her brother George's dearest friend.'

She broke off as the door was flung open with a crash and a woman entered.

'Meg! I can find no one who cares if my head splits with pain,' she announced dramatically in a charming husky voice.

Margaret jumped to her feet and as quickly sank in a low curtsy. Bess, after a startled moment, did the same. 'Dear madam,' Margaret said, rising and going forward. 'How may I help you?'

'Oh, I don't know.' Anne Boleyn looked vaguely around the room. 'I cannot rest with the pain of my head. And my back aches unbearably...'

Margaret gestured towards a low couch. 'Please, madam, lie down. I will rub your temples with warm oil, then Bess shall brush your hair. 'Tis soothing,' she added.

She pulled Bess forward into the light. 'My cousin the Lady Elizabeth de Cheyne, come this day from the west, Your Majesty.'

Anne acknowledged the girl's second curtsy with a wave of her hand. 'Elizabeth—it is a name I am fond of,' she said distractedly, going to the couch and sinking down upon it.

Margaret began preparing the oil, warming it in a little basin over a candle flame, while Anne lay back and looked blankly at the ceiling. Bess considered her silently. The Queen was tall and slender, with narrow hands and feet. Even lying at ease there was a sinuous grace in every line of her body. She wore an exotic nightgown of black satin edged in silky black fur with long pointed sleeves and a plaited gold cord loosely about her waist. There was little evidence of the child growing within her; indeed she looked over-thin to Bess. She had a pale, perfectly oval face in which black eyes were hauntingly large and around her long white neck lay a wide green velvet band from which hung a single tear-drop pearl. Bess thought of what Margaret had said. It was true—in her village at home there were more conventionally pretty girls, but she had never in her life seen a more striking woman. Even pale and listless as she was now, Anne Boleyn sparkled like the handful of stars glittering above the Greenwich church spire.

Margaret bustled back across the room and soon her plump capable hands were smoothing the warm oil gently over the Queen's forehead. After a while Anne opened her eyes and smiled, showing small white teeth. Her charm touched Bess and the room seemed warmer, brighter.

'Would your little cousin brush my hair now?'

Margaret said delightedly, 'She would be honoured, madam.' She arranged the cushions behind the Queen's back and handed Bess the silver brush with an encouraging smile.

Bess stood awkwardly behind the couch and gently lifted the cape of black hair. She drew the brush slowly through the shining mass.

'You have a gentle touch, lady.' Anne yawned, her marked French accent added somehow to her glamour.

Gaining confidence, Bess brushed slowly, rhythmically for a few minutes. She lifted the hair from the white neck and—there was the terrifying . . . thing again. The room became misty and, as though looking into a bright circle of light, she saw in harsh relief the black-hooded man, the flashing blade—— She stood stricken, the hair lying like a length of fine material over her arm.

'Please continue,' Anne murmured. She turned her head and looked up. 'Why, what is amiss? Are you faint?'

Bess laid down the brush with a trembling hand. Margaret came quickly to her side. 'Forgive her, madam. A long journey, many days on the road—and we now await supper for her——'

'There is no need for forgiveness,' Anne said in quick sympathy. 'I am much restored and shall return to my apartments to smack the heads of my lazy women who are no doubt gossiping in some corner...'

As she rose her black eyes met Bess's wavering gaze. She paused uncertainly, struck by the expression in the girl's blue eyes. For a moment they stared at each other in the flickering light, then the Queen shrugged and as Margaret hurried to open the door she swept gracefully from the room.

Margaret turned back to Bess. 'Are you faint, cousin?'

Bess pressed the tips of her fingers to her eyes in an attempt to blot out the horror. 'I am more tired than I supposed... Please forgive me, Margaret. To make such a scene—and before the Queen——'

'Bless you, child. The Queen is but a woman like you and me. But with more cares than we shall ever know, I hope. Now, you lazy boy, how dare you keep us waiting so long? The lady, my cousin, is half starved!' This last as a page stumbled in laden with a tray of food.

Bess sank into a chair by the fire, and ate roast capon and sweet white bread. Margaret thrust a glowing poker from the fire into the cup of wine, grumbling that it was not hot enough, and as Bess drank the steaming liquid she comforted herself. A waking nightmare, that is all it was, she told herself, brought on by fatigue. For how could a madman with a sword come near enough to the Queen's grace to harm her? I was wrong this time. But, said a small voice in her head, you have never been wrong before... I have never been from home before, seen so many strange sights, been so tired. On this thought she set down the tray and with Margaret's help undressed, buttoned herself into the soft lawn nightdress Margaret brought her and got thankfully into the enormous bed

in the adjoining chamber. With a kiss and a promise
that tomorrow she would be strong again Margaret left
her cousin to the darkness. Bess lay listening to the unfamiliar sounds of the palace, the calling of the river
birds outside her window. Now that she was feeling warm
and comforted, her last thought before sleeping was not
of the Queen but of a pair of dark eyes set in a pale
handsome face.

The next day, having enjoyed a hearty breakfast, Bess
felt ready for whatever the day might bring. Margaret,
after a swift survey of the few poor clothes her cousin
had brought with her, produced another of her many
dresses with the tactful explanation that the Queen liked
her ladies to be fashionable and naturally the country
was a little different from London in matters of dress.
So Bess found it easy to accept the loan of a soft amber
velvet gown with a tightly fitted bodice and a skirt which
divided to show an underskirt of paler yellow silk. After
some alterations performed by Margaret's nimble fingers
it moulded her lovely figure perfectly and, although her
mother would have blushed to see the amount of white
breast exposed by her daughter, Bess was content that
this was the expected attire. More rummaging in her
jewellery box and Meg extracted a pair of amber earbobs
and a matching string of beads.

Bess thanked her cousin warmly and Meg said, 'You
must allow me the pleasure of making you a small
present. We have clever needlewomen here at Greenwich
and one of them shall sew for you a new gown—cream
silk, I believe, and,' she narrowed her eyes, 'that lovely
embossed white brocade that is so fashionable just now.
'Tis the Queen's favourite colour after green.'

She hushed Bess's protests. ''Twill be a great pleasure
for me,' she insisted. 'And you will need a fine gown
for the many entertainments—our court is very gay,
especially when madam is entertaining the King.'

Playing with the smooth light beads, feeling them warm to the touch of her fingers, Bess stood by the window and watched a weak January sun gild the dark river. She had been awake since before dawn. The habit of early rising would be hard to break. Meg had woken, yawning, hours later and there had been no sound in the passages outside until a short while before the two cousins had descended to the great banqueting hall for the first meal of the day. Bess had drawn many curious glances from the company as they ate but as the Queen had not attended it had been a short affair and she and Margaret had returned to their chamber without delay. A swift glance around the hall had disappointed Bess, for Harry Latimar was not there. She had never before felt anything but a vague interest in any man save her father, and wondered why she had scanned the faces for him.

'Now to work,' said Margaret, taking her hand and leading her through the passages to the Queen's apartments. 'Each day we examine Her Majesty's clothes, commission necessary repairs and the removal of any stains and suchlike, and order the washing and ironing of her linen. Madam may change her costume half a dozen times a day and she is unusually fastidious in the matter of her personal linen. The fine lace I deal with myself.'

She evidently took her duties seriously.

The royal apartments were stale and heavy from lack of fresh air. The Queen was absent now in the chapel but two of her ladies reclined in the antechamber, languidly trying to decide what costumes they would wear for the masked ball that evening. Anne loved such play-acting, and every lady and gentleman of the court must do their part to add to the entertainment. Meg presented Bess to the two women, who raised their plucked eyebrows and studied her curiously from beneath lazy eyelids. One had a tiny floppy-eared dog on her silken lap and was popping sweetmeats into its mouth. Margaret

introduced them as Kate Mortimer and Madge Fitzroy
and they were to Bess almost frighteningly elegant.

'Meg, where have you been hiding this beauty?' Madge
asked. 'She resembles you not at all,' she added
spitefully.

'She has been brought up in the west,' Margaret replied, ignoring the thrust.

'There is a great likeness to your handsome brothers,
however. I declare I am quite distraught now that they
are from court,' Kate said.

Both ladies looked slyly at each other, their manner
suggesting that they knew these gentlemen very well.

Meg didn't answer but led Bess through the door into
the adjoining chamber.

'It must be very pleasant to have brothers,' said Bess
wistfully.

She had not been lonely as a child—her mother's
brothers had all produced large families and her cousins
had been always in the farmhouse to play with—but she
had always longed for a brother or sister of her own.

'Indeed,' sighed Meg, 'but my brothers are both a sore
trial to my father.' She lowered her voice. 'It was to
remove my older brother, William, from the presence of
the Lady Kate that they have been sent from court to
my mother's estates in the north. However...'

She went to one of the immense oak clothes-coffers
and raised the carved lid to show Bess the sumptuous
clothes within. She examined them with the greatest interest and saw that Anne favoured a few colours above
others; tawny, white, carnation, silver and gold and of
course all shades of green from eau-de-Nil to darkest
emerald. The rich materials took her breath away as she
fingered the taffeta, Genoa damask edged with fur and
lined with silk, the fine lace and rippling satin. Meg drew
out an elaborate silver-tissue gown, embroidered thickly
with gold.

'This madam will wear for the masque tonight,' she
said, 'with the French pearl coronet and silver slippers.'

She turned the dress this way and that and, frowning, discovered a tiny grease spot on one sleeve. She set to work to remove it, directing Bess to gently brush the soles of the satin and kid slippers.

'Shall we attend the ball?' asked Bess.

'Of course,' Meg replied, her head bent over the glistening material. 'The Queen will represent gold and silver—the most precious of all metals—and each lady and gentleman will attempt to wear colours of the jewel of their choice. It is to be on the theme of precious jewels of the world.'

'I have no suitable gown—and no jewels at all save this turquoise ring my father gave me as a keepsake.'

Bess turned the little ring which she always wore on her forefinger tied on with cotton to keep it safe.

'Bless you, cousin, I have the very gown for you. I had in mind that you would look very well representing amethyst. A pretty, modest jewel, I have always thought. And perfect with your lovely fair colouring.'

Bess looked affectionately across at her cousin. Really she was the most generous of women, with both her praise and her possessions. She set to work brushing the tiny shoes, anxious to repay her cousin with her best efforts. As she worked her mind wandered back to the day her father had given her the turquoise.

He had sold his own jewellery to raise money to stock the farm but had saved the little blue ring for sentimental reasons because it had belonged to his mother. Her other more valuable jewels had been inherited by Robert's sister-in-law, but the little blue ring had come into his possession and he had given it to Bess on her twelfth birthday.

'You are like my mother, Bess,' he had said.

They had been walking together along the uneven cliff path a short way from the farmhouse, she suiting her eager steps to his limping gait. It was high summer and beneath her bare feet the headland grass was dry and prickly. Her shoes had swung from one hand and she could remember now how happy she had been to be in his company under a blazing August sky.

'But I don't look like her?' She had seen the little painted miniature of her paternal grandmother.

'Oh, no. She was raven-haired with eyes like green agates. She had come out of Ireland—that wild country—and my father fell under her spell the first time they met.'

'Then how am I like her?'

'In your ways. She was very dainty and sweet but even though I was a child I could feel she was strong—a complete person. She knew exactly who she was and what she wanted from life, if you can understand me, Bess.'

'I think I do... Do you miss her, Father?'

He had stopped and looked out over the sea. On the horizon a ship made tiny by distance moved across the dazzling skyline.

'I was sent from home at eight years old to be a page in my uncle's household. I was miserable and homesick and badly wanted my mother then, but that is the way of things for a boy of good family. It makes them independent, and strong enough to take their place in the world. I knew that later. My mother was strong enough to let me go.'

Bess had been silent, thinking it most unnatural to take a little boy from his mother. She had looked up at the man beside her. He had been still staring out to sea.

'She came to me just before she died. It was most unusual... I was a squire by then, aiming to be knighted soon, and she came riding on a barely tamed horse into the stable yard where I was about my duties. It was a wild stormy day and her hair was wet and curling about her shoulders—— How strange I should remember that... She had come to see if I was well and happy, she said. We talked awhile then she bent from the saddle to kiss me and rode away. Within a month I heard she had suffered a riding accident and was dead. It was

almost as if she knew her fate and had come to bid me
farewell. But that is fanciful nonsense, is it not?'

He had turned his clear blue eyes on Bess. 'For one
cannot see the future, can one, Bess?'

'No, Father.' She had sighed.

'Well,' he had said after a moment, 'that is enough
of such talk for a fine day. Put on your shoes and let
us go home, sweetheart. No doubt it was the little ring
that set me to remembering long-ago things.'

With a start she returned to the present to find that
Meg was at last satisfied that the Queen's apparel for
the coming evening would bring no shame to her
wardrobe mistress and was suggesting they walk in the
gardens awhile. Wearing warm woollen cloaks lined with
fur, the two girls walked sedately arm in arm in the
watery sunshine.

'Walking is a somewhat despised pastime among the
court ladies,' Margaret said wryly. 'They prefer to sit
gossiping and preening and painting their faces. They
have little to do other than discuss their clothes, their
lovers and the private affairs of others.'

Bess tipped back her hood and raised her lovely eyes
to the sky. The formal gardens were unpleasing to her,
used as she was to the rolling green country around her
home, and the sluggish odorous river Thames a poor
substitute for the wild crashing waves on the seashore a
mile from the farmhouse. They came now to the water's
edge, the steps of the landing jetty rimmed with refuse.
A flurry of activity behind them made them step aside
hastily as what looked to be a reception committee
hurried down towards the pier from the palace.

'The King is expected, I believe,' said Margaret,
shading her eyes and looking up-river. Bess looked ex-
citedly and soon saw the royal barge making steady
progress around the bend. Within minutes the King
himself could be seen standing astride in the bows, a
glittering figure surrounded by richly dressed courtiers.
She watched him leave the barge, her eyes round with

excitement. He is truly magnificent, she thought, a head taller than the other men, his clothes gleaming in the sunshine, each hand weighed down with heavy flashing rings. But I don't believe he is kind, she mused, noting the small pouched eyes, the mean mouth.

'And how does the Lady Elizabeth de Cheyne find the King? Is she impressed?'

She turned and looked up into Harry Latimar's smiling face.

'Good day, sir,' she said faintly above a thickening heartbeat.

He was dressed again in silver-grey, a dull metallic colour. His thick hair was simply arranged and he wore no jewels today save a large black pearl in the lobe of one ear. She saw that his eyes were not black as she had thought in the poor light of the previous evening but were of so dark a blue as to appear so. The sun discovered dark red lights in his brown hair and he possessed the pale skin associated with this colour, but not the unfortunate freckles or light eyelashes. His lashes and eyebrows were silky black and would have been womanish in anything other than such a masculine face.

'Are you recovered from your journey?' he enquired, running bold eyes over her.

'Thank you, yes, I——' She stopped as he laid a hand on her arm and gestured behind her.

The King was advancing on them, a jovial smile lighting his face.

Harry bowed and Bess lifted her velvet skirt in a curtsy.

'So, Harry, we are glad to see you here,' the King said.

'Your Majesty is kind,' Harry murmured, his hand still resting on Bess's sleeve.

The King turned his darting eyes on her.

'This is a new face, is it not? And a vastly pretty one,' he added graciously, looking her up and down.

Bess flushed under his frank stare.

'The Lady Elizabeth de Cheyne, daughter of Sir Robert de Cheyne, sir,' Harry said smoothly.

'Robert—— Why, I once knew a Robert de Cheyne.'
The king stood a moment searching his memory. 'Of
course—I have it. He was a fine knight but wounded
severely in a tournament many years ago. A pity; he was
almost equal to myself in skill and strength. Hmm. I
sometimes wondered what became of him and if we
might have granted him some help...'

A pity you didn't voice those thoughts, thought Bess
bitterly. Then perhaps my father could have had a little
dignity in his plight. It had come to her that morning
at breakfast that her father used to be one of the gay
and high-spirited men she saw around her, and for the
first time she had wondered what it had cost him to give
up such a life. She said nothing, however, and the King
had no more time to waste on the trivial matter of the
loss of a man's occupation and pride. He clapped Harry
on the back.

'Come, Harry, a good meal awaits us and we are impatient for it.'

A few fewer good meals might reduce that over-large
bulk of yours, Bess thought sourly as the royal party
moved away. Harry Latimar looked back over his
shoulder and dropped one clear-cut eyelid in farewell.
She smiled back at him.

'Cousin—we must go in now.' Margaret spoke coolly
and Bess knew she disapproved of her exchanging winks
and smiles with a particular gentleman. She slipped an
arm through her cousin's and they walked quickly back
to the palace.

'The King is very grand, is he not?' she said
placatingly.

'He is a fine-looking man,' Margaret conceded, di-
verted from the rebuke she had been about to admin-
ister. All the same, she glanced at Bess's lovely flushed
face and decided she must watch over her carefully. She
herself had been an ardent admirer of Queen Catherine
and, in the days when she had ruled, morals at court
had been strictly observed. They had not been dull days

by any means, for the Spanish queen had loved gaiety and fine clothes and jewels and amusing entertainment, but her staunch Catholicism had disallowed promiscuity among her young ladies and gentlemen, and those who fell short of her high standard had not been welcome for long at court. Those days had gone now and a freer, more relaxed attitude reigned. Meg did not seriously concern herself with Harry Latimar's attentions. In her quiet way she was a shrewd observer and she had seen that his tastes ran to the more sophisticated, worldly ladies who, it must be admitted, made the first overtures. Also, despite his reputation with women and at the gaming tables, Meg rather admired the handsome young man. In an atmosphere of tension, where the stars of the royal court were young and headstrong, she had seen him defuse many an uneasy situation with easy charm and wit. The King loved him greatly, although he probably could not have said why. Meg thought it was because Harry was no flatterer. What he thought he said, but with a disarming candour.

Besides, the only ruling passion in Harry Latimar's life seemed to be gambling; indeed he would wager gold on how long a bird's trill would last—three seconds or four. His friends were the Queen's closest circle—Brereton, Norris, Weston and first of all that dark, caustic young man George Boleyn. Why he loved George Meg could never decide, unless it was that opposites attracted. George's bitter tongue and careless arrogance made him many enemies—his own wife among them—in a way that Anne's similar personality never could, for she was capable of an imaginative kindness that endeared her to those who served her. She too showed great partiality for Latimar, but he did not indulge in the fashionable cult of becoming enamoured with her; he gave his loyalty equally to both his master and his mistress.

* * *

In the great dining hall the clamour had reached a cres-
cendo as the cousins slipped into their seats at one of
the long trestle-tables. A troupe of jugglers and acrobats
performed between the tables for the court's amusement
and the air was thick with the rich smell of food,
woodsmoke from the massive fires burning, and human
sweat. Meg and Bess sat above the salt but some way
from the raised dais on which sat the royal group. Bess
looked covertly along the line of favourites seated near
the King and picked out the handsome figure in silver-
grey. He sat between a good-looking fair man and a
slight, dark man with snapping black eyes. When the
Queen took her place beside her husband Bess saw the
resemblance between Anne and her brother.

George Boleyn, elevated by the King to the title of
Lord Rochford in the first flush of his obsession with
Anne, was an odd combination of dandy and tough. His
face, cast in the same mould as his sister's, was more
sharply defined, each feature chiselled and distinct, and
his beautifully shaped, sensitive mouth was drawn down
in a perpetually sardonic expression which was dupli-
cated in his slanting black eyes. He wore unrelieved black
and the diamonds on his long fingers struck fire in the
candlelight. For some reason Bess found herself reminded of a picture in one of her father's books; it de-
picted Lucifer being turned out of paradise by a band
of angels bearing flaming swords, and the resemblance
between this young man and the dark angel was striking.

His uncomfortably penetrating gaze found her
watching him from the crowd, and she saw him lean
towards Latimar and point her out. Whatever Harry said
in reply obviously didn't interest him, for he removed
his stormy black eyes from her and turned to his sister.

Bess turned her attention to the bewildering variety
of food before her and helped herself to roast swan. So
Harry Latimar was a friend to the brightest luminaries
at court and therefore far out of reach of little Bess de
Cheyne from Devon. She picked at the food and watched

the tumblers performing impossible feats in the confined area. She looked again at the royal couple; Henry showed his wife every courtesy, they ate from the same dish and drank from the same chased silver goblet and yet ... His attention frequently wandered and, following his glances, Bess saw they were fixed on a small girl, plainly dressed in dove-grey, her mouse-coloured hair drawn back from a bland narrow face. Her eyes were cast demurely down at her plate but Bess sensed that she was well aware of the royal attention.

The afternoon passed swiftly, the ladies in a state of high excitement. They fluttered here and there in the fading light, trying on this dress and borrowing that jewel, head-dress, shoes, and arguing endlessly over who suited which colour best. Bess looked anxiously in the mirror, turning this way and that in the shimmering rose-purple silk which Meg had found for her. She wore her hair brushed back and secured behind each ear with jewelled combs. A pendant of amethysts interwoven with gilt flowers hung around her slim neck. Meg, dressed in becoming yellow with topaz rings and bracelets, handed her a little mauve silk mask.

'So—Lady Amethyst and Lady Topaz are ready.'

Bess slipped on the mask. It gave her confidence; she felt no different from the other girls tripping gaily down the cold stone stairway and following the sound of music and merriment below.

The company was very gay that night and more than a little tipsy on the free-flowing French wine. Bess sat nervously on the sidelines. She knew none of the dance steps. Her father, who might have taught her, found even slow walking painful, so she must watch and learn tonight. While Margaret joined in one of the more sedate figures on the arm of an elderly gentleman, Bess surreptitiously drank a cup of wine. As she was used only to weak ale or cider, the ruby liquid ran straight through her warm blood to her head. A sense of extreme well-being flooded through her. She could have stood up and danced alone, whirling to the enchanting music, shouting for joy in being part of this wonderful evening. She quickly drank another and sipped a third.

'Drinking alone is a poor habit, my lady,' said Harry Latimar, detaching himself from the dancers to stand before her.

'Indeed? Well, I am just a country maid. I know nothing of court manners.'

'Will you join the dance?'

'I fear I do not know the steps, my lord.'

'Just follow the others; I will be your honoured guide.'

Tonight he was again in his favoured silver-grey but the sleeves and doublet of this costume were slashed with red tissue, and upon his fingers he wore opals also flecked with red fire. She put one hand on his arm and he swept her into the line of dancers.

She stood uncertainly a moment watching the others. Yes, I see, two steps right and turn, two steps back and turn; curtsy to the gentleman opposite, dance towards him and he swings you high in the air and sets you down. And repeat the movement along the line... She gave herself up to the swaying pleasure. She saw the King swing the plain blonde lady high, holding her a fraction too long, then Bess was opposite him and he lifted her in his great arms before depositing her none too gently on the polished floor. Dizzily she stumbled forward and Harry caught her deftly, lifting her effortlessly against his long body. She looked down and saw his eyes glitter behind the black mask. He set her down and she said breathlessly, 'I feel a little faint...'

He put an arm around her waist and guided her through the dancers, out of the hall, and put her gently into a cushioned chair in one of the curtained alcoves of the antechamber. He sat opposite her, caressing the smoky pearl in his ear with one long finger.

'You have had too much wine, little Bess,' he said reprovingly.

'Two cups only.' She held up three fingers.

He raised his eyebrows. She examined her fingers and laughed.

'Two, three—what does it matter?'

'In the morning it will matter a great deal,' he said, shaking his head sadly.

A burst of laughter came from the hall. Bess removed her mask and said dreamily, 'My cousin tells me you are a rogue, sir.'

'Your cousin is a wise lady.'

'Are you such a disreputable gentleman?' she asked, looking through her lashes at him.

'Playing the coquette doesn't suit you, Bess,' he said abruptly.

'I have no graces as have the ladies from France, you mean?' she retorted.

'You have your own grace, Elizabeth. Simple and innocent, or so I thought last night.'

'You think me just a little country maid.'

'Are you not a maid and also from the country?' he asked gravely. 'All the wine in the cellars at Greenwich will not make you as the other court ladies.' He still wore his mask and she could not see his eyes.

'I disliked being thought a servant by you and your grand friends.'

'I never thought you a servant. Even in your brown homespun you were a charming picture. In fact I think I preferred you so dressed.'

'I'm sure you think your opinion of the greatest importance to me.'

So he thought nothing of her elegant dress and fashionably dressed hair.

For a moment he said nothing, then he rose and offered his arm. 'We must return to the hall. It is discourteous to the King and Queen to leave their presence for too long. Replace your mask—it is the rule until midnight.'

Bess rose too, smoothing her skirts. She felt deflated. I cannot hold his attention for even a short while, she thought, chilled by his polite tone.

They went back to the hall; he took her back to where Meg was sitting and thanked her coolly for her company. Bess took her place under Meg's cold eyes.

'Cousin, I have been most remiss in not informing you of the correct etiquette . . . but I thought——'

'Please forgive me, Margaret; I took some wine and became dizzy. Lord Latimar merely kept me company while I regained composure.'

Meg looked even more shocked. 'Bess——' She paused as a commotion in the hall took her eye. The Queen had risen from her seat and was sweeping from the hall, all eyes upon her. Beneath her golden mask her face was set and pale. Bess looked for the King. As though oblivious to his wife's departure, he was in intimate conversation with the small pale lady.

'Jane Seymour.' Meg sighed and folded her lips together. 'Come—we will see if madam needs us.'

As they left the hall a swarthy thickset man in brown gave Bess an appraising stare. She lifted her chin, resenting his bold stare, and heard him ask the woman he was with who 'the haughty piece in mauve' was.

In her bedchamber Anne was standing at the window, staring out into the night. She turned with a smile as they entered. 'A moment's nausea,' she said. 'Please do not leave the festivities. I shall retire early, I believe.'

'Shall I send your women to you, madam?' Meg asked.

'If you please. Bess—you are enjoying this night?'

'I am, madam.' Bess remained as Meg went out.

Anne went back to looking out of the narrow window. Above the courtyard, its conduit gaily painted in blue, gold and jasper in honour of her coronation, the night skies were thick with stars.

'Look . . .' She beckoned, and pointed up to the dark sky. 'When I was a little girl long ago at Hever I named a bright star the Anne Boleyn. See, it shines brightly wherever I am. And it will shine just as brightly when I am gone. It is a strange thought, is it not, that the stars are the same whoever is looking up at them?'

Standing so close, Bess could smell the perfume on the other woman's hair and on her white skin. A lump of pity rose in her throat.

'You are a kind child,' the Queen murmured as if reading her thoughts, 'but I made my choice and can never regret it. I played the cards I had and seem to have ... lost.'

'No, madam. You still have——'

Anne smiled and laid her hands upon her flat stomach. 'Yes, the trump card. Maybe. A son for His Majesty would win the game and send Lady Jane back to Wolf Hall for good, would it not? But somehow——'

She stopped. 'We all make choices—they should be the right ones, however. I chose to be Henry's Queen at whatever cost and that was right for me. You must be equally sure; for instance, you might think to set your heart upon the wrong man, a man who could bring you nothing but pain. Or you could put that choice aside, enjoy your time at court and go home and forget him.'

The Queen's black eyes had missed nothing that night.

'If that star you spoke of should suddenly disappear from the sky, would you never miss it, or would you search the heavens for it each night?' Bess said slowly.

Anne laughed. 'You argue like those lawyers Henry is always closeted with,' she said, lightly tapping Bess on the shoulder with her white hand. 'Go to bed now and in the morning sun you won't see any stars.'

Bess left the room and gently closed the door. She was still light-headed and wide awake. Should she rejoin the company downstairs? As she stood irresolutely at the head of the stairs one of the ladies she had met that morning, Kate Mortimer, brushed past her. She turned and said, 'Is it little Bess de Cheyne? You are not retiring so early, are you?'

She was a handsome chestnut-haired girl, exquisitely dressed, with an infectious smile.

'I believe my cousin intends to.'

'Oh, Lady Meg is never seen after midnight, but I fancy you may enjoy being merry a little longer. Come—some of us are gathering for a game of cards.'

She took Bess by the hand down the stairs and along the passages to a small room furnished with round tables at which sat some of the younger members of court. Kate drew Bess to a table by the window. The gentlemen rose and bowed as they sat down. Harry Latimar was opposite with his back to the window, George Boleyn on his left. George ran his sharp eyes over her.

'How does my lady sister?'

'She is well enough,' murmured Bess. 'A little tired, I believe.'

'Tired of what, I wonder, or rather of whom?' George said sourly.

Beside him Harry was letting the elaborately painted cards slip through his fingers. His eyes on their bright pictures, he said, 'Shall we play?'

Kate took a little velvet purse from her bodice and shook out a pile of coins. 'I will stake you, Bess.'

'I do not know how to play,' Bess said timidly.

'Watch a while before you begin,' Kate advised. ''Tis very simple.'

Harry dealt the cards around the table. In an undertone Kate explained the rules and Bess's agile mind soon grasped the principles. After two games, both won by Harry, she began hesitantly to play. It was a new experience for her to lay a coin on the chance turn of a card. At home money was regarded with the greatest respect and only parted with for essentials which could not be had by the system of friendly barter between the farms: some cheeses from my dairy for a leg of pork when next you kill one of your pigs and so on. She found it gave her a curious thrill to gamble, which showed in the heightened colour beneath her skin and the added sparkle in her eyes. She began to win. Twenty minutes passed; Harry dealt the cards swiftly, expertly. The air was scented by the smoking candles and at the other tables around them people exclaimed or protested over their luck. Bess did not know it, but the play was light-hearted that night; it was early still and no one had become deeply involved. Many of the serious gamblers were still with the King in the great hall and those present who normally played deep, like Lord Latimar, were content at present to let the cards fall where they would without chancing large amounts.

For once, in any case, Harry was finding himself distracted. He looked across the table at Bess, puzzled by his interest in her. She was not the type of woman he normally found attractive. Firstly she was very young and in his experience youth was overrated and seemed to entitle a girl to be very intense in her invitation to romance but prone to withdraw hastily when the situation became too explicitly physical. Also his jaded palate demanded sophistication; the lady must be witty company and Bess had little to say for herself. She did not join in the banter around the table—an art which Kate Mortimer excelled in—and somehow contrived to look gravely unaware even when Will Brereton became as usual too bawdy. Physically, of course, she was very beautiful. It was the current fashion to mimic the Queen and the ladies dyed their hair inky black and painted their faces a stark white to conform so Bess de Cheyne's ethereal blondeness struck at the senses. But there was something else, something he had felt when he had first looked up at her in the rain the previous night and which distracted his attention now. She looked up and met his eyes and smiled. He lowered his heavy lids without returning the smile and studied the cards in his cupped hand.

A latecomer joined them. 'Is there room for me, gentlemen; ladies?'

Bess looked up and saw it was the man in brown whom she had noticed when leaving the dancing.

'Join us if you will, Tom,' George said.

Tom Spalding brought a chair and placed it between Bess and Kate. They made room for him and he took another long look at Bess while he seated himself.

'I don't believe we have met, lady,' he said, his eyes fixed on her face.

Kate yawned and introduced them.

Tom Spalding had only recently come to court. He was a little older than the others in the group surrounding Henry, but had already made a name for himself for sheer physical courage: on the jousting field and in the hunt he excelled, but he had not made friends of those most intimate with the Queen, particularly Harry Latimar, whose light-hearted approach to life he despised. Lord Spalding was ruthless whether he was testing his skill at a tournament, or riding an animal down in the parkland. He had a heavy hand with women too and the ladies of the court avoided him.

Harry dealt the cards again, including the latest player. Bess picked up her hand and moved slightly in her seat. Lord Spalding was uncomfortably close; he was sweating in the close air and his shoulder was pressed to hers. She decided not to bid and laid her cards face upwards. Tom did the same and dropped his hands to his lap. After a moment under cover of the table he put a hand on her thigh and pressed. Bess sat upright, shocked. She moved further away but he kept his grip on her. She blushed painfully. If one of the boys at home had treated her so she would have slapped his face and complained loudly but here...? Among this company she was reluctant to make a scene but—— She felt the pudgy hand hot and damp through the silk of her dress and was outraged.

She looked around the table; play was still on and everyone was intent on the bidding. She began to feel sick. The wine she had drunk earlier and the acute re-

vulsion she felt at being handled by this man combined
to make her heart beat faster, her head revolve.

A few seconds dragged past then Harry said idly, 'Lady
Bess, I believe you might be more comfortable at this
side of the table. The room is overheated and you are
looking somewhat distressed. There is some small
passage of air through the window here, I think.'

Thankfully Bess prepared to stand up. Tom Spalding
released his grip but made no attempt to rise and allow
her to move her chair back.

'The lady is well enough here, Harry,' he said stolidly.

'I think not,' said Harry gently. 'She is from the west
where the air is sweeter, I suspect.'

'From a farmyard, is it not so? Can the air be sweeter
in a barnyard among the stink of animals?' Tom said
offensively.

Bess paled. In a moment she would forget herself and
smack the man's arrogant face.

'Why no, maybe not.' Harry flicked an imaginary
speck of dust from his sleeve. 'But I believe the animals
there would be kept under some confinement.'

He laid the faintest stress on the word 'there'. Kate
Mortimer laughed maliciously and Lord Spalding took
an angry breath.

Before he could speak George Boleyn cut in irritably.
'Shall we play on or are we to discuss agriculture
instead?'

Harry met Tom Spalding's eyes and held them a
moment, then the older man pushed back his chair and
left the table abruptly. Bess wished the floor would open
and swallow her up.

'You have made an enemy, Harry,' Kate murmured,
glancing sideways at Bess.

Harry fingered the pearl in his ear without speaking.

'Shall we play on?' George said again.

'I believe my concentration is awry now.' Harry stood
up in a graceful movement and bowed. 'I shall retire
now.'

He came around to the back of Bess's chair. 'May I escort you to the ladies' dorter, Bess?'

Bess thought, I am glad to be rescued, but am I to be dragged from the room like a child late going to bed? She raised mutinous eyes to his. George tapped his fingernails impatiently on the table-top.

'Thank you,' she said at last, keeping him waiting while she counted out the money Kate had lent her and picked up her own winnings. She walked with him to the door.

In the passageway she said, 'I would have preferred to remain, my lord.'

'I would not have felt easy about that,' he said teasingly. 'Trouble seems to follow where you go. Unruly horses, unruly men——'

'I do not need your protection, Harry.'

'Have I made an error of judgement? Were you perhaps enjoying the situation? Please forgive me for interrupting——'

He laughed at the expression on her face and tucked her hand under his arm.

'Walk with me a little, Bess.'

They could hear the sound of music from the hall and the muted noise of dancing feet. He paused at the doors and they watched the colourful changeful pattern of the dance.

He said hesitantly, 'Bess—I am not sure why I say this but . . . I was your first friend at court so I feel I may.'

She tilted her head to look up at him. Henry Tudor was a tall man but Harry Latimar was some inches taller.

'Pray proceed, my lord.'

'What occurred in the gaming-room—it was most unpleasant for you, I believe. But . . . you should not have been there.'

She stiffened. 'I did not know I was unwelcome.'

'Don't pretend to misunderstand me, Bess. Your cousin has retired. The other ladies of her kind are still dancing or preparing to leave the entertainment. In a place such as this you choose who you spend your time with and are judged accordingly. I would wish you to choose wisely.'

She withdrew her arm from his. 'I am not a child—I can decide for myself who to make a friend of. I like the Lady Kate; she is merry and good company.'

'Ah, yes. She is good company but...' He hesitated, then went on, 'Her reputation is not unsullied, however. Indeed, your cousin William was frequently in her company and your uncle at some pains to remove him from it in great haste.'

'If what you say is true it hardly becomes you to mention it. To so speak of a lady—and that lady your friend—is not the conduct of a gentleman.'

He raised his eyebrows but said mildly, 'I am not yet ready to take lessons from you in courtly behaviour, Bess. But I agree and am suitably rebuked. It is not my usual habit to criticise a lady, but I feel I must warn you.' He looked uncomfortable, and it was not an expression which sat well with his careless arrogance.

'I can only repeat that I will choose my friends—and can take my place with any lady at this court,' she declared.

'And what am I to make of that statement?'

'Whatever you will.'

'Well... perhaps I misjudged you.'

She said nothing, feeling his words held a double meaning which somehow put her in the wrong. They looked at each other, then he smiled his charming smile.

'Now we understand each other, and since you have no need of my services as escort I will leave you now and wish you goodnight.' He turned and walked away.

She watched until the glimmer of his costume was swallowed by the darkness, then she found her way to her bedchamber. Meg was asleep already, so she prepared quietly for bed. Warm between the sheets, her cousin breathing steadily beside her, she considered the strange day, the unfamiliar sights she had witnessed. Through the hours walked Harry Latimar, slim and graceful, charming and...dangerous. She had an uneasy feeling that she had invited that danger to engulf her and she knew now that he was significant in her life. Perhaps she had known it from the moment she laid eyes on him. She turned on her side and slept.

CHAPTER TWO

HARRY LATIMAR had told the truth regarding the extra cup of wine; the morning found Bess sick and miserable with a persistent demon banging a drum in her head. Meg had forgotten her disapproval of the previous night and was all sympathy and kindness.

''Tis true we learn from our mistakes, coz. You will know now—a little wine for courage but no more.' She laid a cold damp cloth on Bess's aching head. 'You lie here and I will attend to my work. The Queen has sent word she will lie abed this morning; you would do well to do likewise.'

Bess dozed until, presently feeling better, she washed and dressed in the amber velvet. Through the window she could see black clouds gathering over the palace. She brushed her hair and pinched colour into her cheeks. Margaret came back looking troubled.

'Madam is very low this morning. His Grace has shown great displeasure because she left the masque so early last night. But she has learned that the Princess Elizabeth, her daughter, will be visiting Greenwich in a few days. That has cheered her... How cold it is in here.'

She went briskly to the fire and set about coaxing a brighter flame. Bess wandered to the window and sat down. ''Tis raining again, cousin,' she said disconsolately, as a wave of homesickness engulfed her.

Margaret looked over one plump shoulder at her then stood up, smoothing her white hands. She glanced at the clock above the hearth. Bess had noticed it when she had arrived the night before. It was of beaten bronze, very ornate with gilt scrolls and a flower-painted face. It had given her a small measure of comfort then, for it was an exact replica of one her father owned and had brought with him from court all those years before. In the farmhouse it held pride of place on the polished oak dresser.

'It lacks an hour to the midday meal, Bess. Why do you not go down to the solar and acquaint yourself with the other ladies? They gather here at this hour.' She smiled encouragingly at her cousin who looked doubtful. 'Come, do not be shy. You come from a proud family and are as good as, or better than, many of them.'

With this rallying speech to bolster her Bess tidied her hair and walked the passageways until she came to the solar. Resisting the impulse to tap on the heavy door like a servant, she turned the handle and went in. She found herself in a long and narrow room, the walls hung with swathes of embroidered silk, bare of windows except for a small glazed aperture halfway along one wall. It was luxuriously furnished with velvet-covered settles grouped haphazardly along its length on which sat a dozen or so chattering women with tapestry easels before them.

A slender teenage boy with dark curling hair and light grey eyes sat on a stool strumming at his lute. Bess paused in the doorway as the occupants turned their eyes on her with mild interest. Trying to feel as though she belonged there, she closed the door behind her and went forward with relief as Kate Mortimer, who stood at the small window, beckoned to her.

'Look, Bess—have you seen anything quite so diverting before?'

She slipped an arm around Bess's waist and they looked through the window together. To her surprise Bess saw that it overlooked the great banqueting hall, buzzing now with activity as servants flew here and there laying the long trestle-tables with platters of bread, goblets, knives and spoons.

Between two of the tables she saw a grotesque sight: a little man, no bigger than a four-year-old child, so deformed that his bearded head appeared to sprout from his chest, was capering in a mad dance. His arms hung to the floor and as he turned somersaults it appeared from above that a headless monster performed.

'Oh, poor creature.' Bess drew back, distressed.

Kate laughed heartlessly. 'Why poor? There are many who will pay gold to see such a sight. Not at this court, however.'

'Why not here?'

'Oh, Henry has a horror of such people. Any infirmity disgusts him.'

'But they are part of life,' said Bess slowly. 'And they have feelings and should not be made mock of.'

'Oh, to be sure,' agreed Kate, shrugging her shoulders. 'Like the poor, they are always with us. But a sight like that is vastly more amusing than a beggar at the gates.' She drifted away from the window.

No doubt she would find my father with his shambling walk amusing, thought Bess angrily, looking down with a heavy heart. As she watched a group of young men gathered about the freak, laughing uproariously at his antics. They were joined by a familiar figure in grey who watched a moment, unsmiling, then touched the little man's arm and bent to whisper in his ear. Bess saw the shine of gold as Harry slipped some coins into the dwarf's huge hand, then the man with a final bound sprang over a table and left the hall.

Bess turned from the window. She was unaccountably glad that Harry Latimar had not found the pathetic creature amusing, glad he had touched him gently and paid him well and sent him on his way.

'Play some merry piece, Mark. This gloomy weather saddens us all,' Madge Fitzroy said, drawing her needle swiftly in and out of her work. Bess perched on the edge of one of the settles and gave her attention to the music. The boy took up his stance in the centre of the room and plucked the lute with slim fingers. He threw back his glossy head and sang. His beautiful voice was as pure as fluttering snow in the stuffy room. Bess felt tears behind her eyes; she thought of her home, of clear summer skies above the cornfields, the scent of her mother's baking and of her father's musical voice raised in rare laughter. This is magic, she thought—what a gift this delicate-looking boy possessed. She glanced around at the others; they appeared oblivious to Mark Smeaton's spell, whispering and exchanging gossip with each other.

The last note died away, the door opened and the Queen entered. The ladies rose and dropped demure curtsys. Anne wore a fox-coloured gown today—the vivid tawny showed off her transparent skin and contrasted with her black eyes. Around her neck she wore a necklace of pearls from which an enamelled plaque painted with the initial 'B' was suspended. Her hair was pulled back beneath a stiffened pearl-edged cap and hung loose down her back. She had come from a brief sitting with the court painter and declared herself exhausted.

'He said, in the most regrettable English, that he wished to capture my very soul upon the canvas,' she said, seating herself with the elegance Bess associated with her. 'Will those who look upon the result in the future see my soul, do you think?'

The others laughed. Anne's eyes alighted on Bess. 'Can one's soul be transferred to linen, do you think?'

'Perhaps, Your Majesty,' murmured Bess.

Anne's brilliant eyes swept the room. 'It is a sobering thought that the very essence of me will be reduced to a little dried paint, darkened by the years. I feel the hand of death this very moment.'

'It comes to us all, madam,' said Mark, his bright boy's face solemn, his curiously pale eyes fixed on the woman he obviously adored. 'Our destiny is writ before we are born.'

'It hardly seems worth arising each morning and struggling through the day,' said Kate.

'I had not observed you rising before noon most days,' returned the Queen. 'And as to struggle—'tis not a word I think of in connection with you, lady.'

'As many a gentleman at court would confirm,' agreed Madge.

There was a laugh at Kate's expense. Anne sighed. 'But 'twould be so useful to know what lay ahead. If it is forewritten, why can we not know what is in store? We could make each day count for something should we be aware of imminent extinction.'

The other ladies shuddered pleasurably. Bess dropped her eyes and gripped her hands in her lap.

'The cards tell us a little,' one lady suggested.

'Only that which the person giving the reading knows already,' Kate said cynically.

'Some have the sight,' protested another. 'Dorothy has.'

They all turned to look at a little blonde woman, who was working patiently on a tapestry of a hunting scene. She placed her needle carefully in her work and rose.

'Lady Bess de Cheyne is recently come to court,' said Kate. 'We know nothing of her life. Dottie shall read the cards for her and Bess shall tell us if aught is significant.'

Bess coloured with embarrassment, but her protests were ignored. A little table was placed between her and Dorothy Alençon, cards were quickly produced and the others leaned over her shoulder. Mark ran his thumb over his lute strings in a lingering note. Dorothy shuffled the cards briskly and put them into Bess's hands.

'Cut the cards, lady.'

Bess did so. Her hands felt clumsy and damp. Dorothy laid seven cards face upwards and leaned forward to study them.

'I see poverty.' She frowned. 'But much love too.' She pointed to the high heart cards with the tip of her finger. She dealt three more, the dainty Queen of Hearts flanked by two red Knaves. She raised dark eyes to Bess's face.

'You are fortunate, *mademoiselle*. The gentlemen find you most desirable.' With a twist of her wrist she slapped down the final card: the Queen of Spades, her black painted eyes impassive. A little thrill ran round the watchers.

'Is it not the death card?' Madge said with a shiver.

'It can mean many things.' Dorothy's small hands gathered in the cards.

'But in this instance?' asked Anne.

Dorothy snapped the backs of the cards. 'Lady Bess is loved—by her family. And will be loved by several gentlemen. The Black Queen is her own personal dilemma. When she resolves it the way 'lies clear to happiness.'

'Is that all?' one of the ladies asked, disappointed.

'Is that not enough?' Anne said lightly. 'Now is the luncheon hour. We must go down.'

Bess lingered as the others left the solar. Dorothy Alençon covered her embroidery carefully with a linen cloth and bent to collect the spools of silk into a drawstring bag. Was this someone who could also stray off the known path into the unknown? wondered Bess. Could she at last find some consolation in talking to another about her experiences? She went and stood beside her.

'You are talented, Lady Dorothy,' she ventured diffidently.

The little Frenchwoman looked up at her.

'Oh, no. It is just a little game to pass the time.'

'You do not really...see these things you tell of?'

Dorothy straightened up.

'I see a most beautiful young girl in a borrowed gown. With pretty manners and a contented face. This tells me of a happy home—though poor, hence the need for borrowed clothes—where she is thought much of. Last night I saw the attention she received from the court gallants. It is not hard to spin a tale around these observations.'

'But...the cards fall where they will——'

Dorothy shook out her wide sleeves; several cards drifted to the floor. She smiled at Bess's exclamation.

''Tis just a trick, Lady Bess. Nothing more.'

Bess bent to retrieve the cards. 'I see.'

Dorothy patted her arm. 'You are not annoyed?'

'Oh, no. It is just that I thought——'

'No one can tell you what lies beyond today, Bess. And you wouldn't want to know. Not truly.'

'No. Perhaps not.'

Dorothy smiled a charming lopsided smile. She was tiny but very fair and vivacious in the way Bess had noticed was peculiar to the French girls at court. She had intelligent hazel eyes and a wide mouth.

'It is boring at court, Bess, although it may not seem so to you yet. The days grow very tedious, especially in poor weather, and anything that amuses a little is welcome. And this is harmless, I think. But do not tell the others.'

Bess smiled in return. 'Why do you give away your secret to me?'

'I scarcely know. Perhaps because you seem more real than the others. Untouched by the atmosphere at court as yet. And . . . I feel an honesty within you which made me wish not to cozen you. You are like a fresh little breeze from the western sea and I hope we may be friends. Now come—we must go down to our food.'

Among the sea of faces Meg waved and Bess threaded her way through the noisy crowd and sat down.

'You have spent a pleasant hour, Bess?'

'I have. I was less shy than I supposed. One of the ladies, Dorothy Alençon was most charming, I thought.'

'Dottie? Indeed she is most amiable,' agreed Meg.

Over her shoulder Bess saw Tom Spalding's eyes fixed on her. She averted her own, shifting uncomfortably on the padded bench. Why must the man stare at her in that brooding fashion? She shivered, remembering his hand on her at the card tables. She turned her head and directed what she hoped was a suitably repressive glance towards him. He lowered his almost lashless lids and began to eat. Conscious of another pair of eyes on her, she found that Harry Latimar had seen the exchange.

He raised his eyebrows and, putting a hand over his heart, assumed a lovelorn expression. She turned her back and heard his laugh above the clatter of plates and conversation.

'What do we do this afternoon, cousin?' she asked abruptly.

Meg paused in her discourse on the complicated branches of the Alençon family tree, startled. 'I believe madam is to be visited by her dressmakers and some merchants are to offer their wares for her consideration. I shall be glad if you could assist me in noting down her requirements. Do you write a clear hand?'

'Yes, I do. I shall be happy to do that. Forgive me, I interrupted you . . .'

'Oh—yes, now as I was saying, Dorothy's Uncle Louis married a cousin of——'

Bringing the Alençon history up to the present date occupied her until the meal was concluded.

An hour later they were summoned to the royal apartments. Bess and Meg tapped on the door and they entered. Far from being the Queen's private retreat, the vast overheated rooms adjoining her bedchamber seemed very public indeed. Lying on a couch strewn with cushions, Anne held court to any of her friends who cared to visit, and a great many did, drawn irresistibly to her company. Bess seated herself at the solid oak table Anne used for her correspondence. On its shining surface stood a walnut writing box with brass handles, open now, unable to contain the clutter of letters and memoranda carelessly thrust into its compartments. Scraps of paper and rolled parchments had spilled over the table. Looking closer, Bess saw that inset among the decoration on the box was the head of the youthful Henry, his profile as yet unblurred by age. Facing him across the scarred wood was a similarly mounted portrait of his deposed queen, Catherine.

Meg cleared a space and laid out fresh paper and writing materials then busied herself in one of the alcoves in her eternal quest for moths among Anne's dozens of furs.

Bess sat and watched an ever-changing cast of players as they entered the room, exchanged pleasantries, begged favours or brought gifts and left. George Boleyn lounged indolently beside his sister. They were quite extraordinarily alike, her extreme slenderness translated into whippet strength in the man. Both black-eyed; hers overlarge, his narrow in the same pale oval faces. Their sharp tongues were matched too: separately they held their own in witty company; together they were formidably cruel as they mocked those less nimble-tongued. Yet there was about Anne a softness which frequently took the sting from her comments. No such softness was apparent in her brother; Lord Rochford looked what he undoubtedly was; a bitter and disappointed man whose career was only kept afloat by his exalted sister.

Bess's eyelids drooped. She went quietly to one of the windows and opened it a fraction to breathe in a little of the rain-laden air which flowed into the room. Harry Latimar came in, his hand on the studded collar of Anne's favourite wolfhound Urian. It went immediately to its mistress and on her command stretched out at her feet. Harry turned to go.

'Stay, Sir Harry,' the Queen said.

He turned in the doorway. 'You use the same tone to me as to that great beast, madam,' he observed.

'You are not nearly so biddable, Harry.' She smiled. 'But I truly need your advice. I intend to be wildly extravagant with Henry's privy purse this afternoon and add to my meagre wardrobe. I would welcome your opinion on what is on offer.'

'I fear I am not an authority on ladies' gowns,' Harry returned mildly.

'He is more an authority on what is inside them,' said George.

Harry laughed good-naturedly and dropped into a chair. His eyes wandered around the room and dis-

covered Bess at the window. He leaned back and turned
the pearl in his ear.

The merchants, having waited patiently for some
hours, were finally admitted and the floor was soon
transformed into a waterfall of colour. Anne slipped off
one fur slipper and caressed Urian's muscular back with
her toes as she studied the offerings.

'Not the black silk—or that velvet. But this one I
like...' She took up a length of pale green silk and con-
sulted with her dressmaker. 'Lady Bess, come take note
of this.'

Bess came and sat hurriedly at the table. She dipped
the quill in ink and held it poised over the paper. Harry
came and leaned on the corner of the table, laying one
hand flat on the surface beside her. Under his eyes she
wrote at Anne's dictation. 'Twenty yards green silk.'

'You write an elegant hand, lady,' he said.

She could feel his breath on her hair, smell the sharply
scented perfume he used. She dipped pen in ink again
and, returning it to the white page, dropped a blob of
black ink on its purity.

'Had you my tutor your knuckles would be sore now,'
he said idly. 'Do I make you nervous?'

'A little.' Bess bent her head and finished the line.

'I had not thought you timid.' His voice was barely
audible in the crowded room.

'Twelve yards of this sweet raspberry velvet, Bess,'
instructed Anne.

'When you are nervous a little pulse beats just here...'
He touched her temple where her hair curled back under
her cap.

She completed the line.

'And—I think—some of the scarlet tissue. 'Twould
be the very thing for the sleeves of my white brocade
gown.'

Bess began another line.

'Why do you shrink from me? Am I so distasteful to
you?' He leaned over her to pick up a silver paperweight

from the far side of the table. His arm brushed her shoulder and she raised her eyes to his face.

'I am not practised in these...games, my lord.'

He gave the paperweight his minute attention. 'Have you not had your share of compliments, then? I find that hard to believe.'

'Where I come from people have a habit of saying what they mean,' she said hardily.

He laughed. 'It sounds somewhat grim. However, if that is your wish: I find you most attractive, Bess; indeed, you fascinate me. I want to be close to you and know you...intimately. I hope I am not too frank.'

'We are under one roof here, my lord; it seems inevitable we will get to know each other—as you so put it.'

He tossed up the silver ball and caught it. 'Do not commit yourself too deeply.'

'I have committed myself to nothing as yet.'

'Bess, do you have record of the gilded cord?'

'I will set it down, madam,' Bess said.

George Boleyn got up in an easy, graceful movement. 'Come, Harry. My sister seems set on beggaring my royal brother-in-law by buying enough material to clothe all of London. Let us find some more diverting entertainment.'

Harry rose immediately. 'Until later, then, Bess,' he murmured.

As he bowed to Anne she said, 'Do you approve of my selection, my lord?'

'I approve of everything about you, madam,' he assured her, leaving the room with George. After a moment Urian got up from the floor and followed him.

As darkness fell Anne was at last satisfied. Bess gathered up her papers.

'We shall put them in orderly fashion and submit them to Your Majesty tomorrow for your final approval,' said

Meg tactfully. She knew that Anne must account to her royal husband for every claim on his purse.

Anne waved them away. She was tired, her unique vitality drained by her condition. She glanced out at the gathering night. 'Light the candles before you retire, Meg. 'Tis dark now.'

Bess gathered her notes into an untidy bundle while Meg found the tinderbox and soon the room was ablaze with light.

Back in their own room she sank into a chair. She shuffled the papers. Madam had ordered a great deal. The bottom page was folded and of a different parchment. She unfolded it and, frowning, realised she had taken one of the scattered papers from Anne's writing table in error. She glanced at it: a few lines of verse written in a classical flowing script.

'Bess, come—we will visit the chapel before supper.'

She thrust the paper into her sleeve. She must return it later, she thought, following Meg down the stairs and over the slippery cobbles to the chapel.

After the evening meal the two cousins sought the long antechamber to the left of the banqueting hall. This was to be a musical evening. Visiting musicians, from Italy Meg believed, would play for the court. Gilt chairs had been arranged before a raised platform on which the entertainers were already tuning their instruments. Meg spread her skirts and the two girls sat down, looking expectant. An hour later Meg whispered, 'Is it not marvellous?'

Bess nodded, stifling a yawn. She stared about her. The King was present, sitting with his wife at the front of the assembly. Resplendent in crimson and gold, a chain collar of gems on his broad chest, he beamed upon the stage, one hand raised to conduct the melody. He is cultured, admitted Bess, and I am not, for I better prefer Mark's gentle lute-strumming. She sighed inwardly as the assorted instruments built to a climax, then there was a burst of applause.

''Tis the interval,' said Meg regretfully, coming back down to earth from wherever the music had transported her.

Refreshments were served with difficulty along the lines of chairs. A page leaned over them to offer wine and as he did so someone rising from their chair behind him nudged his arm, and one of the heavy cups toppled from its tray and fell between the chairs of the two cousins. Most of the wine poured harmlessly on to the floor but the rest splashed rich red on to Bess's hair and the shoulder of her dress.

'You stupid boy!' Meg administered a sharp slap with a plump hand, further endangering the remaining cups.

The boy's face turned crimson. 'Your pardon, lady.' He produced a less than clean cloth and began to dab at Bess's hair.

'Do not touch my lady's hair with that filthy rag!' said Meg furiously. 'Come, Bess, we will retire. You must change your dress and I will wash out that sticky wine from your hair——'

'Oh, no, Meg,' Bess said, embarrassed, for those nearest were craning their necks to see what the disturbance was. 'You will miss the rest of the performance. See—the musicians are ready to begin again. I will manage quite well on my own.' She got hastily up. 'But your pretty velvet——'

''Tis of no account. It will be as new when cleaned. Choose another from my coffers and use the rosewater in my yew box to cleanse your hair...'

Bess escaped, pursued by Meg's whispered instructions.

She ran along the passages and up to her apartments, which were lit only by rosy firelight. Inside she closed the door and stripped off the damp dress, laying it carefully over a chair. In the bedchamber she found Meg's little yew box and, lifting the lid, searched among the

bottles of perfume and remedies for coughs and colds
for the rosewater. She dipped the part of her hair sullied
by the wine into a bowl of water and poured a little of
the sweet-smelling mixture on to the sticky curls then
rinsed and rinsed again. Still in her linen shift, she sat
on the window-seat and rubbed her hair vigorously with
a dry cloth. Well, she had wished to be delivered from
the boredom of the music recital and she was, and if she
delayed a little longer she would likely find it was over
when she went down again.

The firelight leaped in a sudden draught as the door
to the other chamber opened. Meg, no doubt, unable to
resist overseeing her little cousin.

'Meg?' she called through the open door.

Harry Latimar came out of the shadows.

'My lord...' she said, startled. 'Why—what do you
do here?'

'I was somewhat anxious for you, Lady Bess. I saw
you leave the hall after an accident. It appeared your
head was bleeding...'

He dropped his eyes to the discarded dress and fingered
the dried red stains.

''Tis wine, my lord,' she said coldly. 'Do you have
poor eyesight?'

'No, it is excellent, I believe.' He looked her over
deliberately.

She was immediately aware of her state of undress.
She stood up and sat down again hurriedly.

'May I?' He came further into the room and, lifting
a rose-coloured wrapper from the bed, spread it about
her shoulders. He considered her as she slid her arms
into the cool silk.

'Bess.' He took her by the shoulders and pulled her
upright against him. For a moment they stood thus and
she could feel every bone; he was very thin and the bones
of his hips and ribcage were sharp against her flesh. He
kissed her hair, slipped his hands inside the wrapper and
ran them over the bare skin of her back.

'Harry, please——'

'What do you please, Bess?' he murmured, turning up her face and kissing her mouth.

'Do not——' She laid her hands flat on his shoulders. His lips travelled to her throat. She resisted and his arms tightened about her.

'I say do not——'

They tussled in silence a moment, she struggling as much with herself mentally as with him physically. The sense of destiny she had felt on meeting him, the happiness she had experienced subsequently in being near him, now crystallised in this one moment in time here in a warm dim room with no sound but their mingled uneven breathing. Her body told her that here was the man she wanted.

One of her hands tightened on his arm, her little ring catching on the embroidered silk of his sleeve. The ring her father had given her... She was immediately recalled to sanity; Robert de Cheyne's daughter could not behave in this fashion. She summoned up some remaining shreds of control and said coolly, 'You would not force me, Harry——?'

He released her immediately and stepped back. 'No, indeed.'

Breathlessly she turned away from him. 'I must dress now, Harry, and go down.'

His eyes followed her as she hastily dragged a gown from Meg's chest and stepped into it. It was of a pale blue and cool as running water against her hot skin. It fastened up the back and she struggled a moment trying to reach the buttons.

'Shall I fasten it for you?' he enquired politely, master of himself again.

'If you will.'

As if they were strangers he set to work on the intricate row of pearl buttons. She turned back to face him.

'Harry—you did not truly think me injured, did you?'

'No. I wanted only to be alone with you,' he said, looking her in the eyes. There was a brief pause.

'You had no right to—— What allowed you to think I would be willing——?'

'Why, you did, Bess. You impressed upon me that you preferred honest words and I drew the conclusion that you applied that thinking to actions as well.' His voice was bland; his dark eyes held only candour.

When she didn't reply he said, 'Shall I then escort you back to the musicale?'

'I fear it will be long over now.' She picked up the amber velvet and stared at the wine stains. As she did so she heard the crackle of parchment and, reaching into the sleeve, withdrew the folded paper which she had put there that afternoon.

'What is it?' he asked her.

'Oh . . . I took it by mistake from the Queen's apartments.' She unfolded it. ''Tis lines from a poem, I think.'

He took it from her and tilted it so that the page caught the light from the fire. He scanned the lines. 'A love poem, not, I think, yours.'

'Of course not. As I said, I took it in error from the Queen's writing desk.'

He handed it back, an odd expression on his face. She carried it to the fire and read slowly:

And graven with diamonds in letters plain
There is written her fair neck around,
Noli me tangere, for Caesar's I am
And wild for to hold, though I seem tame.

'It is beautiful, and sad,' she said.

'All unrequited love is sad, I suppose.' He spoke from the darkness across the room.

'It was written for madam, of course.' She refolded the paper. 'I feel sorry for the author. Do you know who penned it?'

'I would guess it was Tom Wyatt. The Queen's cousin. Don't waste your sympathy, however; I imagine he has relinquished that particular dream long ago.'

'It is very moving, though.'

'Oh, yes, Tom has the knack of setting down in words what the rest of us can only half feel.'

Bess crossed the room and tucked the poem carefully into her prayerbook.

'I will be sure to return it safely tomorrow.'

'I'm sure it is one of many such expressions of love with which Anne is showered each week.'

'Are yours among them?'

He laughed. 'No, little Bess. I prefer my women to be more . . . available. But courtly love is still fashionable.'

'Courtly love?'

'To profess love for someone you know you can never have, admire her from afar. To live for her glance, her careless touch, a kind word.'

'It seems rather unsatisfactory.'

'I agree; reality is much more exciting.'

She turned to the door. He was there before her to open it. 'You really are very sweet, Bess,' he said quietly. There was a regretful note in his voice as he stepped aside to allow her to go through the doorway. They descended the stairs without speaking, Bess willing her senses to return to normal. She was innocent enough, but her re-action to this man had been nothing short of shameful and had frightened her. He is dangerous to me, she thought. When he is near me, when he touches me, I lose all cool judgement.

She glanced over her shoulder at him. His handsome face was impassive. He could have taken me there in that firelit room without a thought, as he had no doubt tumbled many of the court ladies. Then he would have rearranged his fine clothing, run a white hand through his shining hair, and rejoined his friends, thinking it no more than a pleasant diversion. Resentfully brooding on

this, she slipped on the smooth stone steps and would
have fallen had he not swiftly caught her arm.

'You must be more careful, Bess. If you lose your
balance 'tis a hard place to fall.'

The winding stairway stretched dark before them. True
enough, my lord, she thought ruefully. I must keep my
head and avoid such temptation in the future.

When they reached the hall the company was streaming
out and Bess fancied several pairs of sharp eyes noticed
their arrival together. The ready colour stained her face
as Harry excused himself and moved against the tide
thronging the doorway to join his friends grouped around
the King.

'Ah, Bess.' Meg came to her side. 'You were long upstairs.' She surveyed her cousin critically. 'But you have
managed, I see. Your hair looks very well and that gown
becomes you. It is growing late, love; shall you retire
with me or find some other amusement?'

'I shall retire with you, Meg,' returned Bess firmly. 'I
had thought to write some message to my father.'

'Of course. Your parents will be anxious for some
word, and I will arrange for the next traveller west to
take it in his baggage. 'Twill be some weeks before it
arrives, however.'

What would she say in her letter to her mother and
father? wondered Bess as she and Meg linked arms and
went up the staircase. That she was well and happy? Oh,
yes, she could put that down with truth. For she was;
the life at Greenwich pleased her very much; the
company, the luxurious furnishings, the delectable food
all satisfied something in her. But with the pleasure in
her surroundings flourished the strange plant of her fascination with Harry Latimar. In spite of her simple upbringing, her association only with men more concerned
with wrenching a living from the earth than with ro-
mantic love, some part of her recognised and acknowledged him. She had apparently conveyed some invitation
to him which he had acted on tonight when he had come
to her room. She did not yet know the rules of that par-

ticular game and must be more careful what she said. It occurred to her that she had in some way been protected at home, perhaps by the fact that, although as hardworking and often poorer than the other girls, she was her father's daughter and therefore different. She had no such protection here for, from what she had observed and heard from the sly whispering about, there were many ladies of equally noble birth who would have been only too glad to have Latimar show such interest.

She spent the rest of the evening writing a cheerful, loving letter and talking to Meg beside the dying fire, then went to bed and fell instantly into a deep dreamless sleep.

The following morning she and Meg were occupied with the Queen. The Princess Elizabeth was expected at the end of the following day and the royal nursery must be scoured and aired and made ready. Today Bess saw a facet of the Queen she had not seen before. Eager, anxious, loving, Anne Boleyn cast off the arrogant cloak she usually paraded in and became just another mother looking forward to seeing her child again after long absence. Her ladies looked on with tolerant amusement as she fussed over the warming of the huge feather mattress, examined the minute clothes laid in lavender in the coffers, and interviewed a harassed cook with a long list of the small princess's likes and dislikes regarding her meals.

'Why does madam not have her daughter with her always?' Bess asked Meg eventually.

'It would not be seemly,' answered Meg, shocked. 'The Princess Royal must have her own establishment. Naturally.'

Naturally? thought Bess, trying to imagine her mother allowing some other woman to care for her beloved Bess. As far back as she could remember Joan had been there, in the night to soothe her after a nightmare, comforting her after a fall in the yard and raising her voice in anger should anyone dare to upset her little daughter. But this was not the way for those highborn. Most of the women she knew now at court had spent their childhood among strangers. Anne herself had been only a child when she had sailed for France with Henry's sister, Mary, to take up duties for the new Queen of France.

By mid-afternoon even madam was content that nothing else could be done to prepare for the Princess and Bess was free to leave the nursery and have some little time to herself. She ran back to her chamber, retrieved the scrap of parchment bearing Wyatt's mournful poem, and hastened to the Queen's rooms. She pushed open the door and saw that the room was empty. She ran quickly to the table and, opening the writing box, slid the paper inside. The poem had touched her heart and Harry's explanation of courtly love had interested her. His earlier display of a very different kind of affection had excited her senses. She would wish for a combination of the two emotions, she decided.

Once she was outside in the corridor again Kate Mortimer came tripping up to her and took her hand. 'Lady Bess, what a morning! I declare madam is quite beside herself. Had I to listen to another eulogy on the two-year-old paragon I would have turned lunatic. I am ready for a little more mature amusement. Come with me to the tennis courts. The gentlemen are to engage in a lively game, I hear.'

She pulled Bess along in her laughing wake and they settled in the gallery overlooking the covered courts, waiting for play to begin.

'Bess, can you do me a small favour?' Kate whispered after a few moments.

'Of course.'

Bess looked into the pretty face beside her. Other women at court were more elegantly beautiful but none were so mischievously attractive as Kate. As Harry had told her, Kate had a not entirely pure reputation at court, but she could turn the dullest assembly into a riot and Bess admired her. She had confided to Bess that she was betrothed to a man that her parents had chosen for her long ago and would be married at the end of the year. Meanwhile she had said gaily she would have as merry a time as possible.

'Will your husband not mind your—er...?' Bess had asked, blushing.

'The wicked loss of my virginity, mean you?' Kate had asked, laughing. 'Dear Bess, I doubt he will ever be able to find out, for he is in his dotage and only wishes me for his wife to combine his estates with those left me by my grandfather. So I must have a little fun before being shackled to him...' Now she explained to Bess what she wanted of her.

''Tis this: tonight we—a few friends and I—perform a short play to amuse the court. An old traditional story of good versus evil, you know well the kind of thing. Well, that silly miss, Mary Townsend, has turned her ankle dancing and we are without a lady to perform her part. Can you help us?'

'Of course, Kate,' Bess said quickly, 'but is there time for me to study lines?'

'Oh, this part has no lines to say. You must only look beautiful and aloof and that I think you will do very well.'

Bess looked sideways at the other girl. Was she mocking her? But she saw only friendly enthusiasm in the bright hazel eyes. 'Very well, I will do my best.'

'Good. Come with me to the solar after the tennis and we will go through the play together. Sssh—play is now beginning...'

Bess turned to look down into the court. She had never seen or even heard of this game before. The sandy area below with a sloping roof inlet at either end formed two rectangles divided by a taut cotton net. The players stood at either side and hit a ball to and fro across the net with paddle-shaped bats.

'Two gentlemen play each other, then two more. The winners of each game play again and the victor of that game plays the victor of a further game,' Kate explained. 'They must place the ball within the marked lines only—anyway, you will see. 'Tis most exciting.'

Bess watched with interest. It was exciting—the ball flew back and forth pursued by the agile players. After several games there was a stir and the King appeared and took his turn on the courts. He was good-humoured this afternoon and, although overweight and slowmoving compared to the younger opponent, he was a skilful player.

'He will wish to impress with a certain lady in the audience,' murmured Kate, looking across the gallery.

Bess turned her head expecting to see that Anne had joined the ladies, but saw instead the slim pale Jane Seymour. She was dressed in a sombre blue gown and as she leaned forward to observe the play Bess saw a jewelled plaque slung on a thin gold chain swing out from beneath the folds of material at her breast. Even from the distance separating them Bess could see it was a painted likeness of Henry, framed in a square of large diamonds.

'She is not cautious,' commented Kate.

''Tis shameful,' returned Bess angrily.

She fixed her eyes on the scene below as Harry Latimar faced George Boleyn across the net. Now she saw the game as it should be played; the two men were well matched and the contest lasted longer than any previous game. Neither man was willing to concede a point. Bess could not take her eyes off the slim figure in grey hose and loose-fitting cream shirt. She had heard many things called beautiful but surely nothing was as beautiful as the broad shoulders and slim waist and long straight legs of this man as he ran gracefully around the court in the last of the January afternoon light slanting in through narrow windows. Kate nudged her.

'He must play the King now in the final match.'

Bess saw that the bout had finished and George was clasping his friend's hand in defeat.

'He will naturally allow His Majesty to triumph,' the lady on Kate's other side suggested.

'Harry never gave up victory naturally in his whole life,' Kate said cynically.

There was a short break while Harry refreshed himself, then the two men came back on court to loud applause. At first it seemed that Latimar must win; he was the younger, fitter man. But Henry was a wily opponent— he could place his shots just so and soon had Harry chasing here and there while he himself seemed scarcely to exert himself.

'He is most able,' said Bess judicially. 'I fear he must win.'

'Why Bess, surely you are not hoping your King will be vanquished?' Kate teased. 'If you are you will be disappointed—see, the contest is decided. His Majesty has won.'

The King acknowledged the applause and put his arm around Harry as they left the court together.

'Now,' Kate said, rising, 'come to the solar and we will have our rehearsal. The other ladies will be awaiting us.'

The other ladies were waiting impatiently and reacted with some enthusiasm when Bess was brought too. 'She is just perfect, Kate,' exclaimed Madge Fitzroy. 'Much more the part than Mary, who could not look virtuous in ten million years.'

Amid laughter greeting this comment Bess saw that neither Meg or Dorothy or any of the more sober ladies were present and misgivings assailed her. 'What part am I to play?'

Kate opened her eyes wide. 'Why, you will be Lady Virtue, of course. It is quite easy, dear Bess. You must just stand upon the stage and look your own sweet self while the rest of us act out our parts. Oh—here are our costumes.'

Two needlewomen entered, their arms full of glittering materials. Kate seized one of scarlet spangled lace. 'Here is mine. Is it not naughty? I am Lady Fallen from Grace.' She laughed.

The others held their outfits against them. Bess looked doubtfully at hers. It was a mere shift of fine white lawn with a girdle of thin gold chain.

'It is scarcely decent,' she protested.

'The stage will be softly lit,' Kate reassured her. 'Now let us proceed.'

An hour passed, at the end of which Bess was totally confused by the contrary directions she received. Madge thought she should drift up and down the stage looking distraught; another lady was sure she should kneel in timid supplication centre stage, while Kate was quite determined she should stand quite still upon a stool and assume as haughty an expression as she could manage.

'The Four Temptations—all played by gentlemen— will appear and try to coax you from your pedestal, but you will have naught to do with them,' Kate explained.

The heated discussion went on until Madge caught sight of the clock and exclaimed, 'We must go about our duties, ladies.'

They each took their costumes and hurried to the door.

Kate said to Bess, 'Now come to the far chamber in the west wing, beside the chapel, at ten o'clock sharp and do not worry—it will be the greatest fun.'

Bess ran up to her room with her costume and hastily washed her face and hands and brushed her hair. She was wearing the blue silk again today while the velvet was sponged and pressed and Meg had lent her a pair of sapphire earbobs in the shape of daisies hanging from a chain of diamonds. She brushed her hair off her face and fastened it under her cap the better to show them off. She shook her head and admired them as they danced and sparkled in the candlelight; how quickly she was growing accustomed to the wearing of fine clothes and jewels, she thought. In the glass the vision of herself arriving at court dressed in homespun rose before her. Could she have changed so much in three days? Even the trace of West Country in her voice had faded. She shrugged impatiently; whatever she looked like, sounded like, she was still Bess, was she not?

She went swiftly down the stairs again. Would Harry take part in the play? She had not spoken to him that day; indeed he had seemed to avoid her, leaving any group she joined. Perhaps he was angry with her for rejecting him last night. But was it not best that she should have little contact with him?

The Queen looked very happy that night at supper, straining eagerly towards tomorrow's reunion with her child. She sat beside the King as usual, her eyes alight with happiness. Harry Latimar sat next in line and he looked at Bess but gave her no salutation. She turned her back on his intent unsmiling glance and continued her meal, dreading the moment when it would come to an end and she must take part in the entertainment. All too soon Meg touched her arm and told her she intended visiting the chapel before retiring. She was disappointed when Bess did not offer to accompany her.

'I have promised to help the ladies with their play.'

'Oh?' Meg frowned. 'Let us hope it will be more decorous than those performed of late.'

'I hope so too,' murmured Bess, fearing it would not.

When she reached the makeshift theatre it was in turmoil. A curtain had been hung before the hastily erected stage and behind the painted backcloth the would-be actors struggled into their costumes with the help of their patient maids. Kate took her in charge. 'You help Lady Bess now, Philippa. I am ready.'

She was dazzling in her clinging low-cut dress, a coronet of red stones and brilliants on her cloud of auburn hair.

'The wages of sin should not be rubies, Kate dearest,' said a man in a hideously painted mask and the costume of a nightmare animal.

'If you will step out of your gown my lady,' Philippa
requested wearily. She had been on her feet since first
light, and although the ladies and gentlemen were en-
titled to enjoy themselves she wished only to get to her
bed.

Bess took off her dress and the maid began to slip the
white lawn over her head.

'No, no, it will be all wrong over your petticoat, Bess.
Take that off too.' Kate waited impatiently while Bess
contrived modestly to remove her undergarment while
pulling on the costume at the same time. 'There—fold
it here and here and fasten the chain so...'

Bess was relieved to note that as far as she could see
she was covered from neck to ankle in the fine soft stuff.
She had an uneasy feeling, however, that among the other
ladies' elaborate costumes hers made more of an attack
on the imagination simply because it was so modest.

'Where is her wreath of flowers?' demanded Kate. 'She
should have flowers in her hair.' The wreath could not
be found.

'Well...' Madge considered. 'If we loose her hair it
will have the right effect.' She took the pins out and the
mass of silvery hair tumbled down.

'I look ready for my bed,' protested Bess.

'I was thinking the very same,' said a man in gold
tissue with horns upon his head.

Kate and Madge giggled but Bess turned away. She
did not like any of this. She remembered what Harry
had said about choosing one's friends carefully and was
dismally aware that if Madge and Kate had lived in her
village they would have been in danger of being whipped
through the streets for harlotry. However, it was too late
to demur now. A stool covered in silver cloth was placed
in the middle of the stage and she was helped on to it
with final instructions from Kate to 'look as cold as ice'.
She was cold enough in truth with fright as the curtains
were pulled back and for a moment she was alone on
the stage looking out over the audience. A ripple of an-

ticipation travelled through the onlookers. Then Will Brereton as narrator introduced her as Virtue and invited them to witness the cruel temptations which would plague her. The play began. After she had overcome her first terror Bess could listen to the lines and appreciate them. It was a clever piece, witty and amusing despite being shamelessly bawdy. She could almost have enjoyed being a part of it had she not, as soon as the curtains opened, seen Harry Latimar seated directly before her, his arms folded, an inscrutable expression on his face. She wondered what was on his mind as he watched the play unfold. He could at least testify that she had the right to be cast as Virtue, she thought wryly.

The seats in the theatre were full; it was evidently an amusement that the court enjoyed. The King was not present but Anne and her brother were there. Anne loved such entertainment and frequently took part herself, and tonight she was prepared to enjoy herself. Bess heard her distinctive laughter above the other merriment.

The man in gold appeared, laid an open chest upon the floor and, seizing a handful of gold coins, held them up to her while he begged her for her favour. Bess looked suitably unaffected and he took his treasure and left. Next came Lust, the man dressed in animal skins, his face even more horrific in the sole flickering lamp. He had Kate in tow as an example of what could happen to a maiden who should succumb to his heady emotion and even Bess could hardly keep from laughing as Lady Fallen from Grace acted out her part. Kate was a born actress, loving the appreciation of the audience and being the centre of attention. She left the stage reluctantly to rousing cheers and Lust lurched around Bess so enthusiastically that she was almost toppled as she shrank from his clutching hands. He was banished at last and Bess righted herself. She looked over the edge of the dais at Harry. He still sat with his arms folded, surveying her gravely. He had been joined by Tom Spalding and Bess shuddered inwardly as Tom leaned forward in his seat and did not remove his eyes from her even while the other actors played out their roles around her.

In the last act Love came softly on to the stage. Was it just chance, wondered Bess, that he wore a floor-length swirling grey cloak and silver mask? He spoke gently to her, coaxingly, in a vibrant voice she did not recognise, of the scent of night flowers under the moon, of a man and a woman meant for each other, of the ecstatic union of two lovers. He cast an almost magical spell and involuntarily Bess looked down at him and the audience chuckled knowingly. Love reached up at last and lifted her from her perch and left the stage carrying her aloft, exposing a good deal of Virtue's pretty legs as he did so. The curtains closed and the audience applauded and shouted. Love deposited her upon her feet.

'Well done, Bess, you were excellent. It was the greatest success, I believe,' Madge congratulated her.

'I was not expecting to be swept away in that manner,' said Bess, adjusting the skirts of her draperies.

'Love is famous for taking us unawares,' laughed Kate.

The man in the grey cloak removed his mask, becoming just another passably attractive young man.

Politely refusing a warm invitation to join the players for a late supper, Bess re-dressed and left the theatre.

Outside her chamber the wind howled around the windows and flung a handful of raindrops against the tiny panes. The fire was barely alive and, shivering, she added an apple log and warmed her hands before seeking her warm bed.

CHAPTER THREE

BESS was awake early the following morning but Meg
was already about in the adjoining room before she had
washed and dressed her hair. She greeted Bess distractedly. 'Good morning, cousin. I trust you slept well.
Come and give me your opinion of this.'

In her hand she held a little cap of stiffened lace sewn
with a piping of cream silk and studded with pearls.

'It is beautiful, Meg.' Bess turned the lovely piece of
work in her hands.

'It is for the Princess. Madam commissioned it,
sending a woman to Hatfield to take measurements from
Elizabeth and choosing the pattern and matching the
pearls herself. I hope it will please the babe.'

'It would please any child,' Bess assured her, remembering that when she had once been given a length of
pink ribbon it had delighted her for days. This costly bit
of frippery would have transported her.

'Mmm. Well, do you carry it to madam for me. I must
look over the Princess's wardrobe once again.'

She replaced the cap in its cocoon of fine tissue and
put it into Bess's hands.

The Queen was in conversation with her brother when
Bess came hesitantly into the room. 'I tell you 'tis not
to be borne, George—each day she pushes me further
from Henry's affections——' She looked up and saw
Bess. 'Lady Bess—what have you there?'

Bess guessed that Anne spoke of Jane Seymour and
she put the little cap into the outstretched hands with
an expression of mute sympathy. 'It is the gift you ordered for your daughter, madam.' Bess dropped a neat
curtsy.

'Oh, let me see... Oh, yes, it is quite perfect. Will it not look adorable on Elizabeth, George?'

George agreed it would look very well on his niece. His narrow black eyes between luxuriant lashes roved speculatively over Bess. 'Your performance last evening was enchanting, lady,' he said. 'We gentlemen were quite agog.'

Bess flushed. His tone was polite but his eyes the reverse.

'Do not tease little Bess, brother,' Anne admonished him. 'She is not one of your doxies. I have already a great affection for her.'

'As do we all,' said George. 'The more we see of her, the more we care for her.'

Bess blushed a fierier red, remembering the manner in which the play had ended.

When George had left them Anne said 'Do you have pressing duties, Bess, or can you spend the morning with me?'

'I am at your disposal of course, madam,' Bess replied immediately.

'It will seem a long day for me, anxious as I am to see my sweet daughter.' Anne laid down the cap and began to pace restlessly to and fro. In her violet bedgown her pregnancy was finally apparent. 'And 'tis the most inclement weather for a child to travel.'

Rain coursed down the leaded windows and bounced off the sills. There was a light tap on the door and Harry Latimar came in. He bowed to Anne and cast an enigmatic glance at Bess.

'I have come to take Urian for his constitutional, madam.'

The huge black dog uncoiled himself from under a couch and padded towards him.

'Oh, 'tis a poor day for walking,' Anne said.

'He grows fat and lazy, madam. I think he would do better in the stables with his peers.'

'Do not chide me, Harry; I like to keep him here. I have need of all my friends around me just now.'

'You cannot make a lap dog of a hunting hound,' said Harry, running his hand across the dog's muzzle and receiving a swift caress from the long pink tongue.

Anne sighed. 'You're right, my lord.' She looked up into his dark eyes and Bess felt a stab of jealousy.

Latimar looked his Queen over with affectionate eyes. 'You are low in spirits on this dismal day, but I believe before long you will be happier.'

'Yes, indeed.' Anne moved away and sat down at her virginals. She pressed a key and listened to the note resounding in the air. Harry leaned over her and turned the pages on the music stand. Bess watched them. They were less like Queen and subject and more like—what? Anne was quick-tempered and always conscious of her hard-won position; she could be devastatingly cruel to the men she thought over-familiar. But Harry was more than equal to her, for he seemed always to regard her as a woman, to be respected, of course, but not to be ruled by. Bess wondered if she held the fascination for him she did for his friends.

Anne looked over at her. 'Do you know this, Lady Bess? I believe it comes from the West Country.'

She began to play, the ivory keys several shades darker than her white fingers. Bess went and stood by her. She knew the air very well, for it was an old Cornish harvest song. She hummed, then sang, her throat thickening, for it reminded her so acutely of home. After a moment her sweet untrained voice became less husky and she carried the jaunty melody perfectly to its conclusion.

Anne clapped her hands. 'That was splendid—you have a most pleasing voice. Has she not, Harry?'

'As you say, madam. Now have I your leave to take that poor brute out for some fresh air?'

'Of course.' Anne stared after the two shapely animals as they left the room. 'We are dismissed, I fear, in favour of more manly pursuits,' she said with a short laugh.

'Sir Harry is your loyal servant, I am sure,' Bess said gravely.

Anne laughed again. 'He is my husband's loyal servant and never lets me forget it.' She looked at the silver face of her clock for the hundredth time. 'Now if you will send in my ladies I will dress. It is almost time. You have been most amiable in assisting the minutes to fly.'

Bess curtsied and left the room. When she had found Anne's women she put on her cloak and went down to the ground floor and out into the gloomy day. For an hour or more she walked without thinking of anything at all under the dripping trees.

As she was returning, driven in by the driving rain, she witnessed the arrival of England's tiny heir. Elizabeth Tudor was lifted carefully out of her velvet-padded carriage and carried into the palace half asleep, her little booted feet dangling. Bess glimpsed a triangle of white face crowned by a blaze of red hair before she was hurried up to her anxious mother.

Two days later, after she and Meg had breakfasted, a page brought word that Lady Bess might visit the Princess.

'It seems she has a great liking for you, coz,' Meg said, pleased, 'for Elizabeth is her most precious concern. Go now and don't keep little madam waiting.'

Bess sought out the royal nursery. She was glad of the diversion; Harry continued to avoid her in the most unobvious manner but often, turning suddenly, she would find his dark eyes on her with a reflective expression in their brilliant depths. He did not invite her to join him in the dance or at the games the young courtiers played; she felt his withdrawal and suffered. The weather had at last relented and the strong winds and storms abated; today a bright morning sun lit the stone corridors.

Little Elizabeth's wails of rage could be heard as she entered the richly appointed rooms. The nurse turned a harassed face as Bess came in.

'She will not be dressed, my lady, until her father visits and he is out riding this day and will not return until dusk. Madam is feeling unwell and I am at my wits' end.'

Bess stepped forward and curtsied to the little figure whose feet were planted in a stance ridiculously like her father's.

'Is it not delightful that you and I should bear the same name?' she said gaily. 'I am indeed honoured, Your Highness.'

Elizabeth stopped screaming and studied the face bending over her. Liking what she saw, she reached out and clutched a fistful of the shining hair. 'Your hair is like pieces of silver, lady. But red hair is better.'

'Oh, yes, Your Highness. Red is my favourite colour. The colour of wild strawberries and sunsets in summer and ...' she looked at the dress in the nurse's hands '... that charming gown you will soon look so beautiful in this day.'

The Princess's eyes crinkled in her father's swift smile; she knew she was being cajoled but the flattery was irresistible. She allowed the nurse to dress her in the red velvet dress, its full skirt parted to reveal a kirtle of cream silk embroidered in gold. It was an exact replica of one that Bess had seen among the Queen's gowns. White stockings and black kid slippers completed the outfit and she was ready to begin her day.

She ate her breakfast of bread and milk with her eyes on her new acquaintance. She was a fascinating child, this royal princess, a curious combination of her parents, her father's looks dominant. Not altogether ideal for a girl, mused Bess, but the grace and charm of her mother were evident too. At little more than two years old, she was extraordinarily forward in speech and tall for her age. The Princess Royal cast aside her breakfast bowl.

'The Lady Bess shall now take me walking in the gardens,' she announced grandly.

So Bess must rush to her rooms and collect her cloak to please the small tyrant.

Out in the brisk air the Princess's cheeks turned vivid red, her small blue eyes sparkled as she skipped along the formal gardens, the beds bordered with low hedges of yew, rosemary and lavender. Some of the yew trees were tortured into shapes of birds and animals which Bess disliked but still found fascinating. Little Elizabeth was surprisingly knowledgeable about the gardens; she pointed out with pride the strange plants and shrubs transported at great cost from France and Italy and Spain.

'My father is concerned with many important affairs, but even a plant has his close attention,' she told Bess with satisfaction.

She took Bess's hand and swung on it, a baby once more. Bess held laughingly on to the sturdy hand as they progressed.

'Oh, look, Your Highness, this milder weather has brought forth early flowers.'

They bent together and Elizabeth put out a hand and clutched at the little group of snowdrops, their fragile white heads drooping as if they knew they had come too soon. The ornate over-large gold bangle she wore on her wrist slipped off and fell with a tinkle on to the path. Bess retrieved it.

'Keep it for me, Lady Bess,' Elizabeth said carelessly. She turned as a group of courtiers came in sight. Bess saw that Harry Latimar was among them. Seeing their Princess, the gentlemen stopped and saluted her. She acknowledged them with regal dignity and, taking her Uncle George's arm, moved off with the gay party. Harry and Bess looked after them, Bess uncertain whether to follow, reluctant to leave the man beside her. But the child did not look back and appeared to have forgotten her.

'When I close my eyes to sleep I see nothing but your face. Whoever speaks to me, I hear only your voice,' he said abruptly, his eyes still following his comrades.

She looked up at his profile, seeing the shapely nose, the stubborn chin, the curve of thick lashes on his cheek. He turned to her.

'Bess,' he said as though in anger, 'you have enchanted me. I can think of nothing but you. It is most . . . inconvenient.'

After three days of being ignored by him, his words set her alight. Her musical laugh rang out. 'Oh, Harry, are you trying to say you have fallen in love with me? "Inconvenient"? 'Tis a strange word to describe love——'

'Oh . . . love. I know nothing of love. This is more like a malady—a sickness.'

'Love is often so described by the poets, I believe,' she said demurely.

'Are you really so innocent, Bess?' he demanded suddenly.

She said uncertainly, 'I don't understand you, sir. I thought you spoke of love——'

'Why do you keep repeating that word? I speak of quite a different emotion. I would ask you to be my mistress,' he finished quietly.

'Your mistress?'

'Why, yes, is it so unexpected? Surely not?'

She looked at him. The sun struck his hair, accentuating the reddish tint, played over the jewels about his throat and on his hands.

'What did you expect, Bess?'

She said slowly, 'Some small measure of respect, perhaps. I believe I made my feelings clear on the night of the musicale. The night you attempted to force yourself upon me——'

'Your words made it clear but your response did not. And I have never forced myself on any woman.'

In the trees above a bird began to sing, an endless musical note in the clear air. When she did not reply he said, 'I am always confused in conversation with you, Bess. You play the innocent today but it scarcely can be genuine after your display on the night of the play.'

'Display? I thought it most clever and was pleased to take part. I am sorry you did not find it enjoyable.'

'No man could help but find the sight of you half clothed enjoyable.'

She drew back outraged. ''Twas merely appropriate costume for my role. There were other ladies less modestly attired.'

'I saw no other ladies.'

Their eyes clashed. Then he said gently, 'Bess, an arrangement such as this is quite usual, I assure you——'

'Usual for the half-dressed painted ladies of this place but not for Robert de Cheyne's daughter,' she returned furiously.

He looked at her, and from within him an unidentifiable emotion stirred. He said coldly, 'Then there is nothing for us, lady.'

She fixed her clear eyes on his face. 'I see that now. You follow each lecture with an attempt to molest me, it seems. You pretend concern for me, Sir Harry, with your stern criticism of my friends and my behaviour, but wish merely to take advantage of our friendship to make this insulting proposal.'

'There is no insult involved. I offer you my protection in return for your favour, that is all. And should you continue to conduct yourself in a certain manner it will be the first of many proposals.'

Immediately the words were spoken he regretted them. It was not in his careless easygoing nature to taunt a less able opponent and now, as he saw the tears spring to her eyes, he was instantly repentant. He put an arm about her shoulders. She shook it off and straightened her back.

'Then this will be the first of many times I give this answer: whoever my friends, whatever my behaviour, the only proposal I will ever consider will be an honourable one.'

He considered her silently a moment. 'You speak of marriage, then?'

She flushed but said steadily 'I do. There will never be anything else between me or any man. And I will not be Harry Latimar's little country-maid mistress hiding in dark corners, creeping into vacant beds——'

'Then there will indeed be nothing between us. For I am already betrothed,' he said flatly.

The blackbird had ceased his triumphant song. A cloud passed over the sun and a fitful wind began to blow up from the river.

'You are to marry? Who? Is this lady at court?'

'No, Bess, she is not at court. Indeed, she is still in the schoolroom. It is the Lady Katharine Bonney. She is but nine years old.'

'You are betrothed to a child of nine?'

'You don't understand these matters,' he said, at last stung by her tone. 'It is arranged between her father and mine... and the King. Henry has interested himself in me——' He stopped, unsure why he felt the need to defend himself.

'I see.' She turned away, twisting the turquoise ring in a nervous gesture. 'No doubt you think me a fool.'

'I could never think that.' He was watching her. Watching the way the wind lifted her hair from the pulse beating in her temple. What was it about her that had haunted him in the last few days and nights? Whatever it was, it seemed he could not possess it. He was angry with himself, and with her for provoking him to declare himself only to be so summarily rejected. He was not accustomed to losing this kind of skirmish.

She turned abruptly and walked quickly down the path away from him, not noticing that the sky had darkened and a fine rain was falling. After a while she felt the

insistent drops and stopped. Glancing back, she saw that
the palace was a long way off. To her right the river
tossed angrily in the gathering storm, and a flash of
lightning lit the sky, followed by a roll of thunder.

She looked desperately through the curtain of rain and,
seeing a stone summer-house built by Henry so that he
could enjoy the river view without risking the elements,
she hurried towards it. Pushing open the door, she
brushed aside the cobwebs and saw that she was not the
only refugee to seek shelter. The figure turned and removed his hat.

'I beg your pardon, sir, if I disturb you,' she said.

'Not at all, mistress. Richard Woodville at your
service. Is it not a wild day?'

Again a streak of lightning tore at the sky and above
the answering thunder she told him her name.

Richard Woodville drew a wooden chair from the wall
and flicked at the dust with his riding gloves. 'Please be
seated.' As she sat down she saw that her host was very
young, probably not much older than herself, and had
an unfashionably sunburnt face beneath thick honey-
coloured hair, unevenly cut. He was plainly dressed in
a dark brown jerkin and doublet with a soft hat and
scarred leather boots. He was as different from the
gentlemen of the court as was a sparrow from a darting
dragonfly.

'You are not with the court?' she asked him, loosening
her cloak and brushing raindrops from her face and hair.
His eyes on the bright strands escaping from her hood,
he said, 'No indeed, I am just come from Cornwall with
a gift from my father to the King.'

'I too am from the west,' she said, pleased to discover
a comrade.

He smiled, revealing white teeth. They talked easily
together for a while. He told her that the King had heard
of a splendid strain of horses bred by his father, a country
squire, and had expressed a desire to own one. There
being no one who cared to undertake the journey at such
a hazardous time of year, he had volunteered.

'I wanted to see the King—and a royal palace—for myself,' he said shyly. 'But since I came here I have been somewhat lost. There is again the question of clothes. They do dress most fine here.'

Bess smiled sympathetically. 'I understand; if it were not for my cousin who is most generous I would be in similar case.'

She noticed however that his clothes, although not grand, were of the best quality and immaculately cut.

They talked on, two young people with a home in common, and outside the clouds chased each other across the river and a pallid sun came out. Bess stood reluctantly. 'I fear we shall be late for the midday meal.' She was glad of this encounter; it had enabled her to recover a little from her distress.

'I will escort you back to the palace,' Richard said, opening the door and letting in the damp air. They walked slowly back to the palace and at the entrance to the main hall separated, with a smile. Bess watched him make his way through the crowd, his diffident manner and dull brown costume setting him apart.

She found her place and apologised to Meg for being late. Margaret examined her rain-soaked cousin. 'I declare you are always damp, Bess,' she said, amused.

Bess told her about her meeting with Richard Woodville and pointed down the hall at him. Meg leaned forward slightly and looked curiously at him. 'Woodville? I think I have heard mention of that name somewhere. His family I believe, although not noble, are very wealthy.'

Privately she mused that it might well be a good thing if Bess were to form an attachment with a well-to-do young man from an estate near her father's home. One who would not expect a dowry as someone from a grander family would. Under her careful supervision, of course. She had grown very fond of Bess in the short time they had been together but, really, the girl seemed to grow prettier by the hour. Her countrified ways had fallen away like the husk of a nut and her lovely face and charming manners drew the attention of the young men like a magnet. Two ladies had remarked to her that morning that Bess seemed a little wild. It was lucky for her that no one had thought to inform Meg of the *risqué* nature of the play, but she did know that Bess's disappearance with Harry Latimar on the night of the masque and the subsequent scene in the gaming-room had greatly annoyed a number of ladies and there was jealousy also over the Princess's insisting Bess accompany her on her morning walk. Such things were very petty, but court life could be made desperately miserable for any girl who offended the high-born ladies with whom most of her time would be spent. The fact that many of them behaved with even less restraint was irrelevant—Bess was as yet an outsider.

Meg sighed, conscious of the hot glances straying towards her cousin who, unaware of this attention, ate her meal, her thoughts occupied with what had passed between herself and Harry. Her cheeks burned as she went over the scene in her mind. What had possessed her to let him know she believed he thought of marriage in connection with her? What an unsophisticated little fool he must think her now. But in country areas such a thing would not be unusual; men and women made up their minds about these matters quickly. There was little time to waste on lengthy courtships when every moment was devoted to working and making a living.

Almost she wished she had never come to court, never laid eyes upon him. Now every man she met would seem insignificant and shadowy beside him. Raising her eyes, she caught Richard Woodville's intent gaze on her and half smiled. He nodded gravely and she found it oddly comforting.

The long meal, with its many courses, dragged on. She leaned her chin on one hand and looked about her. The Queen was absent in the nurseries with her daughter; the King's place too was empty. Without knowing why she did so she glanced towards the Lady Jane Seymour's chair; she was not there. The air thickened as the afternoon wore on, the rushes covering the floor giving off their sweet scent as servants trod back and forth from the kitchen area, screened by heavy oak, bearing laden platters of food which were half cold by the time they reached their destination. The younger members of the court, their master and mistress absent, were noisier than usual. Only Harry Latimar sat quiet and unsmiling, his eyes on the silver goblet of wine he turned thoughtfully in his hands. She wondered what his thoughts were. She had touched him—of that she was sure; how much or how deeply she could not say. He was accustomed to getting what or whom he wanted, obviously. That was evident in his arrogant manner. But beneath that assured charm Bess felt a quality both sensitive and delicate. A quality which she identified with.

Around her people yawned behind their hands, their eyelids drooping after too much heavy food and strong wine. At last the plates of sweetmeats and bowls of apples and nuts which signified the end of the meal were carried in. Relieved, Bess nibbled a honey cake baked hard and studded with gilded nuts. She studied the pretty confection, imagining the faces of the village children at home if presented with such a treat. She looked at the flushed and sweating faces at the table. They eat too much, they have too much, she thought resentfully. Why, the silver bowls on which the rosy winter-stored apples were heaped would keep the families at home for years. She smiled wryly to herself at her foolish notions and, glancing up, found Harry's brooding eyes on her. He raised his wine goblet in an ironic salute and at this safe distance she could look all she wanted at him over the heads of the crowd. She was angry and insulted but...the most desirable man at court wanted her and despite her spirited refusal she was flattered.

Meg said, 'Come, Bess, we will return to our chamber now.'

Passing the nursery, she remembered the Princess's little bangle and Meg left her as she knocked timidly on the heavy doors. A nurse admitted her with a finger to her lips. 'Her little Highness is sleeping.'

The Queen came through the draped curtains of the bedchamber. 'Come in, Bess.'

Bess explained about the bracelet and laid the trinket in Anne's outstretched hand.

'Thank you. Now come and see her.'

Together they went to look at the little girl lying asleep, one plump hand clutching a fiery strand of hair. 'Is she not sweet?' Anne asked fondly, drawing up the coverlet under her daughter's rounded chin.

'Very, Your Majesty.' Bess gently touched the thick red hair.

As she did so the room darkened and Bess knew the familiar swirling of her senses. The sleeping child vanished and in her place grew a ball of light in which Bess saw a woman. Tall, richly dressed in unfamiliar clothes, the fabulous material encrusted with gemstones, a curious standing lace collar starched and edged with gold thread framing her face. On her curled and jewelled head was set a heavy crown. All these things Bess noted, but most of all she saw the woman's eyes. Immense dignity showed in their bright depths and the habit of command; sadness too. But, above all, Bess felt, a great happiness in fulfilling a destiny——

'Bess! What do you see?'

'I, madam? Why…nothing. Forgive me; my thoughts were elsewhere.'

Anne let fall the coverlet and left the bed. She crossed the room and turned and surveyed the disconcerted girl. 'You're a strange child,' she said, her dark eyes thoughtful. 'I think perhaps you see things the rest of us do not.'

'No, madam, I see…nothing.' Bess pressed her hands together, her heart beating wildly, remembering her mother's anxious words.

Anne was silent a moment, then, 'I have been called a witch,' she said, fingering the wide band of velvet at her throat. ''Tis all foolishness, dreamed up by my enemies, of course. I am no witch. But I know there are those who have a—power. If you have that power it could only be good. No one could look at you and think otherwise.'

'I...thank you, madam. But I have only the power of daydreaming when I should not.' She stumbled a little over the words.

'Very well.' The Queen shrugged her shoulders with one of her unmistakably French gestures. 'You may go.'

Bess left the nursery. She knew she had disappointed the woman she was growing to admire. She would have liked to tell her that her beloved daughter would be a great Queen some day. But she dared not admit to another soul that she could see what others could not. There was mortal danger in these times for anyone who claimed to possess such a gift. It did not seem strange to her, for she had grown up possessing it. For as long as she could remember, every now and again, usually with the touch of another person, she saw a small piece of their future and, whether it be something pleasant or not, it had always been proved true.

As children did she had assumed when very young that everyone had this sight, and it was not until she was around four years old and had been listening to her mother gossiping with one of the neighbouring farmers' wives about her hopes for her daughter to marry a certain boy that she had realised they did not. When the woman had gone, Joan de Cheyne had been idly speculating on whether there would be a June wedding, when Bess had announced confidently that the girl was not going to marry her childhood friend in June or any other time. She would be married when snow lay on the ground and her new husband would work with fire and horses. She had insisted that she had 'seen' it but her mother had laughed and given her a stern lecture on the difference between making up stories and telling downright lies. Two weeks later a wealthy man, with a flourishing blacksmith's business, had fallen in love with the girl in question and the following snowy February had seen the grandest wedding in those parts for a long time. Then Joan had had a long talk with her little daughter and had turned white at what was revealed. Bess undoubtedly had 'the sight' as country people called it. She recounted to her mother without guile a dozen or more instances of this power, convincing Joan that the only way she could have known such details of their neighbours' lives was if she had indeed 'seen' them, and looking into her child's innocent face Joan felt a certain awe, along with terror that anyone else should know and put the usual interpretation on such a gift. Such a gift belonged only to long-dead saints; anyone in ordinary life who possessed it could only have had it bestowed upon them by the Devil himself.

But Joan was a woman of sound common sense; she knew that not everything in life could be explained—no one could believe in any religion and think that. You had to have a little faith, and she knew that Bess was wholesome and no more in league with devils than she was. On the other hand she had no intention of allowing witch-hunting fingers to be pointed at her child, so she impressed upon the little girl that this was something to be kept secret. A wonderful gift maybe, but secret, secret. She had reinforced this year by year and always hoped it would be something she would grow out of, like the sore throats she suffered during the cold winter months.

She could guess from where Bess had inherited her strange gift. Not from her mother's prosaic ancestors with their inability to see beyond the next sunrise, but from Robert de Cheyne's mother, Caitlin; she had been wild enough, it seemed, from what little her husband had told her.

Joan Beechwood had been fifteen when Robert de Cheyne had taken up residence on the bordering farm.

He had hired Joan's eldest brother Jonas to make some sense of his new career while he continued his convalescence. Jonas Beechwood could easily be spared from the family farm; there were six other sturdy boys with Joan in the middle, the only surviving girl. This was unusual in days when infant boys appeared to have a less tenacious hold on life than their sisters, but Joan had grown up quite content to be the only girl in the noisy male-dominated household.

When Jonas had become established and had brought home the news that the knight farmer was a true gentleman, Joan had been sent by her mother with neighbourly offerings of meat broth and custard to the invalid, and on seeing Robert de Cheyne propped up on a makeshift bed in the kitchen of the neglected farmhouse had been dazzled by his beauty and his complete unlikeness to her brothers. He was the very opposite of her hard-working, uncouth family, and something unexpected in her unromantic nature had reached out to grasp this glamour for herself. She had nursed him tenderly all through that summer while he had treated her with vague courtesy and never for a moment indicated he might consider her as a future wife.

With the coming of autumn she had resolved that she must make the first move. Even now, eighteen years later, the glow of a late summer sunset and the sound of dead leaves rustling underfoot would take her back to the day she had brought this about. He had been gaining back his strength slowly, painfully, a little more each passing week, and had in the last few days been able to walk with difficulty about the yard. He would never be straight and quick-moving again—the fractured bones and damaged muscles had knitted badly—but he limped with an odd grace despite this. As he came across the uneven ground towards her with the sun behind his fair head Joan had been overtaken by such a longing to belong to him that instead of standing aside to allow him to pass through the narrow doorway into the kitchen she had reached out and drawn him into an embrace unmis-takably explicit to such a sophisticated man. The result of the next magical hour had not been pregnancy for Joan, and there had been no necessity for him to ask her to marry him. But he had asked, and made her feel that she honoured him with her acceptance.

He was a younger son; his brother had inherited all his father's estates and since died leaving it to his only son; his sister had disowned him because of his strange behaviour and his only portion had been title to the land he now farmed. He was no great catch, he had told her frankly. Especially for a girl pretty enough to marry well even without the marriage settlement her father had let it be known would go with her. She had scarcely taken in any of what he said. What did she care for money? She was young and strong and a clever manager. And she would have the man she wanted; they would be suc-cessful. Which they were, in a very small way. And if he sometimes thought about the elegant soft-skinned scented ladies he might have married and she sometimes felt she had caged a unicorn when a carthorse would have suited better, neither said any such thing or re-gretted their choice.

But any unexplained element in Bess's personality Joan instantly attributed to her husband's forebears; after all, Beechwoods could be traced back over hundreds of years and had always been good fellows, modest hardworking women, farming the land with never so much as a petty crime laid at their doors. The de Cheynes were surely a different matter. Robert himself was different. One of the intimate possessions he had brought with him was a small painted miniature of his mother in an oval silver locket, and Joan often looked at the pictured face of Caitlin de Cheyne with mixed feelings. Certainly the lovely face was beautiful and kind, but within the sea-green eyes the artist had captured an inner quality of waking dreams and, put together with the occasional tales Robert told of his mother, Joan thought that had she been an old and ugly woman living in this remote area she would have been feared and shunned, or worse. Her own mother still remembered two old crones who had been swum for witches twenty years ago. She was consequently vigilant about Bess in her early years.

So Bess had kept it to herself. Sometimes in the early days it had been very hard; surely the knowledge that something good was about to happen would be pleasant to look forward to? Of course if it was something distressing then it was obviously better not to know. One thing was certain—what she saw came about as surely as day followed night. When she helped her cousin Sally sew clothes for her expected baby she could have told her she needed two of everything, but had pretended to be as surprised as everyone else when the twin boys were delivered. And when John Hobday put a fork through his foot digging onions she could have told Peg Hobday that the ointment sent hastily by Joan was useless and she should summon her sons to say farewell to their father.

Soon the habit of saying nothing and showing no more than momentary vagueness at what she saw had become very strong, and after a while she was able to experience these strange visions with a fatalistic view that what she saw she could not change and must therefore disregard it. Often she would wonder why she was singled out for this unique power and often she resented it, but on the whole she could accept it as as much a part of her as her unusual silver hair. In the past few years if her mother had fearfully referred to it Bess had, without actually lying, led her to think that it was practically a thing of the past. And curiously she never saw anything about her own life—that particular book was closed to her inner eyes.

The next few weeks were very gay at Greenwich; the Queen had thrown herself into a campaign to amuse and divert her husband and her infectious charm lit up the court. A day must not go by without some interesting activity or entertainment planned for him. Despite her simple upbringing, governed very much by the fact that rising with the sun, working hard all day and knowing you had to do it all again the next day meant that you slept thankfully as soon as it was dark, Bess discovered that here she could dance all evening and still have the energy to play all the next day after very little rest. There were so many varied things to play at; she learned archery, and the rules of the games she was spectator at such as tennis and wrestling. She was soon dancing the latest figures with elegant grace and dabbling again in the endless gambling the Tudor court so enjoyed. Backgammon, dicing and shovelboard whiled away the daylight hours if rain fell, and often continued on through the night until dawn. She showed a talent for these games: she had a quick mind and a cool head and there was not a woman, or a man for that matter, she could not best at these pursuits which combined skill as well as chance. Except for Harry Latimar. He was a league ahead of her and all others because he seemed prepared to stake everything he had on the roll of a dice, the flick of a card. It was this quality which kept him in turn fabulously rich or disastrously poor depending upon how the pendulum of luck swung for him.

If the weather was kind, and it was unusually so in the beginning of that year, then there were outdoor games and even fishing. Henry had stocked the lakes and ponds for the amusement of his court. And Bess became rather popular with both the men and women at Greenwich. The ladies soon found that she was no competition for them with their lovers and the gentlemen found that although she turned aside their advances she always managed to do it so charmingly that they had no need to feel spurned. She had a great many admirers, most of whom pursued her in a light-hearted but dedicated fashion. Only Tom Spalding proved a constant thorn in her flesh; he would not or could not accept that she had no liking for him and would attempt to behave in the most unseemly fashion whenever he caught her alone. She dealt with this by contriving never to be alone with him, or even near to him in a group, but she resented his attentions; there was something of the wild animal about him, thinly disguised beneath his ponderous manner, and she feared him.

George Boleyn was another she feared, but for different reasons. He was never physically a nuisance to her—he was too fastidious ever to put himself in a position to be refused by any woman—but she was frequently the target for his waspish tongue. He called her the little Devon duchess and enjoyed embarrassing her with his sarcastically outrageous conversation. A more experienced woman would have known that this attention masked an interest in her that he would not pursue. And the reason for this, a more sophisticated girl would have suspected, was the result of a restraining influence: Harry Latimar, still angry with himself and with her, yet kept a watchful eye upon her. But she fell into the habit of being with George and his friends and soon George found himself making a friend of Bess de Cheyne as did his sister the Queen. But Bess remained the same modest girl who had come so reluctantly to court and no amount of flattery could change her, although she flourished and grew more mature in this company.

Even Meg could find no fault with her conduct now, but she followed her private plans to make a match between Bess and Richard Woodville and brought them together as often as she could. She knew that although the young nobles might fuss over Bess and profess extremes of love their intentions did not include marriage: Richard Woodville was obviously the answer for a girl without money behind her. Richard could not, of course, penetrate the intimate circle around the royal favourites, but he managed to be near Bess when she was walking in the grounds or in the palace gardens. His feelings towards her became stronger every day and she felt she could have cared a good deal for him had not a slim silver figure always overshadowed him.

Harry Latimar kept his distance during these weeks; he never sought her company at the dancing, or spoke directly to her when they found themselves together. Bess's newly opened eyes noted that he was often with a new lady at court. Thomasina Beauchamp had recently come from France and caused a stir even in this glamorous company. Her clothes, her jewels were of the finest quality and her long green eyes almost immediately alighted on the most attractive man in the assembly. She had an elderly husband tucked away in Kent somewhere but this did not impede her progress and Bess, more worldly now, soon saw all the signs of a grand affair. It made her desperately unhappy to know that Harry and Thomasina were engaged in a passionate intrigue, but she would not let it show. She danced more spiritedly, laughed more joyously.

As the month continued fair Bess began to feel restless. Her nature, although appreciating the luxury and colourful pageant of life at Henry and Anne's court, demanded some constructive occupation. And there was little to do but enjoy herself. The extraordinarily mild weather put everyone in a holiday mood.

The King and Queen appeared as any other married couple, seemingly happy to amuse their little daughter, a little more content in each other's company. Henry took the greatest delight in Elizabeth; he was seldom seen without her in his arms, or by his side on these sweet sunlit days. Whatever his differences with Anne, he appeared to show her every consideration as her condition became more obvious in her thickening waist, and in her face, in which the sharp planes had been most attractively softened. She was blossoming a little more each day and was unusually tranquil, her unpredictable temper smoothed away by motherhood. Bess held a curious attraction for her, more so than the glittering ladies she

normally spent time with. This was of great satisfaction
to Meg, who thought her gentle cousin's presence a good
influence on her quicksilver mistress.

Bess noticed with relief that Jane Seymour's sly personality was absent from Greenwich and was glad for
Anne's sake, but she herself was increasingly nervous
and shying at shadows. She knew the reason for this:
Harry Latimar had apparently completely accepted her
passionate rejection of him and no longer felt the need
to avoid her but now treated her with a distinctly
brotherly affection. Perversely, this annoyed her, especially as she knew where he spent his nights and with
whom. While she knew this was the more practical, the
only sensible course for them, she resented his calm acceptance. At every gathering her eyes sought him, a day
when she didn't see him was wasted, and to herself she
no longer bothered to deny that she loved him.

Midway through the month Henry decided that they
should take advantage of the clement weather and spend
a whole day out of doors. A picnic was arranged. Bess
was amused by the ensuing excitement. At home she was
accustomed to her mother wrapping some food in a
napkin and sending her out into the fields or to the seashore on fine days to enjoy the modest fare. Here the
spoiled men and women behaved as though a great treat
were in store. To have a meal away from the great stuffy
hall was different and therefore exciting. The company
would ride out into the parkland, tether their mounts
and eat in the shelter of the great trees planted long ago
by another queen, whose love of the unconventional
would have made her smile on such free and easy behaviour. A small army of servants were dispatched in
the early morning with wagons of more food and wine
than could possibly be consumed.

Bess borrowed a green and tawny costume from Meg.
The custom for riding astride had lapsed now and each
lady must acquire the skill of riding side-saddle, and
naturally a suitable riding habit had been designed. Bess

surveyed herself in the glass and thought it became her
very well. The velvet jacket buttoned up to the neck over
a dull yellow skirt, less full than normal wear, and polished leather boots gave her a rakish air. The boots were
a little tight—Meg had enviably tiny feet—but she
thought she could bear the discomfort for a while for
the sake of fashion.

Meg placed a jaunty little hat, complete with curled
feather, on her cousin's head. 'There, you look just right
now, Bess.'

'Thank you, Meg. Oh, I wish you were to come with
us. Will your poor head not allow?'

Meg pressed her hand to her forehead. She suffered
from periodic agonising headaches which she bore
bravely. 'No, it is still banging and I feel a little sick.
But I shall do very well here. I shall lie down presently
and one of the maids shall rub my temples with a little
raw alcohol. I shall be recovered when you return. Do
you go and enjoy yourself.'

Bess took a last look in the mirror, kissed Meg and
ran down to the stable yard. Richard Woodville approached her tentatively. 'Lady Bess, I have taken it upon
myself to choose a mount for you.'

She smiled at him; he was too shy to meet her eyes
but the wind blowing through his thick hair and his gentle
hands on the horse's neck touched her.

'Thank you, Richard, that is most kind.'

'You have not ridden in this way before?' he asked
anxiously as she looked apprehensively at the unfamiliar
saddle.

'No, indeed.' At home she would simply have flung
one leg over the bare back of one of the farm horses
and jogged on her way, clinging to his mane. The grey
palfrey was laden with what appeared to be a small
leather chair, at its rear a rigid, shaped back, at the front
a wooden pommel.

'It is quite simple,' he assured her gravely. 'You merely sit in the saddle as though it were a chair and place one leg around the pommel...' He blushed.

A page obligingly brought a stool and Richard lifted her from it into the saddle. She arranged her skirts and straightened her hat, quite at ease. He put the reins into her gloved hands. 'I will follow close behind, Bess—you need not fear.'

She smiled again, looking down at him. The company were moving out now and she saw Harry and Thomasina, well matched on gleaming black horses, ride out together. She kicked gently on the satin hide with her heels and the little mare followed the others quite meekly. Bess discovered quickly that balance was the key to riding side-saddle and soon was able to take her mind off the new experience and take pleasure in the outing.

Nature was still convinced that it was winter and showed her bare brown trees, their branches etched against a radiant sky, her earth below as hard as iron. Only the soft sun-filled breeze tried to persuade the harsh landscape that early spring might be just around the corner. Kate Mortimer on a wild-eyed piebald rode alongside her for a while.

'Is this not a pleasant change, Lady Bess?'

They had not spoken since the night of the play as Kate had just made a prolonged visit to her family. Bess was glad to see her back at Greenwich. Last night had seen a lively exchange between Lady Kate and Thomasina Beauchamp and Bess had been privately satisfied to see the lady from France bested in the argument. Now she agreed that it was indeed pleasant to ride out in the countryside.

Kate glanced at her enviously; the morning light full on her face, so damaging to her own attractions, showed up the perfect skin luminous around Bess's fine eyes, the glint on the silvery hair, already escaping from the little hat.

'What do you put upon your face Bess—some country remedy perhaps?'

'On my face? Why, nothing, Kate. Save water, of course.'

Kate sighed. It should have been easy to be jealous and spiteful towards Bess de Cheyne but somehow one couldn't be. She was so unassuming, so eager to please, and her dignity was not to do with her startling good looks but sprang from an inner pride.

'I have heard my mother say that good fresh vegetables and dairy food are good for the complexion,' said Bess helpfully. 'And fresh air too.'

'Indeed?' Kate resolved to pay more attention to her diet, and maybe take a turn around the palace grounds more often. Her horse tossed its head impatiently, resenting the slow pace of the palfrey.

'Ride on, Kate.' Bess smiled. 'I am but a beginner and must make my way carefully.'

She watched Kate canter ahead to join the royal party, the nucleus of which was the King. Anne had not wished to jeopardise her condition so had stayed in the palace, but the Princess Elizabeth sat before her father, encircled by his arms, bouncing in the saddle and trying to take the reins in her small hands.

'May I ride awhile with you Lady Bess?' Richard Woodville brought his mount up alongside her.

'Of course,' Bess said. Looking ahead, she saw that Harry on his unruly black stallion was as elegant on its back as on the dance-floor. In a short time he and others surrounding Henry gained a copse of trees and disappeared from sight. She admired Richard's horse, out of his father's famous stable—as was the mount Henry rode that day—and commented on its delicate strength, but after that they fell silent. Richard had no talent for small talk and in any case he asked nothing more than to be by her side, to be able to look at her, smell the scent of her. Unlike Harry Latimar, he was not puzzled by her attraction for him, for she symbolised all he had ever dreamed of in a woman: she was beautiful, soft-spoken and gentle. And she seemed to look upon him kindly. Meg had spoken to him about her, albeit obliquely, and he felt confident that their attachment was favoured by the one relative Bess had at court. But a girl like Bess could not be hurried, must not be frightened away by a too eager suitor. If he had been given to analysing his feelings, which he was not, he would have known that it was her air of being untouched by the way he obviously felt about her that attracted him most.

For a year now his mother had tactfully brought to his attention a number of girls she thought suitable to wed her son. She had invited them to lunch and tea and they had arrived knowing they were on approval and anxious to do their best to ensnare the young Woodville heir. He had felt quite hunted for some time now.

His lack of enthusiasm for any of them had not worried his mother; sooner or later one of the pretty fresh-faced daughters of the Woodvilles' wealthy landowning acquaintances would strike the right note; meanwhile she was content with his bachelor state. She had not realised that she had produced a strong desire in him to choose his own wife.

Presently they came to the area designated for the picnic ground. A score or so of servants scurried here and there, serving ale and wine, carving the vast succulent joints of meat and cutting pies and cakes and tarts into generous slices. The ladies and gentlemen stood about, their horses' reins looped over their arms, a goblet of wine in one hand, a pastry patty of goose or beef in the other.

Bess accepted some wine and Richard went to get her some food. She turned smiling eyes on Elizabeth, who, having been set down, darted about, forgetting her royalty as she filled her hands with sweetmeats. Anne's black hound, who had stubbornly followed Harry out of the stables, put up a questing nose to the gingerbread she held. Although the dog reached her shoulders and was four times her weight, she thrust him impatiently aside without fear.

What a Queen she will make, mused Bess.

'You are thoughtful, Bess.' Harry was at her side. She started guiltily. 'What?' he asked, observing this. 'Were your thoughts not suitable for me to hear?'

He was happy today, without a care, his eyes a darker blue than the sky and his manner towards her teasing and friendly.

'My thoughts were quite idle, my lord. Which proves I am learning the ways of court.'

He laughed delightedly. 'Your words are prickly, Bess, and that is strange as your appearance makes one think only of softness.' He touched the smooth velvet of her sleeve. She took a half-step away from him, seeing Richard returning with a plate of delicacies which he was carrying carefully over the rough ground. He handed her the plate and bowed to Harry, who looked over the other man's shoulder with supreme disregard.

'Harry!' George Boleyn called, the inevitable dice cupped in his hand.

'Forgive me, Bess.' He excused himself.

Kate Mortimer picked her way delicately over the heather towards them. She ran a calculating eye over Richard and Bess introduced them. Richard, blushing, spoke politely and the conversation turned to horses, a subject which appeared to painlessly overcome the difference in their ranks. Bess found a tree stump and sat down to eat. It was true that food eaten out of doors was more tasty and she found an appetite that she had not had since coming to the south. While she ate her eyes rested on Richard. From his expression Bess could guess that Kate had tired of the equine discussion and was practising her own brand of flirting, and Bess felt a wry sympathy for him. Her gaze slid past him to where Harry threw back his head and laughed as he picked up his winnings from the dice game. He stood talking to the King, turning the coins over in his long fingers. He and Richard could not be more dissimilar, she thought: Richard still sunburnt from the past summer; Harry pale, untouched by the sun or rough winds. Upon the younger man's shoulders was the unmistakable mark of hard work and responsibility, on Harry's nothing more cumbersome than a mild interest as to where the next amusement lay.

'Lady?' She turned to find one of the stable boys at her elbow.

'Your palfrey is lame, my lady—we think she has picked up a stone in her hoof. I fear there will be no riding her today.'

She looked at him, nonplussed. 'Is there some other mount I could ride back to the palace? Or perhaps I may be taken back in one of the wagons.'

The boy looked doubtful. It was not his position to make decisions; he had been given a message for the lady with the silver hair and had delivered it.

'Is there some problem, Lady Bess?' Tom Spalding came over to them. She stiffened. 'Thank you, Lord Spalding—'tis of no account.'

'The lady's mount is unfit, my lord,' volunteered the boy, relieved to have the presence of someone in authority.

'Then you'd better get back to care for the beast.' Tom dismissed him. 'I can help you, Bess. Two of my squires can ride double, leaving a fine mare at your disposal. I will see that she is later saddled with your rig.'

'Thank you,' Bess said distantly, rising and looking around for Kate and Richard. Lord Spalding laid a heavy hand on her shoulder.

'You do not look overly grateful, Bess.'

What was there about him that made her shrink? He was not ill-looking and was obviously well bred... It was a mystery why one man's touch should fill her with loathing while another lit a fire. Again her glance strayed to Harry Latimar. As if he knew he was observed he turned towards them, the faintest frown marked his white forehead as he saw Tom Spalding standing close to her, then he turned attentively back to Thomasina.

The afternoon progressed; over the scene hung a warm blue haze. Games were played and Bess, forgetting herself for a time, became joyously involved in the high-spirited romps. But all too soon the light began to fade—early twilight denied the warm day. Tom led up a tall black mare and helped Bess to mount. 'She is named Sprite and is gentle enough if carefully handled. I shall in any case be close to hand.' He made it sound more like a threat than a comfort.

He accompanied her as the revellers left the clearing and streamed down the slope into the wood. The mare was a harder proposition to handle than the grey and it was dark among the gently waving branches. In the un-canny way horses had of sensing their riders' state of mind Bess's inexperience was instantly communicated to Sprite and from the start she was unsure in her steps. The riders called to each other as they took different bridle paths in twos and threes. Tom Spalding kept close to her as Sprite picked her way nervously along the stony ground until a bird, startled by the activity below, cried out and noisily beat its wings. Sprite hesitated, then lowered her head and shook it restlessly. Tom leaned over and patted her neck, speaking gently. Bess could feel his wine-soured breath on her face then he took his hand from the mare, lifted her chin and attempted to kiss her. Bess tightened the reins and swayed. Sprite took fright and danced sideways.

'Be careful, Bess,' said Tom sharply, 'you are making the beast nervous.'

Where was everyone? The wood was suddenly very quiet, the blanket of darkness all-enveloping. Looking ahead, she could just make out a faint lightening at the edge of the trees. Grasping the reins firmly, she drove one heel into the sleek black hide and Sprite leaped forward. Within seconds Bess gave up all pretence of controlling the terrified animal and clung to the pommel.

As they crashed out of the trees a low branch swept her little hat from her head, scratching her cheek and making her eyes water.

Sprite bolted down into the valley and Bess heard cries of alarm from her right. Almost blinded by her hair, she saw a figure detach itself from the bulk of riders and an age later she heard hoofbeats thudding on the heath behind her. Harry passed her at full gallop, pulled up his horse sharply and, leaping from the saddle, turned to face the oncoming horse. He reached up and caught the reins, bracing his shoulder against Sprite's heaving chest. It was a bold move but to try to check the frightened animal while mounted himself would have been disaster for Bess.

He lifted her from the saddle and turned to the trembling horse, running his hands reassuringly over her while Bess stood gulping air. At last he turned to her. 'You are a danger to yourself and those around you, Bess. Not least to this poor creature. To ride in semi-darkness at such a pace invited injury to both of you.'

'I had little choice. Is it not obvious that she had bolted?'

He looked her over critically. 'Your face is bleeding.' He took a square of linen from his jerkin and held it out to her. It was still warm from his body as she pressed it to her face. 'What were you about, riding such a temperamental beast?'

'My palfrey was lame. Lord Spalding provided Sprite for me. She became . . . frightened in the wood and . . .' She shrugged and spread her hands. 'I must thank you for your prompt action. 'Twas brave of you.'

Full night had fallen now; under the pale half-moon they might have been the only two people alive.

'Let me see that.' He uncovered the scratch and lifted aside her hair. 'It is not deep, I think. You are lucky.' He replaced the linen and applied firm pressure with the tips of his fingers. They stood silently for a few seconds.

'Did you not leave the picnic with Lord Spalding?' he said.

'I did. We were separated in the wood.'

'Is it possible you were distracted from the business in hand by something more entertaining?' he said challengingly.

When she didn't reply he said slowly, 'You have a habit of being involved in dangerous situations, Bess. Do you provoke them, I wonder?'

'In no way that I am aware of,' she said coldly.

It seemed to him that for the first time in many days he was really seeing her, allowing himself to see her. For him it was a disturbing moment: he had thought himself free of her but when he had seen the horse and rider breaking out of the trees and recognised Bess a wild emotion had taken hold of him. Abruptly he took a step backwards and the stained cloth fell to the ground. As she bent to retrieve it he put his hand on her head, his fingers in her tangled hair. She stood up and faced him, but before he could speak they heard voices out of the darkness behind her and the jingle of spurs and harness.

'The rest of the party has caught up with us,' he said.

Bess heard Dorothy Alençon's concerned voice. 'Thank God, all seems to be well.'

She saw Richard, his face a white disc in the moonlight, her hat crumpled in his hands. Tom Spalding dismounted beside them and he said heavily, 'What happened, Lady Bess? You should not have left my care.'

She said wearily, 'I am not skilled enough to manage a mount such as Sprite. Fortunately she has suffered no hurt.'

'But you have,' interrupted Dorothy. 'Put her up behind me, gentlemen and let us get back—it is striking cold and the child is shivering.'

Before Tom could touch her Harry stepped forward and lifted her on to the broad back of Dorothy's bay. 'We all learn from our mistakes, Bess,' he said, his lips against her hair. 'Next time you will be able to identify a wild animal even in the dark.'

She gripped the back of the saddle, the darkness masking the quick colour in her face. Did he think she had gone willingly into the dark woods with Tom Spalding?

Dorothy chirruped to her horse and they moved off. She heard Kate Mortimer's amused comment. 'What a truly heroic gesture, Harry. What will be your reward, do you think?'

Harry's answer was lost in the wind blowing over the heath, but she heard his ironic laugh.

All that week she was dispirited and Meg was quick to find excuses for her. ''Tis natural you are still homesick, Bess. The life at court is strange to you and you are missing your home. I find when I am a little discouraged with life there is strength to be found in prayer.'

Bess smiled and kissed her anxious friend. The long scratch still stood out on her face like a livid weal. Meg had applied balm and dressed her hair to hide it and Bess had washed out the linen Harry had given her and laid it under her pillow, despising herself while she did so.

She suspected that Meg did not altogether embrace the new faith; she had spent too many years in Queen Catherine's gentle presence and her former mistress's devout belief in the papist religion was firmly engraved on her meek soul. However, God was apparently God to Meg; all-seeing, all-caring and all-comforting for whatever ailed. Bess would have been more inclined to believe in a sympathetic idol had there not been quite so many wretched beggars around the gates of the palace and had she been able to see any form of Christian behaviour around her. The court paid lip-service to the Protestant faith but most failed to apply it to their everyday lives. However, she supposed they had more personal problems to concern them.

Anne certainly had, for Jane Seymour was back at court again, commanded there by the King. She had, thought Bess, only a ghost-like attraction, but then ghosts could be as intimidating to the living as a warrior with a sword, and Anne reacted aggressively when she should have been scornfully dignified, and paid attention when she should have ignored.

Henry had returned to the chase with enthusiasm and showered gifts and attention upon the girl. She refused the gifts with downcast eyes and protestations of modesty but the attention she appeared to gain some form of life from: she could achieve some small animation when Henry was nearby, like an anaemic flower which gained sustenance from the sun. It was not in Anne's nature to be complaisant and the court was an uneasy place with its mistress constantly in turmoil.

Anne drew strength from her friends and Bess had rather reluctantly become one of them. Reluctantly because she felt ill equipped for such promotion among that heady mix of the physically beautiful and the verbally outrageous, and because it threw her into constant contact with Harry. He was dealing with what he had felt on the evening of the picnic by paying more attention to Thomasina; Bess had to witness this and it frequently made her as miserable as Henry's attachment to Jane made Anne. And without the same right. Every day she became more attached to her black-haired, vividly absorbing Queen. She found it incomprehensible that Henry should prefer a frail slip of a girl like Jane when within his reach was someone as fascinating and vital as Anne. So as long as the Queen gained support from her she would be there.

One evening, attempting to follow Meg's advice and find comfort in prayer, Bess sat in the chapel. She tried hard to communicate with God but her own thoughts kept getting in the way. She thought suddenly that her father would be celebrating his birthday that week and she would not be there to offer her good wishes. She wished he were here and, with his knack of being objective, could advise her on her problems. A sound on the stone floor of the aisle disturbed her as Lady Jane Seymour slid into the pew beside her and knelt for a few seconds, her blonde head bowed. Obeying her immediate instinct, Bess rose to leave, but Jane stood too and said tentatively, 'Lady Bess de Cheyne, is it not?'

'I am, my lady,' Bess said shortly.

Jane smiled. She had rather prominent front teeth, a childishly unformed chin and very pale blue eyes. Close to she was obviously older than Bess had thought, misled as she had been by the tiny stature and immature body.

'I have seen you about and admired your looks.' Jane's voice too was that of a child, rather breathy and light.

'Indeed?'

Jane sat down and indicated for Bess to do the same. Reluctantly she did so.

'You disapprove of me very much, do you not?' Jane asked. So she could be plain spoken.

'Should I not?'

'None of this—this predicament I find myself in was of my choosing,' Jane said slowly.

'No explanation to me is necessary, lady.'

'No. Of course not. I hardly know what prompts me to engage you in conversation. Except that my enemies do not accuse me to my face and my friends support me without discussion. So I seldom have an opportunity to arrange my thoughts. I suddenly wished to speak those thoughts aloud. While I was at prayer it came to me that I am like the flotsam on the Thames beyond the pier. Where the tide flows I go too. Women are a frail species, are they not?'

'It is possible even for a woman to resist the tide and strike out for a different shore.'

'For a strong woman maybe. But I am not naturally combative. I conform to the wishes of those most forceful around me. And there is of course the problem of being so in love...'

'You love him?'

'Oh, yes! Why are you surprised? Is he so unlovable?'

Bess was silent. Jane went on musingly, 'I think maybe
I bring out the best in him. He is by nature a man who
wishes to be dominant and of late he has had too many
personal battles to fight, added to the demands of ruling
a country such as ours. With me he can be quiet and
easy for an hour now and again.'

'He should possibly seek those quiet hours with his
wife, who is at this moment carrying his child.'

'Is Anne quiet and easy to be with? I think not. Rather
she is a high note on a musical instrument, very thrilling
if one is feeling lively but discordant when one longs
only for peace. You, I think, admire her greatly?'

'I am her friend,' Bess said simply.

It was growing dim in the chapel, the candles were not
yet lit and the linen on the square of altar was an
unearthly shade of white. High on the west wall light
still flowed through the coloured glass windows and one
of the ruby panes threw a patch of rosy colour across
Jane's face. She sighed. 'Truly I am ill cast in my present
role of temptress. I would that Henry were a modest
country gentleman, unmarried and free, so that I could
most gladly accept him.'

'You would give up the chance to be Queen of England
so lightly?'

'Have Henry's queens been so enviable?' asked Jane
wryly. 'Catherine died in miserable circumstances; Anne,
although I have no liking for her, I can find it in my
heart to pity. No doubt that sentiment from me would
annoy her greatly.'

A black-clad priest had entered now and was moving
quietly about the chapel igniting the white candles. He
did not glance their way.

'You could, if you so desired, insist upon leaving
court,' suggested Bess.

'Perhaps I could. And maybe in time Henry would
grow tired of beating at the door of Wolf Hall. But it

would be of no great comfort to Anne, for there would soon be another woman, another, I suspect, very like myself. He has wearied of her, I fear. She cost him too much; in precious time, in those who opposed her and died, and most of all in his pride.'

They were quiet for a time, letting the minutes slip away and then Jane said, 'I must return now.' She put up a hand to readjust her headdress. The elaborate button in her close-fitting cuff caught in the gauzy material and she fumbled a moment to free it. 'Lady Bess, could you please...?'

Bess took hold of the fine stuff and had time only to think, Oh, no, before her inner eye fixed on the picture within the dazzling light. Jane lay on a vast bed propped up by many pillows. She was deathly pale and beads of moisture stood out upon her brow. In the crook of her arm lay a babe new-born; red and wrinkled, it whimpered and turned its mouth blindly to its mother's breast. As Jane smiled down at the infant the church bells rang out to celebrate the birth of a future king of England.

It was no more than a flash of moving colours, then Jane said, 'Can you not free it?'

Bess unwound the shining threads from around the button with shaking fingers and they both got to their feet. As they left the chapel Jane Seymour said, 'I thank you for your company, Lady Bess.' She smiled gently. 'However reluctant it was, you have a sympathetic heart and listened kindly. I wish you happy in your life.'

They left the chapel and walked back to the palace door. Bess thought: I have seen the pieces of a pattern fashioned by some divine hand; Anne's death; Jane's son destined to sit upon the throne of England, and ultimately Elizabeth reigning supreme, but I can say nothing, change nothing.

They entered the palace in silence and Thomas Seymour appeared instantly and took his sister's arm. He nodded briefly to Bess and hurried Jane away. At the foot of the stairs they encountered George Boleyn descending. The Seymours stood back to allow him to pass and he gave them a mocking smile. Rochford watched them ascending the stairs then turned to Bess. He said softly, 'Consorting with the enemy, Bess?'

''Tis hard to think of her as that . . . we but passed a little time together in the chapel.'

'And she took advantage of an opportune place to . . . convert you to her cause?'

'No one could convert me to any cause which would hurt madam. You know that full well, Lord Rochford.'

His black eyes softened. 'I do. You have proved yourself a loyal friend, Bess. And you are a beautiful woman. Were it not to tread upon the feelings of a friend of mine, I would not rest until I had possessed such beauty.'

'I cannot imagine what you mean, sir.'

George laughed. 'Which part of my remark can you not imagine, Bess?'

'Either part. The first is obscure, the last offensive.'

She brushed past him and began to climb the stairs. He leaned his back flat against the wall and watched her ascend. 'I believe my friend may have met his match at last.' His teasing voice followed her as she swept around the bend in the stairway. She had seen visions which foretold a part of a great country's history, but George's words floating up to her were somehow more important and meaningful to her.

CHAPTER FOUR

BESS was in the Queen's bedchamber on the morning which saw the events which most effectively sealed Anne's fate. Anne was fretful and inclined to sudden furious rages. Unusually for her, normally a careless but kind mistress, she had reduced her women to tears several times that day and Bess could see that nothing would please her but to make those around her as miserable as she felt. As another lady left the room red-faced and struggling to control herself, Bess said timidly, 'Is there something I can do for you, madam?'

Anne sat down on a couch opposite her mirror and stared at her reflection in the glass. 'There is nothing anyone can do for me, Bess. I am quite beside myself, as you see. Oh, Bess—just look at me. I am carrying Henry's child; it should be a peaceful time for me but everywhere I turn I hear whispers regarding Jane Seymour and Henry, and nothing I say or do wins me the slightest attention from him. And I am ugly now, more swollen every day—'tis no wonder I cannot keep my husband.'

'You are not ugly, madam,' said Bess quietly. ''Tis natural to carry extra weight at such a time. Any husband should be proud for the reason.'

Anne half turned on the couch. ''Tis the nearest you have come to criticism of His Majesty, Bess. Has he tried even your gentle heart?'

'I cannot help but criticise anyone who makes you unhappy,' said Bess shortly.

Anne released her heavy hair from its night-time plait and shook out the black waterfall. 'I look in my glass and wonder what Henry can find so appealing about that whey-faced miss. What do you think of her, Bess?'

Bess hesitated. 'I think she is weak, Your Majesty. It is her brothers who are promoting her to...distract His Majesty.'

'You are right. The Seymour brothers. They will not be content until they have thrust their sister on the throne at Henry's side.' Anne began viciously to drag her brush through her silky hair.

'They can scarcely do that, madam,' Bess said gently. She came to Anne's side and took the brush from her hand. 'Please, let me do that for you—you will hurt yourself.'

She began to brush out the tangled mane, her mind sweeping back to the evening she arrived at court and had seen the fearful vision while performing this same task. She bit her lip and forced her hands to be steady, her face show nothing of what she thought.

'It is another pleasant day. Will you wish to walk in the gardens a little? My mother holds that to walk at such a time is good for a prospective mother.'

'Mmm? Oh, yes, perhaps I should. Help me dress and we will brave the outdoors together,' Anne said idly.

Bess helped her into a simple gown of vivid scarlet and bound the black hair up beneath its cap. She noticed again the slender neck, white as milk and longer than she had seen on any other woman. She put a fur cloak tenderly around the Queen's shoulders and opened the door for her. They walked slowly down the corridors and down the short flight of steps to the next floor. It was unusually quiet and they passed no one on their way. As they drew opposite one of the heavily curtained alcoves set into the wall they heard low laughter and Anne glanced at Bess and smiled. 'Lovemaking at this hour of the morning? It seems my court grows unruly.' They walked on, and then Anne paused and turned back. She walked to the alcove and drew aside the velvet hangings.

Before her shocked eyes Henry was revealed seated close to Jane Seymour, his arm about her shoulders, his head bent to hers. Anne turned pale, then brilliantly red.

Before Bess could reach her she put out an arm and grasped the other woman's shoulders and pulled her to her feet. She administered a sharp slap to Jane's pale face and would have dealt her another had not Henry stood up and taken her wrists. Jane Seymour, after a quick terrified glance at Bess, walked quickly away and up the stairs.

'You forget yourself, madam,' Henry said through clenched teeth.

Anne gasped. 'I forget nothing. How dare you behave so, in broad daylight? 'Tis you who forget you have a wife, and it is one of her own waiting ladies you amuse yourself with.'

'You had no right to treat her in that manner, to dare to strike her——'

'I would dare a great deal more than that. Fetch back your hussy, Henry, and I will show you how I would take that smile from her sly face——'

Henry's great hands tightened on the slender wrists; Anne cried out in pain. Bess stepped forward. 'Sir, I beg you to remember madam's condition.'

Henry released his wife and turned to her. For a moment there was such anger in his face that Bess thought he would strike her, then he said, 'Take your mistress to her rooms. We do not wish to see her about us again this day.'

Bess took Anne's arm and pulled her away down the passageway. Henry looked after them for a moment, then he turned on his heel and walked away in the direction Jane Seymour had taken.

In her bedchamber Anne let her cloak slip to the floor. She was calm now but shivering. Bess took her to the bed and made her lie down. Pulling the cover over her she said, 'I will fetch my cousin. Meg will know some soothing cordial to give you——'

The Queen lay staring at the ceiling. 'No, Bess, tell my ladies Leicester and Fitzroy to attend me. And advise them that my pains are begun——'

'Oh, no, Madam! 'Tis too soon.'

'I know that, Bess. 'Tis too soon and too late,' Anne said incoherently. Bess ran to the door and called—within seconds the room was filled with fluttering women. Meg took her by the arm and hustled her to the door.

'Come, Bess. It is not our place to be here now. Come with me.' Protesting, Bess was led away.

Hours later as the moon rose over the palace the Queen most painfully miscarried her child. It was of course stillborn, and the boy that Henry had so much longed for. Bess was not present at the interview the King had with his wife but she heard the door slam on his departure and was consumed by a cold anger.

Furious with Anne, Henry gathered together his gentlemen and spurred for Whitehall. Those left at Greenwich talked in hushed whispers. Bess was frankly bewildered. Was it madam's fault she had lost the child? No, it was the distressing scene caused by the King that had provoked the tragedy. The King should be ashamed to treat her so at such a time, she said stoutly for all to hear.

Meg hushed her nervously. 'Bess you must not speak of the King in that way. It is dangerous.'

But Bess, forthright and loyal, could not be silenced.

As if matching the King's mood, the weather turned sharply back to winter. It became bitterly cold again and snow fluttered over the palace. Henry rarely visited and between the royal couple was a rift as wide and glassily icy as the frozen palace lakes. He spent more and more time away from Greenwich as February passed slowly by. Anne was quietly but desperately unhappy now and gloom invaded the court. Bess was scarcely more cheerful herself, for Harry Latimar was one of the gentlemen whom Henry chose to accompany him on his visits to his other palaces, and when he was at Greenwich he spent his time with Thomasina.

Anne recovered slowly from her ordeal and was rarely present at the evening entertainments, which Bess attended, for want of something to occupy herself and for a half-ashamed desire to be in the same room as Harry.

On a day which followed a full week of sleet and snow she borrowed Meg's riding habit and requested permission to ride out with one of the grooms. Feeling she must have fresh air and solitude for once, she was in the stableyard awaiting her mount when Richard Woodville found her.

'You ride out today, Bess?'

Of late he had taken to accompanying Meg and Bess on their customary excursions around the garden, seeming always to know when they were to take the air.

'I thought to, yes, Richard.' A groom brought her mount, a gift from Anne who had selected from her stables the little chestnut mare for its gentle nature. 'You seem always to know my movements. Do you have a spy report regularly to you?' Her desire to be alone made her sharp-tongued but her smile took the sting from the words.

He coloured. 'I met the Lady Margaret just now and she advised me of your plan. You should not in any case ride alone and unprotected.'

She contemplated him a moment. 'The groom would of course have gone with me. But no doubt he will be glad to be relieved of duty on such a cold day.'

She turned with another smile to the shivering lad and sent him back to the smoky fire in the kitchens.

Richard helped her to mount. He wore a buff costume which she guessed he had had made since coming to Greenwich. It was quite plainly cut but the cloth was very fine and smooth.

She said, 'Let us make a start then, shall we?'

He leapt into the saddle and they clattered over the flags and out of the quadrangle under the arch of the main gateway from which spears of ice hung, frozen swords above their heads. They rode in silence for a while, soon arriving at the entrance to the park. Her riding had greatly improved and she felt a certain pride in her handling of the elegant creature. As the horses gathered speed on the flat heath the wind brought a flurry of snow. Bess raised her blue eyes to the sky.

'I think it will snow before long. Perhaps we should turn back now.'

'There is shelter in the trees ahead. And although cold it is not an unpleasant day.' He had no intention of giving up the next half-hour or so in her company. In the last few days he had managed scarcely a word with her. Soon he must go home—he knew that he had already stayed longer than his parents had anticipated. They would be watching the roads for him each day now.

'I have been eager for conversation alone with you, Bess.'

'You do not join the company each evening for the dancing or gaming, Richard,' she said, knowing she was only putting off the moment when she must listen to what he had to say. 'I myself have learned the steps of the dance and it is an agreeable way to be with one's friends. I get great enjoyment too from watching the play of cards and sometimes indulge myself if I have a little money.'

'I could scarcely ask you to join me when I see you always taking the floor with the Queen's brother or his friends. I doubt if I would be welcome at the card tables—I have not the temperament in any case to risk my silver in that way.'

Bess was silent. She could not deny it; she was accepted partly because of Anne's patronage and partly because an extra woman, especially if she were pretty and lively, could fit in anywhere. A man—and one like Richard—was a different matter. She frowned slightly.

'And yet I do not really belong to their circle, you know.'

'No, indeed,' he agreed vehemently, 'you are quite different—more thoughtful and kind than any of them . . .'

'You think you know me very well,' she said gently, 'but might it not be that you wish to believe me so?'

'I do know you,' he said firmly. 'I have seen you turn aside in distress at a servant being cruelly beaten or some scornful comment of Rochford's or Latimar's directed at some unfortunate.'

Even his name heard on the frozen air could bring the heat to her face. He glanced sideways at her. 'There is no special arrangement between you and Sir Harry Latimar, is there?'

'Have you observed anything to make you think there might be?'

He made an impatient movement with his hand. 'I cannot take part in these word games, Bess. I can only say simply that, feeling as I do for you, your attention to this man is obvious to me.'

Bess considered his words—she could understand them. Harry might pretend indifference to her, she might do the same, but there was between them an almost tangible link. She hesitated; her impulse was to tell him to mind his own concerns but...could such sincere affection be scorned?

She said slowly, 'There is nothing between us but—I think—some mutual attraction. Sometimes it is that way, Richard.' It went against her honest nature to deny what she really felt for Harry and she wondered why she did so.

'I know that.' He reined in his horse on the high ground. The parkland lay spread before them, bleak and patched with snow. To their right the frozen lake reflected a sombre sky. No bird sang and there was an eerie stillness. 'But such attraction is not a basis for anything firm and lasting. Not without respect and kindness. And Latimar is not kind, I think.'

'You don't like him, do you?'

'I cannot say that. But he is of this court. I have eyes, I see what they are. Like his friends he is mocking of all the virtues I hold dear. That day he saved you when

your horse bolted he remarked to Lady Kate that he had
merely saved you for another fate. The implication was
most distasteful...'

She shifted her weight in the saddle; her horse, not
liking to stand in the freezing wind, tossed her head.
Bess stroked the cold mane. 'Perhaps we don't understand them, Richard.'

'I understand decency, I hope.'

She laughed—the musical sound was torn away in the
wind. 'It does not suit you to be pompous.'

'Well—perhaps I am pompous. But I still say you and
I are alike, Bess. And I wish to say something else to
you. Something of great importance to me.'

She gave him her full attention and under her eyes he
forgot the carefully planned speech. 'Even in the short
time since we met I—that is I have never seen a lady I
wished to...' He stopped then started again. 'I have
spoken to your cousin and she has given me leave to find
out if you... Bess, I feel sure you must know what I
want to say,' he finished desperately.

At last it had decided to snow in earnest and a fine
veil of white flakes swept over them.

'I know it is too soon, but I must go home shortly
and I would wish to, hope to, take a kind word from
you with me.'

'I cannot promise...anything, Richard.'

'Not promise, Bess. But say you will keep in your mind
what I have said, how I feel.' He reached forward and
caught one of her hands. 'Say it, Bess——'

'Very well, Richard. I will keep what you have said
in my mind. Now I must go back to my duties. The King
is expected and madam may wish my services.'

He had to be content with this. They turned their
horses and rode quickly back across the ground they had
just covered, now under a fine dusting of snow. As they
left the park and turned in to the palace grounds Harry
Latimar came riding out on his great black horse. He
was bareheaded and melted snow shone on his face. As

he passed them he saluted Bess with one gloved hand and then raced out against the wind, Urian barking at his horse's heels.

'Sir Harry takes a chance riding into the storm,' Richard said disapprovingly. 'A soaking can result in the joint sickness catching one.'

Bess thought privately that Harry was not in any danger of being caught by anything. He was moving too fast.

The old adage that March roaring out like a lion must bring April timidly in like a lamb proved wrong that year, for the palace was still white with snow in the weeks that followed. Henry made only spasmodic attempts to be with his wife and rumours that he sought a permanent split with her abounded. Bess continued to support her royal mistress and was still vehement in her defence.

Fine drifts of snow still lay on the ground when Margaret and Bess took their afternoon walk one day in late April. Bess had been deep in thought and started nervously as Harry Latimar stepped suddenly out in their path. She had not known he was back at court, for Henry had spent the last weeks at Wolf Hall.

'I would speak with Bess, if you please, Lady Meg,' he said to Meg, who walked on a little way, hovering uncertainly.

'Bess,' he said without preamble, 'I have heard of your support for the Queen and I have come to tell you to be careful what you say.'

'I am not the only one who speaks so, Harry,' she said slowly.

'You are the only one who matters to me,' he said evenly. 'I ask you to remember that when the net is flung the little fish as well as the big are trapped.'

'Are you turned fisherman, then, Harry?' she asked mockingly.

A faint colour showed beneath his pale skin. He took
her by the shoulders and seated her roughly on a wooden
bench overgrown with ivy. 'The King is ruthless in dis-
posing of those whom he is angry with.' He lowered his
voice but spoke very distinctly. 'Whether they be queens
or waiting ladies.'

'Queens?' Bess faltered. 'But Harry, is the King so
angry with madam?'

'The King means to marry Jane Seymour, whatever
you or I may say or do,' he said flatly.

'And what do you say and do, Harry? I have not seen
you lately in the Queen's company. The Lady Jane has
your full attention now, no doubt.'

He stood looking down at her, his eyes brilliant with
anger. 'If I have turned fisherman you are acting the
fishwife, Bess.'

She rose to her feet. 'Which would not appeal to you,
sir. I observe that your tastes are still for the lady from
France.'

'While you show undue interest in country yokels.'

'How dare you call Richard a yokel? He is a
gentleman.'

'Richard, indeed. You are very free with his name—
are you free in other ways when in his company?' He
glanced at Meg, still standing uneasily a little way away.
'I hope the lady your cousin will soon enquire as to his
intentions towards you.'

'His intentions towards me are honourable, which
cannot be said of yours.'

Abruptly the anger died in him and he relaxed. 'Oh,
Bess, Bess,' he murmured, 'must we always wrangle like
this? I have been so hungry for the sight of you in these
last weeks.' The words rose unbidden from within him.

'I believe you were a mere hour's ride from Greenwich.
At Wolf Hall, was it not? Had you wished you could
have satisfied that hunger quite easily,' she said coolly.

'The King would not allow me leave to visit,' he said
almost sulkily.

'Oh, the King would not allow. Then of course I understand. Indeed, we all understand that for Latimar to offend the King would be impossible. And might endanger his ambitions.'

She spoke the harsh words but his closeness was almost unbearable. She had an insane desire to put her arms around him. A moment passed while this was communicated to him, then he caught her against him and kissed her on the mouth, his arms like iron about her body. She pressed herself to him then after a breathless time he released her and she stood trembling, at a loss for words. Then she slapped his face.

'You are a little late in your maidenly struggles, as always,' he said coldly. He had had no intention of touching her but still something in her aroused his usually controlled nature and he had been overwhelmed by the need to hold her, to handle her. He was puzzled again by the effect she had upon him.

Meg hurried up. 'Bess...my lord—this unseemly brawl——'

'You are quite correct, lady,' Harry said. The imprint of Bess's hand was outlined on his face. 'I ask your pardon.' He bowed mockingly at the still speechless Bess, then turned without another word and left them. As he strode down the path his head brushed an overhanging branch and a sparkle of frozen snow drifted down on to his shining head.

Meg hustled Bess angrily back to their apartments and raised her usually soft voice in an angry lecture.

'Oh, Meg, everything you say is true, but——'

'There can be no "buts", cousin; as if we had not enough trouble without you roistering in the bushes with Lord Harry——'

'Roistering...' In spite of herself Bess smiled, and Meg smiled faintly in return.

'Seriously, dear coz, you must contain your actions—and your words. There are grim times ahead. But even were all normal Sir Harry Latimar would be a flame too hot for you to linger near.'

'I can't seem to help it, Margaret.' And neither could Harry. She knew now that he was as involved with her as she with him. The invisible thread which had linked them from her first night at Greenwich had grown stronger.

'And what of Richard Woodville?'

'Richard is my dear friend.'

'I think he looks for more than friendship. He thinks to talk to your father when he returns home,' Margaret reminded her. 'It is a very... safe future he offers you.'

Safe. Bess picked up her string of amber beads and sat running the smooth beads through her fingers. Yes, Richard was safe. Warm and solid and very like her in interests and background. If her father had not had his misfortune Richard would never have looked so high as a knight's daughter, but as things were... How pleased her mother would be, how much she could help her family, her village. Richard would be an indulgent husband, she was sure. But...

The last rays of light slid in through the windows and fell on the blade of the knife with which Meg idly peeled her apple, turning it to a glittering weapon. She thought of her cousin's words on Anne Boleyn and her head drooped. She felt she was constantly cutting her heart on Harry Latimar's bright sharpness.

Greenwich had been a dull place with the vibrant presence of the King so often withdrawn. Gloom hung over the palace beneath the leaden skies; would it never be spring? asked Meg. But now the King returned for the May Day celebrations and Anne made yet another attempt to please her royal husband. A tournament was planned for that afternoon to be followed by a grand ball. The cooks were endeavouring to lay before the company an exotic feast and a group of travelling players had been summoned to perform. There would be as much gaiety, the Queen decreed, as could be possible, and everyone was to don their finest dress.

That morning the little Princess Elizabeth had left in her velvet-lined litter, another sad parting for her mother, thought Bess, watching the little hand fluttering in farewell. But Anne, determinedly cheerful, turned her attentions to her arrangements to amuse the King.

'She covers up her misery,' Meg said, hurriedly refurbishing the Queen's favourite green silk gown. 'But everyone knows what is happening.'

'What *is* happening, Meg? People whisper and hint but Harry—Harry told me plainly that the King would marry Jane Seymour. How can that be?'

Meg sighed as she lit another candle. Outside a bitter wind lashed the grounds. She sat down again and raised her sewing closer to the flame. 'It has happened before, has it not?'

'But Anne would never allow herself to be divorced. She will think of her daughter, and it is not in her nature to give up what is hers.'

'Queen Catherine had a daughter too,' Meg reminded her. 'And it will be easier to put aside madam, who is not royal. Almost I pray she will be . . . sensible. If she is not, I fear for her——'

'In what way do you fear? They are most legally married and even Henry cannot keep divorcing his wives when they displease him.'

Meg looked up from her work. Bess's face was turned away and her profile was cameo-pure, outlined against the grey light coming through the window. Meg continued with her sewing. 'Well, let us hope that there may be a reconciliation, dear cousin.'

She finished her work and laid it aside. 'We must prepare for the tournament, Bess. 'Twill be a long day with the ball to come tonight.'

While Meg carried Anne's dress to her Bess sat on at the window looking out over the calm water. The tournament would be a friendly affair—an exhibition of skill, nothing more. She was undecided what to wear; in spite of her level-headedness she was very feminine, and the other ladies had so many fine clothes to choose from... She drew an impatient breath, annoyed with herself, and shook out her amber velvet.

Kate Mortimer came in yawning, wearing a silk wrapper loosely held about her body, her face still wearing last night's paint.

'Oh, la, Bess, not that gown again. I am as tired of it as you must be.'

Bess flushed; it was not pleasant to have one's thoughts expressed by another. 'It is well enough for me, Kate,' she said stiffly. 'My lilac silk suffered a mishap last night—a gentleman spilled wine upon its skirt and I will not ask Meg to lend another of her gowns——'

'Now I've offended you.' The other girl laughed. 'I had no such intention, you know.' She sat on the settle by the window and glanced out at the blustery day. She had more than a sneaking affection for Bess now—at first she had despised her for a little country miss, but it was becoming obvious that Lady Bess was not to be underrated. Her spirited defence of her Queen was admired by many—Kate herself did not have the courage for such championship—and there was the fact that, where Bess was, the liveliest gentlemen were to be found also.

'I have a charming black velvet I never wear,' she mused. 'It makes me look sallow but 'twould be perfect with your fair colouring.'

'Thank you, no, Kate. I am content with what I have——'

'Oh, come, Bess, to please me? 'Tis on my conscience, for it cost a great deal and I feel guilty every time I see it in my chest. It is usual, you know, to dress quite grandly for these occasions. Also,' she added slyly, 'I have just been admiring Lady Thomasina's new gown, worn for the first time today. She is very beautiful, is she not?'

She looked speculatively at the other girl but Bess's face remained impassive. ''Twould be fun to steal a little of that lady's thunder; has she not stolen a little from you?'

Bess dropped the amber velvet and stood up. 'I do not understand you, Kate,' she said shortly.

'Oh, come, Bess, we are but poor simple women together. Can we not discuss a problem and perhaps solve it?'

'I think you are neither poor nor simple, Kate,' Bess said slowly, 'and I do not know to what you refer——'

'I refer to Harry Latimar,' Kate said, polishing one of her rings on her wrapper and holding it up to the light to admire the diamond.

'Harry Latimar is nothing to me and I am nothing to him.'

'Is it so? Then I would advise you to try a little harder to rearrange that.'

'To what end? I believe he is betrothed.'

Kate looked up in amazement. 'But that will come to nothing for quite some time. Meanwhile . . . Truly, Bess, do you not desire him at all? He is as skilled, I would wager, in love as in every other sport he takes part in.'

'Do you speak from personal experience?'

Kate laughed, a little discomfited. 'Why, no, but I will admit to you that I find him as distractingly handsome as all the ladies do. However, beneath that indolent manner Harry is as resistant as steel to doing anything he does not desire to.'

'That being the case, then, we must assume he is quite content with his present . . . arrangement,' Bess said with finality.

Kate was silent a moment then she said with unusual seriousness, 'You're a fool, Bess de Cheyne. Anyone with eyes in their head can see what you feel for each other. Do you have so much that you can afford to deny yourself a little heaven on earth?'

When the other girl didn't answer she got up. 'Well, you know your own business best, but I will not take no for an answer regarding my pretty gown. I think it most uncharitable of you not to ease my conscience.'

Bess sighed. 'Very well, Kate. I should not wish to be responsible for that.' She gave a half-smile. 'Truly, 'tis kind of you.'

'Then I will fetch it now. And my conscience will trouble me no further. You, of course, have a pure and spotless conscience. I shall pray it keeps you warm on these cold nights.'

At two o'clock Bess took her place in the stand above the covered jousting area that Henry Tudor, so loving the sport, had created. She was aware of looking her best—the stark black velvet accentuated her stunning fairness, she wore no jewellery and had bound her hair simply with a narrow velvet ribbon to match her dress and presented a picture of unadorned elegance. A great number of appreciative eyes followed her to her seat. Above her on the luxurious cushioned dais the Queen and King were both present. The King wore a disgruntled expression; at the last moment his leg, injured in another tournament and as yet unhealed, had been too painful to allow him to take part. Beside him Anne, dressed in tawny yellow, her hair loose and strung with topaz beads and ribbons to match her dress, made every effort to amuse and cheer him.

One by one the contestants entered the arena, their plumed horses dancing, and reined in before the royal dais. Bess fixed her eyes on Harry, easily recognisable even before he lifted his visor because of his height and graceful management of the tall black horse. The knights called for favours from their favourite ladies and a ripple of excitement ran around the assembly. The Queen was naturally overwhelmed with requests and smilingly took some of the ribbons from her dress and hair and threw them down. Bess, looking at the King, saw a brooding expression in the small eyes as he noted the gentlemen lucky enough to receive his wife's favours.

Harry looked up directly into Bess's eyes. 'May I have the honour, my lady?' His clear voice carried above the noisy chatter.

Bess coloured and her pulses raced; swiftly she tore the black ribbon from her hair and sent it flying down, one long strand of silver still attached. Harry caught it deftly. As he did so a woman behind Bess said in her ear, 'I believe my lord was speaking to me, lady.' Bess turned to find Thomasina leaning forward, her green eyes narrowed in anger. She wore violet that day and she stripped off an amethyst bracelet and carelessly tossed it down. Henry turned in his saddle to catch it and then hesitated, holding both ribbon and bracelet. As he hesitated Tom Spalding's horse jostled his and the man in brown reached out his gauntleted hand and plucked the ribbon from Harry's hand and tied it clumsily on to his lance.

Those seeing this gasped: it was a calculated insult.

'Begin, begin,' the King shouted testily.

With an angry gesture Harry turned his horse and brushed past Lord Spalding, almost unseating the heavier man.

Bess sat back, her face burning. Behind her she heard Thomasina's spiteful laughter. Looking over her shoulder she caught Anne Boleyn's black eyes and their expression of wry sympathy. Bess watched the proceedings in silence; what had possessed her to act so? Had she imagined he spoke to her? In her dreams Harry Latimar was hers, but in reality he belonged to the worldly beauty seated behind her or, in the end, to the child Kate Bonney. The bouts below her continued; each match was hotly contested, riders were unseated and defeated as the medieval pattern dissolved and reformed again and again.

Anne's brother George and Harry Norris the King's groom took the field in gleaming armour, and theirs was a hard-fought contest. From where she sat Bess could hear Anne's excited exclamations and, when Norris was painfully thrown to the hard ground, her cry of concern. Bess glanced again at the royal couple; Henry's eyes were not on the tourney below but upon his wife, and what Bess read in them chilled her. Norris regained his feet, removed his visor and raised a hand to Anne in an oddly intimate gesture to signify all was well. They show their fondness too well, thought Bess, and what husband could tolerate that? Not Henry, who felt his increasing years magnified by the good-looking talented men with which his wife surrounded himself. Tom Wyatt's bitter poem had been well expressed—it was dangerous to attempt to aspire to Caesar's wife.

At last only two knights still fought for the ultimate winner's laurels: Latimar and Spalding. Again and again they brought their sweating horses to mock battle. Harry was the more controlled, the more technically gifted combatant, but Tom Spalding was an experienced warrior; he had seen bitter fighting in Scotland and today seemed inspired. The final clash came and both riders were toppled to continue with short swords on the ground. Henry Tudor leaned forward, heavy hands on his knees, his eyes shining; this was a fight to watch. Round and round in the cumbersome armour the two figures revolved, the last of the sun flashing on the blades of their swords. At last a roar from the crowd and Latimar was down. He lifted off his helmet preparatory to conceding defeat. Spalding drew his short dagger and held it against the exposed white throat. The crowd half rose, Bess's heart beating wildly in her throat, then the King stood up. 'Enough,' he roared and Spalding sheathed his dagger and put out a hand to help his opponent to his feet. Harry was up in one graceful movement, ignoring the outstretched hand, there was thunderous applause and the tournament was over.

Bess got to her feet with the others, her hair without its confining ribbon streaming over her shoulders. She left the tourney ground and went straight to her bed-chamber. Later she attended the Queen as she prepared for the ball. Her ladies whispered among themselves. The King would not remain for the feast; he had left Greenwich immediately the tournament ended, had given Anne no explanation and had not invited her to ac-company him. She was pale and listless and Bess did what she could to comfort her.

'I am ready now to go down, Bess. You go and prepare yourself.' Anne smiled up at her. 'I have set myself to put on a magnificent show and would that someone at least enjoyed it.'

Bess did not at once begin to dress but sat and looked out into the night at the wind sweeping over the bare trees. There was a knock on the door and a page stood before her, in his hand a little package for her. She opened it and her black ribbon fell out. She read the parchment note.

I have retrieved this from my Lord Spalding who had no right to it and return it now to its owner. The more precious favour I have kept for myself.
                                        Harry.

The silver curl was missing from the velvet knot.

Bess blushed, then paled. What had Harry done to...retrieve her favour? Tom Spalding was a powerful man, rich and influential. He was also known to be a ruthless and unscrupulous opponent. She glanced out of the window again. When darkness had fallen so a chill had overtaken the palace—it seemed that winter would never relinquish its grip in favour of spring. What lay behind Harry's gallant gesture? she wondered. After weeks of treating her casually had come the scene before Meg in the gardens; now this. Perhaps his assumed in-difference to her was not proof against his dislike of Tom Spalding.

Meg came in shivering and stirred up the fire. As Bess slipped the ribbon and note into her bodice she came

and sat with her cousin in the window seat. ''Tis so cold.'
She hugged Bess. 'You are very pale, poppet—is all well?
You missed a pretty scene below.'

'A scene?' Bess asked without interest.

'Latimar and Spalding—throwing dice like all possessed. And Sir Harry without a penny to his name at
present and his creditors hounding him——'

'What happened, Meg?'

'Oh, I left before the end of the encounter. A crowd
had gathered and 'twas most unruly. I know not how it
finished. I went then to the chapel and became quite
chilled at my prayers.'

Bess listened to her cousin's gentle voice with half her
mind. So that was how Harry had won back her ribbon.
In a dice game. How typical. She would have had more
respect for him if he had taken Tom by the scruff of the
neck and shaken it from him. She cut short Meg's
chatter. 'I hear the King has left court suddenly, Meg.'

'It seems he is angry with madam again; some incident at the tourney displeased him. I fear she can do
little right these days,' Meg said sadly.

'Everything she does is right; she tries to please him
in every way. He behaves like a spoiled child at every
turn,' Bess replied scornfully.

'Bess, Bess, you must not speak so. However, I will
not scold you now. 'Tis time to dress for the evening.'

Meg prepared herself, putting on a modest dress and
leaving Bess to take her turn with the warm water brought
by the page.

She washed her face and hands, blinking through the
water like a child. She disliked the habit of the other
ladies of never washing, but soaking themselves in
perfume and painting their faces layer upon layer. Their
clothes were rich and fashionable but underneath... She
wrinkled her nose scornfully. They were like the life
here—shining and bejewelled where one could see, but
below the surface corrupt and unclean.

She put on the new white dress Meg had had made for her: the creamy silk with its stiffened bodice and underskirt sprinkled with tiny seed pearls, the overskirt a more brilliant white which gleamed in folds about her slim body. She put on little gold slippers and arranged her hair under the three-cornered cap also studded with pearls. Her reflection shone in the dim room. Meg came back to fetch her and hand in hand they descended to the banqueting hall.

Bess's glance found Harry immediately in a costume of silver-grey shot with purple. He was seated next to Lord Rochford as usual and did not look her way during the lengthy meal. She noticed that while George only picked aimlessly at the fabulous food *he* took nothing from the proffered platters. His wine cup was filled again and again, however, and even from a distance she could see he was becoming slowly but steadily drunk. Halfway through the meal she saw George put his thin hand over Harry's goblet and apparently remonstrate with his friend. Harry knocked the hand away and the other man half rose, his black eyes flashing. Those around them stopped eating to stare at this unusual display, then Rochford's face relaxed and he sat down again and put his arm around his friend's shoulders. Anne leaned across him to speak and Harry smiled unwillingly.

An atmosphere of desperate tension had invaded the hall in spite of the strained laughter of the Queen and her ladies and the jocular efforts of her gentlemen.

What a sorry coil women made of their lives, thought Bess. Anne Boleyn should have been content to leave the King to his royal wife and she, Bess, should be content with a Devon squire. She looked down the laden table and found Richard's brown eyes on her as usual, their expression patient and loving.

The evening moved on. An amusing and imaginative play was performed and applauded, but nothing lightened the gloom. The hall was illuminated by hundreds of wax candles, their light reflected in the solid

gold and silver plates adorning the walls. The flames
leaped in the draught, throwing grotesque shadows on
to the tapestries, and mirrored themselves as points of
light in the Queen's brilliant eyes. Bess thought the whole
scene like a fantastic animated embroidery, constantly
changing. She drank a cup of wine and the picture
swayed before her eyes but her spirit did not lighten.

She and Meg joined the dancing later and George
Boleyn led her out on the crowded floor. 'You are more
beautiful than I have ever seen you, Lady Bess,' he said.
He had his sister's unique grace at the dance.

'Thank you, Lord Rochford.'

Harry had left the banqueting table at the end of the
meal and she could see neither him nor Thomasina now.

George said, as though he had not noticed her swift
perusal of the dancers, 'Harry is depressed tonight and
thinks to lighten his heart gambling.'

'Indeed, that is surprising.'

He laughed. 'I despair of you two ever coming
together. Those warm looks of yours cannot possibly
conceal a cold heart.'

The habit of sparring with him was strong but she
smiled as she said, 'Why should you interest yourself in
us, my lord?'

'Perhaps I would perform one good deed before
eternity overtakes me.'

'Why do you talk of eternity?'

George caressed her back with his slim fingers. 'I love
life as much as any man, Bess. But lately I have felt a
cloud descending. I am fanciful, do you think?'

'You have a long life before you, I imagine.'

'Perhaps. My sister is quite determined you can foresee
the future. Do you perceive a long and happy life before
me?'

A cold finger touched Bess's heart. 'Why should that
not be so?'

'I have cast my lot in with Anne. What happens to her will inevitably happen to me.' George's voice was no more than a sigh above the music.

'You are the best brother a woman could have, George.' It was the first time she had called him by his given name and her voice was gentle.

'Dear Bess. I have very little affection for the women I know but I could fall in love with you. I fear the competition is too great, however.'

'You speak of Richard Woodville?'

'I speak of Latimar. Open your eyes, Bess—you are a woman such as one seldom meets and Harry is such a man. To say that you are made for each other is to understate the case.'

'He perhaps does not have your clear sight.'

'Harry is confused. Do not commit yourself to any other until that confusion is no more.'

The music ceased and the dancers applauded. Bess lifted a hand and laid it against George's white cheek. They didn't speak, but something passed between them before George bowed and left her.

Bess danced awhile until the musicians packed away their instruments and the company split into groups, most gathered around the lute player, a new face at court. Bess looked for Mark Smeaton; she felt a sudden need to be soothed by the magical quality of his singing, but he was nowhere to be seen.

She drifted into one of the ante-rooms where several lively games of cards and dice were in progress. A number of people called and invited her to join their game, but as if drawn by an invisible magnet she went and stood near where Harry sat, deep in a game with Tom Spalding. It was an unfamiliar game to her and she did not understand the play but she knew that Harry's luck was out that night. The other man was keeping a precise note of his winnings and his column of figures grew longer as she watched. Harry held the ivory dice in his open palm before throwing them on to the painted board in his casually reckless fashion. He lost again.

Thomasina, standing directly behind him, tapped his shoulder with a pointed finger. 'Come, Harry, retire now. Lady Luck is not smiling on you tonight.' Earlier on Bess had seen her dancing with her green eyes constantly on Harry as he sat over his wine, angry that he would not join her. Now she leaned over him and put proprietorial hands on his shoulders. He glanced up at her and then past her to where Bess stood. Then he got up and, pushing past the sympathetic spectators, left the room. Bess paused a moment, then followed him. She kept him in sight as he moved swiftly through the throng in the hall and out into the long gallery. A cold wind blew sharply through the new-fashioned windows, which jutted out to allow light from three sides, and the points of the candles in the embrasures danced as she walked. Harry was standing in one of the stone alcoves staring out at the dark gardens, the dull silk of his clothing agleam.

He turned his head to look at her and she saw that the clear-cut eyelids were heavy over his navy eyes. 'Why have you followed me, Bess?' He spoke carefully but the words were slurred.

She scarcely knew why herself. 'I am . . . concerned for you, Harry.'

He laughed and put up one white hand to caress the flawless black pearl in his ear. The wind tore at the windows; the candles in their metal-branched holders sank and died. In the chill darkness he said, 'You are like a ghost in that white dress. I am haunted by you, heaven knows.' He spoke absentmindedly.

She thought suddenly, He has changed greatly since we first met; the gay high-spirited man has disappeared, leaving behind a stranger. They looked at each other.

'Oh, Harry,' she said helplessly. 'What is to become of us?'

Again he spoke in that strange detached way. 'Of us, who knows? But George and the others... It is rumoured that they will shortly be arrested. Anne too. Mark Smeaton is already taken and it is said that he has made some iniquitous statement.'

Fear clutched at her.

'Don't worry on my account, dear Bess. There is no such rumour of arrest concerning myself. It appears I lead a charmed life. That can change at any time, of course. It seems no one is safe. Henry is angry with me already—my staying here looks to him like a...choosing of sides. He has ordered me to rejoin him tomorrow.'

'You are more the King's friend than the Queen's,' she said slowly.

'Which no doubt has saved me. Small comfort when George and my dearest friends are in such danger——'

'What will happen to him—and the others?'

He turned heavy eyes on her. 'They are to be charged with treason. And the Queen too.'

She remembered the flashing blade and shuddered.

'You're cold, Bess. Go back where it is warm. If you are sensible you will seek an even warmer place in Devon with Richard Woodville.'

'I would rather be here in the cold with you, Harry.'

She saw his white teeth in the darkness as he smiled ironically. 'In a dark corner with a gentleman of my reputation?'

At the far end of the gallery a laughing group drifted out of the hall and stood talking noisily. Harry drew her to his side so that the wall shielded them from sight. Pale moonlight spilled over her face and he put a hand on each shoulder. 'Lovely Bess, you're not quite real in this light.'

'I am real enough, Harry.' Maybe this would be the last time she would see him, touch him. She bent her head and pressed her lips to his hand.

As if reading her thoughts he said, 'A kiss for the condemned man?'

She said abruptly, 'What we spoke of—in the gardens those weeks ago. I was wrong to turn you away. Even a little love is better than nothing. Even one night.' She flushed in the cold light.

He looked down at her consideringly. He was fast becoming sober; the wine had left a stale taste in his mouth. 'Come, Bess, you're distraught. And after all your fine words and heroic resistance——'

'It all seems unimportant now, Harry. I am changed in some way.'

''Tis only the atmosphere lately, the uncertainty. These are strange times but when all has righted itself you will regret this.'

The colour left her face. 'Never. I will regret nothing. I know that I love you, Harry, and it is right that we should be together for however short a time. Just this one night, if that is all there is for us.'

He hesitated. An age ago he would have thought this moment a victory, but if she had changed, so had he. She was more than just flesh and bone to him now; her personality had invaded his life.

She raised her eyes to his face. 'Shall you reject me, Harry?'

'I question only this sudden about-face. You have been so anxious in the past to evade an encounter such as this.'

'I know that. And you must think me contrary. But tonight I feel differently. I have thought about it and I feel ... differently,' she said simply.

Despite the physical electricity between them he was amused. She had thought about it and felt differently, and so came to him in her forthright fashion to tell him. It occurred to him suddenly that he had come as near to liking Bess de Cheyne as any other woman he had known. She was naïve, she refused to play the game of love by the rules set down at court. She was maddeningly loyal to her friends, be they the Queen or that hussy Kate Mortimer. She concerned herself with things no lady should bother about; the poor, the needy drew her compassion and more than once she had drawn Anne's attention to some deserving cause. She could display a devastating clear-sightedness which was why George, who had no time for fools, was interested in her. Most intriguing of all, she had so many parts to her personality that one could fumble with the pieces for an age before finding the complete Bess.

There was demure Bess extending her hand to Richard Woodville when they met in the gardens, looking kindly on his devotion, there was ice-cool Bess outfacing all others in a game of chance, joyous Bess romping with little Elizabeth, haughty Bess dealing sharply with the boorish Tom Spalding——

And now she would offer herself to him. What man could resist her? Not he, still a little dazed from wine and with catastrophe around the corner.

They crossed the gardens to the stone summer-house in silence. The wind had dropped and above them stars pricked the sky. It was still bitterly cold but there was now a subtle change in the weather which reminded one that spring was due. Bess pressed open the door and they stepped inside. It was dim among the cobwebs and dust; the yellow light from the moon could scarcely penetrate the window openings. She turned to face him and in a swift, decisive movement took off her little cap. Her hair tumbled down over her shoulders, the shining mass catching what light there was.

His eyes travelled over her but he made no move towards her and after a moment she went to him and touched him gently. He took her in his arms then and kissed her forehead, the eyes, her mouth.

She did not hear the door open but he drew back immediately. A figure was silhouetted against the darkness. 'Bess...' Richard Woodville said. 'I saw you leave the palace.'

Irritation mixed with affection swept over her. 'Richard, you had no right to follow me here, no right to spy on us.'

'No right?' he repeated slowly. 'I was concerned for you.' Her own words to Harry a short while ago.

'You're intruding, sir,' Harry said, a cutting edge to his voice. 'This lady is in my care.' The gulf between their ranks was suddenly apparent to Bess in Harry's aristocratic drawl; he was casually at ease before Richard's youthful uncertainty.

Richard faced him; he was the smaller of the two men but more sturdily built. 'I am Richard Woodville, sir, of Devon, and I have hopes that this lady will one day be my wife.'

'Indeed?' Harry turned in mock enquiry to Bess. 'Are you then betrothed to this gentleman, Lady Bess?'

'I am not. And you both know it,' she said shortly.

There was a brief silence, then Richard said, 'Your cousin may have need of you, Bess. The Queen's brother is just now arrested and two other gentlemen with him.'

Harry drew a sharp breath. 'Is it so? And the Queen?'

'She is confined to her apartments, I believe.'

Harry turned back to Bess. 'I must go back, sweetheart.' He was trembling, whether in anger or fear she could not tell.

'Of course. We will all go back.' She raised her hands to arrange her tumbled hair, replacing her beaded cap with the eyes of the two men on her.

Harry took her arm across the gardens but his face was set and pale and they parted without speaking at the entrance to the palace. Richard followed her to the foot of the stairs. 'Bess—I know you are displeased with me. But I truly had only your well-being in mind.'

She thought, If I tell him now why I went alone to the summer-house with Harry, indeed initiated our visit there, he will never speak of marriage again, never look at me in that special way. Instead she said, 'We cannot talk now, Richard. I must go to Meg.'

She ran swiftly up the stairs to her room; it was empty so she went from there to the Queen's apartments. She found Meg in the antechamber—she was a deathly white. 'Where have you been, cousin? I searched for you.' Without waiting for an answer she continued. 'Help me with these, please.' She had an armful of gowns and cloaks and furs and walked distractedly in a circle looking for a place to lay them down. A heavy brassbound trunk with an entwined 'H' and 'A' emblazoned upon it stood half full in the middle of the room. Bess took the muddle of velvet and silk from Meg's arms and put them on a chair. 'Be calm, Meg, and tell what is happening.'

'Lord Rochford is arrested and the Queen expects to be taken at any time. Oh, Bess, we will all be questioned.'

'About what?'

'They must prove madam unfaithful...' Meg whispered.

Bess laughed aloud, ignoring the fear which crept over her. 'How ridiculous. They can question us all for a hundred years and never prove that.'

'You don't understand. They *must* prove it. They have tried all else and one way or another it will be done. 'Tis the only way they can cry treason. And Mark Smeaton has already confessed.'

Mark Smeaton. Had his infatuation for Anne tipped his imagination into running riot and so endangered the woman he loved? 'Where is the Queen now?' she asked.

Meg raised her finger to her lips and glanced at the closed door of the bedchamber. 'She has taken a sleeping draught and two of her ladies are keeping watch. I was instructed to make ready her travelling trunk.' There was no sound from behind the panelled oak doors.

They stared fearfully at each other. It was very warm in the small, richly furnished room. Burning logs crackled in the fireplace and the flames exaggerated the shadows in the corners of the room. Then Meg swallowed and withdrew her hands. 'Help me with the trunk, Bess, then at least when they come—if they come—my

lady will be comfortable wherever she is taken.' She was
back to her own calm self again; the moment of panic
had passed.

For an hour they brushed and folded and packed, then
Meg fastened up the trunk with the leather straps and
smoothed her hair. There was still no sound from the
adjoining chamber as they went out and back to their
own room. Bess lit candles and Meg stirred up the dying
fire. Then they sat either side of the blaze and stared
into the flames. By unspoken agreement they made no
preparations for bed but simply sat in the firelight and
waited.

As a grey dawn crept into the room Bess awoke with a
start. She could hear the tramp of feet outside in the
passage, then a ruthless battering on the doors of the
Queen's apartments. She and her cousin sat up, listening
for a moment, then Meg ran to the door and opened it
a little. Bess followed her and, hearts pounding, they
heard the dreaded command from Lord Norfolk's lips
for the Queen to accompany the King's guards to the
Tower. They heard Anne's musical voice murmur in reply
before she went without protest, then only the hysterical
sobbing of those ladies she had left behind.

Meg closed the door slowly. 'The Tower...' That dark
and horrible place. Bess pictured it as a nightmare prison
of grey stone, the only sound the scurrying of rats and
the lapping of chill water on the steps of Traitors' Gate.

She went to the window and drew aside the velvet
hangings. Some miracle had been wrought during the
long night; spring, so long delayed, had come at last.
The sun was rising into a blue mist and the air flowing
in was gentle and mild.

'Well,' Meg said with an effort, 'we must go down,
Bess. Perhaps we will learn something new while we eat.'

Bess changed out of her white gown and into the amber
velvet. She brushed out her hair and wound it into an
unfashionable coil at the nape of her neck. She saw from

her mirror that she was pale, and violet shadows darkened the fine skin around her eyes. She thought she looked plain and much younger than her seventeen years.

It was a subdued assembly who broke their fast that morning. Bess forced herself to eat. She looked to the top table but saw that Harry was not there—indeed it was empty of all its usual gay occupants. Richard was in his place, however, and gave her a quick unsmiling glance. She noted that he was dressed for riding and guessed that he planned to leave the court that morning. Many who had no official business to keep them at Greenwich would no doubt do the same. It was a cheerless and dangerous place now, despite the advent of spring beyond its walls.

Listlessly Bess fetched her cloak and walked in the grounds with Meg. No one had seemed to know what the next step for their royal mistress would be; indeed there was a reluctance to discuss the matter at all, as if not talking of it would somehow protect them. Everywhere about them was evidence of the dramatic change in the seasons: green buds had sprouted seemingly overnight, the pale shoots of spring bulbs pushed up through the brown earth. The sun was warm on their backs as they walked slowly away from the palace to the riverbank and along to the end of Queen Margaret's pier. The gamine French wife of Henry VI had loved Greenwich and built the long finger of wood out into the wide river to enable the easier embarking of the vast river barges she loved to travel to and from the capital in. She had believed that the river breezes kept the palace and its grounds sweet and it certainly seemed so on this glorious morning. Even the constantly floating refuse had been swept away in the recent storms and the water was dazzlingly clear under the sun. Bess thought that had she been at home now how delighted she would have been with the mild weather, the gold of daffodils in the Devon valleys. A wave of homesickness engulfed her. She heard footsteps behind her and, turning, saw Richard

hurrying towards them along the boardwalk. Meg looked
at his face and then moved back down the pier a little.

'I must speak with you, Bess.' Richard took off his
hat and turned it in his hands. 'I am leaving for the west
today. I have come to say goodbye.'

She smiled at him without speaking. He looked young
too this morning, but his brown eyes were steady. 'I mean
to see your father and ask for you. May I tell him you
are of the same mind?' He spoke with determined
confidence.

Bess turned to the glinting water. 'That would not be
true, Richard,' she said gravely. 'You would not want
to marry a girl who loved another, surely?' She could
put it into words now; what was the use of denying it
to others when she could not deny it any more to herself?

He flushed. 'I don't believe you love him, Bess. You
are just . . . dazzled by him. If you would just go home,
back where you truly belong, all would be different.'

'No, Richard,' she said gently.

'He'll not marry you, Bess,' Richard burst out. 'Even
now he is riding for Whitehall to show his loyalty to the
King, while his friends rot in prison. He's worthless with
his silk clothes and white hands. A gambler, a high-born
wastrel. He's no use to a girl like you. Whereas I—I will
work for you, build a good life for you——' He stopped.

She sighed. 'I know, Richard. Everything you say is
true. You are good and kind and I value your proposal
but . . .' She watched a bird swooping over the water, down
to the wavelets and up again into the pure blue sky.

'I won't give up, Bess. When we rode together that
day you promised to keep what I feel for you in your
mind. I hold you to that promise.' He took her arm and
turned her to face him. At his touch the dizzy feeling
took hold of her, the gardens faded, the river was blotted
out and she looked into the circle of light. Richard was
there, older, much lined, his fair hair iron-grey. He knelt
on one knee before a graceful house, his arms around
a child; a boy, himself in miniature. As she watched the

child turned its head and he and his father both smiled at a woman coming out of the house through the rose garden towards them. Bess narrowed her eyes; the woman's face was in shadow——

'Bess!' Richard gripped her. The picture faded. 'Bess, are you ill?' She put one hand to her face.

'No. No, but you must go now, Richard. You have a long and difficult journey.'

He looked at her, nonplussed. 'Say you'll think of me, Bess. Say you'll consider again my offer.'

She smiled but only said, 'God speed, Richard.'

He released her, looking steadily into her face a moment, then turned and left her.

Meg rejoined her. 'You foolish girl,' she exclaimed irritably. 'I hope you realise what you have thrown away. He truly cares for you, and has more to offer you than a tarnished reputation.' It was as near as she would go to mentioning the relationship she suspected had developed between her cousin and Latimar. She was glad that his unsettling presence was removed from court and hoped he would stay away until she could persuade Bess to return home.

'Don't lecture me, coz. I know what a trial I am to you,' Bess said, still thinking of what she had seen.

'No, not a trial. But I am worried for you. In the days to come you must be careful. What you say, what you do.'

'If asked I shall tell the truth and that is all,' Bess said shortly. 'Is that not enough?'

'I shall pray the enquiries only touch those who have known the Queen longer than you have, dear Bess,' Meg answered. Something in her cousin's face prevented her from saying more. She took her arm and together they left the peaceful river and returned to the palace.

CHAPTER FIVE

Two days later Meg's fears were confirmed and Bess was summoned before Thomas Cromwell. She was in the solar with the other ladies when the request that she 'attend upon Master Cromwell without delay' came, and she laid down her embroidery, outwardly calm but inwardly trembling. Meg was not present but Kate Mortimer accompanied her to the door and instructed her in a whisper, 'Say as little as possible, Bess. Volunteer no information, for they have a way of twisting the most innocent remark into something vile. I swear that by the time they had finished with me they thought me half-witted—so long I took to answer even the question how old was I! But after an hour they lost patience and let me go.'

She spoke with her usual careless manner but Bess could see under her make-up that the freckles she sought so vigilantly to conceal stood out like scars. She is frightened for me, thought Bess, following the page, and I am frightened for myself. Brave words are one thing when uttered to friends, but will I have the same courage when questioned by a man such as Cromwell? Many of the court had been quizzed and had returned trembling and reluctant to tell of what they had been asked. Some had not returned at all, and one could only guess at their fates.

The page directed her to a small room and opened the door for her. Although the day was warm and the sun shone the room was almost dark, the heavy drapes pulled across the windows and only one candle burning on the table before the chair in which Thomas Cromwell sat. He did not lift his head from the papers he was studying so intently but gestured with his hand towards a stool.

She sat down, arranging her skirts with care and taking deep breaths. A few moments passed and still he sat with his head bent, apparently in no hurry to get to the business in hand. Bess straightened her back and folded her hands on her lap.

Eventually he collected the papers together and laid them aside.

'I have note here of a valuable horse being given to you by the Queen. Why was this gift bestowed?' He did not look directly at her.

For a moment the apparent irrelevance of the question and the abrupt manner in which it was asked confused her.

'A horse——?'

'Yes, my lady. An expensive animal formerly from the King's own stables.' Still his eyes were fixed on some point beyond her left shoulder.

Bess took another breath. 'Oh, yes. Her Majesty gave me the mare as I had none of my own and wished to ride.'

'You have been at court a short time only. You will admit that it is unusually generous to give such a costly present to a mere acquaintance.' Now he turned his eyes full on her and allowed himself to study her carefully. He was not a good-looking man, being very short and plump with large muddy-coloured eyes. He was dressed as though for a winter's day in thick fur-collared robes and a rich velvet cap.

For some reason now his attention was completely upon her she felt more at ease. She looked him in the eye. 'Her Majesty is well-known for her great generosity, sir.' Her voice was gentle and rather expressionless.

He linked the fingers of his capable-looking hands together and leaned slightly forward. This was one of Latimar's little light of loves, he pondered. Not the usual type that young man favoured. Beautiful, yes, in a rather virginal way, but quite lacking in vivacity.

Bess sat calmly under his scrutiny, her hands still folded, her eyes only mildly interested.

'It was perhaps payment for some service rendered?' he continued.

'Service?' Bess said blankly.

'Some favour you performed for the Queen which she returned with this costly gift.'

'Favour?'

'Do not repeat every word, lady. I think you must know what I mean.'

'I am afraid I do not, sir. We all serve the Queen, do we not?' The faintest note of reproval crept into her voice. 'And expect no payment for it.'

Cromwell sighed. He hitched his robes up and got to his feet. He moved the curtaining a little and peered through the gap. 'I will give you an example. Let us say that the Queen had asked you to take a message for her to a member of this court at some time.'

'I have often taken messages for madam. To her ladies, her dressmaker——'

'To a gentleman?'

Bess frowned. 'A gentleman?'

Cromwell let fall the curtain and returned to the table. 'Yes, lady to—let us say—Lord Weston, or Brereton.'

Bess's face cleared. 'No, indeed, sir. Not on any occasion have I delivered a message to either of those gentlemen, or indeed to any gentleman at all.'

Cromwell sat down heavily. He had questioned dozens of the court; some had been fearful, some frankly terrified. Some had said too much, others had been apparently struck dumb, but all had shown some emotion. This little girl sat as though invited to a chat about the weather. And yet . . . He had seen her in the company of all the men he was at pains to incriminate, had seen her in many a conversation with George Boleyn. He contemplated the rings upon his fingers and began to turn the emerald on his forefinger, watching its sea-green glitter in the candlelight.

'You have often, I am sure, witnessed the conduct of the Queen with her brother Rochford?'

'Conduct?'

'Are we back to the little game of repetition?'

'The Queen is often with her brother,' she agreed after flushing a little at his reprimand.

'And can you describe their behaviour?'

'Their behaviour is as would be expected,' Bess said equably.

'They are fond of each other?'

'Indeed. Second only to the King, the Queen is fondest of her brother.'

Cromwell ceased turning the ring. 'You have observed an intimate affection between them? Unnaturally so?'

He had laid his cards upon the table now and she raised her eyes to his. Had he gambled with her he might have been a little wary at the candour in them.

'No.'

'No?'

'Never at any time have I observed anything other than the normal affection between brother and sister,' she stated flatly.

'I see. And no other gentleman has been entertained by her in...intimate circumstances.'

'Not to my knowledge, no.'

There was a short silence. The air in the room was lifeless and stale. But Bess remained cool, her hands still demurely clasped in her lap, her blue eyes holding nothing more than a faint puzzlement at the turn the conversation had taken.

'And the Queen gave you the mare out of the kindness of her heart?'

The interview had revolved full circle. 'Yes, Her Majesty is most generous in that way. I recall a lady of the court finding herself in straitened circumstances due to the death of her husband, who had left many debts. Her Majesty paid those debts and——'

'Thank you.' Cromwell cut into her ingenuous account. 'You may go now, lady.'

Bess looked startled then got to her feet. She lifted
her skirts in a curtsy, opened the door and closed it gently
behind her. In the cool passage she swallowed. Her heart
pounded and for a moment she thought she must faint.
But the moment passed and she returned to the solar
and picked up her embroidery with a steady hand. Kate
sat beside her. 'So?'

'Master Cromwell asked a number of curious questions and I answered them as best I was able.'

Kate surveyed her friend. 'I am sure you were more
than a match for him, darling.'

Bess threaded her needle with scarlet silk. 'There was
no question of any contest, Kate. But the interview made
me afraid for madam.'

'We all share that sentiment,' Kate said gloomily.

The next days dragged by. Nearly a fortnight passed in
a flurry of rumour and speculation. No one knew exactly
what was happening, but one thing was certain: the
Queen was to be brought to trial and her court was to
be disbanded. Meg would soon leave to join her mother
in Kent and Bess would no doubt be sent home.

'The King will want no reminders when Lady Jane is
mistress here,' Meg said grimly to Bess as they made
ready to leave Greenwich for Hampton. They and four
other ladies had been commanded to the river palace by
order of the King, the reason for which they had yet to
discover. Kate had whispered to Bess that one of the
other ladies insisted it was to stitch on Lady Jane
Seymour's wedding-gown. Bess would have marvelled
at the irony of making a wedding-dress for a new wife
while the husband's present wife sat in prison, had the
whole situation not horrified her. She thought often of
Anne, imagining her alone and forlorn in the Tower. As
she had sat in the fading light, staring out over the black
water at Greenwich, she pictured Anne gazing at the same

placid river, her heavy hair about her shoulders and that curious sparkle of high courage in her black eyes.

Bess and the other ladies waited impatiently at the pier for the barge to carry them to Hampton. It was another golden spring day, the air soft, the breeze as gentle as a caress. The sun shone down on Bess's uncovered head, turning it to silver. Meg had pleaded with her for hours the previous evening to go home, but Bess had refused stubbornly. Eventually her cousin had given up. 'We will all be sent from court soon enough, anyway.'

That was no doubt true, thought Bess, watching the oars cut the water in swift clean strokes, but I must see Harry once more before I go. Just once more. She could never have him, she knew that now, but she could not go home without saying goodbye to the man she loved. Meg spoke of the court being disbanded and this was what would happen but Bess could not be sorry, for the light had gone out of the assembly for her. She missed Anne's vibrant presence in her life and that of the handsome talented young men who shared her imprisonment, but most of all she hungered for Harry Latimar, a hunger made greater by their brief passionate exchange in her room on the night of the musicale, and in the summer-house. Now she closed her eyes and let the sun warm her face. Around her the other women chattered, tossing this and that rumour around like a child's ball.

'...and they say that Jane Rochford herself swore that her husband had been unfaithful to her with his own sister.' Gasps met this disclosure.

'I do not believe it,' Kate declared. 'George is a strange man, but that—never.'

'That view was confirmed by Latimar,' said Madge Baldwin, 'and his refusal to confirm this piece of evidence has cost him his little heiress.'

Bess opened her eyes slowly and looked at the speaker.

'Ah, little Bess takes notice at last.' The woman leaned towards her, lowering her shrill voice a little. 'Yes, Harry

Latimar's punishment is the breaking of the marriage contract with little Kate Bonney.'

'He is lucky if that is the only punishment,' Meg said fearfully.

'Lucky indeed,' agreed Kate. 'Of course the King loves Harry too well for aught else, but it is punishment enough for a gambler who was hoping to set his debts straight with a handsome dowry and to continue his soft living with a rich little wife.'

'Lord Harry was no doubt defending a lady's honour,' said Bess. 'It seems she has no one else to speak for her now.'

'A lady's honour is not a subject normally close to Harry's heart,' said Mary Leicester spitefully.

'Come, Mary,' interposed Kate hastily. 'Bess is only suffering what most of us have suffered around Latimar—an acute attack of love.'

There was general laughter and Bess turned her burning face away and looked out over the shining water. So Harry was released from his marriage contract, for all the good it would do her. For the first time in her life she longed to be rich, not just passably wealthy so that she could have her share of pretty dresses and jewels, but fabulously rich so that a man like Harry Latimar could be hers. As this thought crossed her mind it was met by another: you would not wish to buy him, surely? Bess de Cheyne was good enough for any man just as she was.

Eventually the mellow red brick towers of Hampton Palace, crimson in the sun, came into view. Bess gazed at the imposing building, once owned by one powerful man, coveted and soon taken by another even more powerful. They left the barge and proceeded towards the palace, six pretty women dressed in bright colours, fluttering across green lawns like exotic birds. As they stepped across the stone bridge over the moat the King appeared and cast a bad-tempered eye over their respectful curtsys. He was dressed elaborately in cloth of gold trimmed with lynx fur and looked red with heat. He was surrounded by his gentlemen, one of whom was Harry Latimar.

As Bess rose she looked at him and he gave her his ironic smile. The King walked on and Harry took her hand and lifted it to his lips. 'How are you, Bess?'

'Well, thank you,' she replied gravely. The late afternoon sun shone full upon him; on his auburn hair, his brilliant smile. Although she had thought of him for two weeks and worried about him, now perversely she was angry with him for looking so well and handsome. While she felt plain and tired and marked by recent events he, if anything, was more clear-eyed, more beautiful, more... Oh, she could not describe to herself the needle-bright aura surrounding him. As if he had not a disquieting thought in his head.

He looked at her, sensing her antagonism.

'Although,' she continued, 'it is difficult to be unmoved when a lady whom one admires is subject to such trials. I fear that Anne is in desperate straits.'

The use of the Queen's first name was unusual for Bess; his eyes registered this and an expression of pain clouded their blue depths.

In the silence between them Henry could be heard laughing at some pleasantry from one of his gentlemen.

'Loyalty is a quality much to be admired,' Harry said, slowly releasing her hand.

'Come, Bess.' Meg took her arm. 'We must go in now.'

Looking back over her shoulder, Bess could see him standing looking after them, the usual mocking expression gone from his dark eyes.

There was no mention of wedding-gowns that evening. Jane Seymour was there, however, making an effort towards friendship with the ladies from Greenwich. She was as always sombrely dressed in lavender-grey velvet and wore no jewellery except for the diamond-studded miniature of Henry around her neck. She was well enough, thought Bess. Pretty and modest and self-effacing and no doubt, as she had declared to Bess when they had met in the chapel, swept into her present position by stronger wills than her own. But comparison between her pale charm and another woman's dark enchantment was inevitable. The light had gone out of the royal court; a new era was emerging. The music was slower, laughter softer and even the colours of gaiety were muted. The King wore a now familiar brooding look that night at the evening meal. He was attentive to Jane but he lacked the challenging air Bess had seen about him a month ago. If Anne had produced a boy for him, she mused, they would have remained together, probably, in the amicable enmity which most long-married couples eventually came to. Now it fell to Jane to bear Henry's son and achieve the invulnerable position that her predecessors had sought.

Harry Latimar shone like a bright star in this dull company; dressed in silver with diamonds glittering on his white hands, bright hair shining in the smoky candlelight, he drew the eye like a dark jewel. He was drinking heavily again that night and Bess wondered if he imagined himself for the first time an outsider. He had been granted exemption from the dreadful fate of his friends but he had the air of a man who despised himself for accepting such a gift.

'Bess.' Meg broke in on her thoughts. 'I shall not linger when the meal is over. I am tired after our journey and shall seek sleep before the other ladies come to bed.'

Here at Hampton she and Bess had no pleasant rooms to themselves, but were sharing a bedchamber with the others who had come from Greenwich. Beautifully appointed though it was, with comfortable feather beds and every amenity, it was still difficult to get used to washing and dressing among the constantly bickering and gossiping women. Bess could not blame her cousin for attempting to find a little rest before Kate and Madge and their friends came noisily to bed after an evening of drinking and dancing. For this evening was no dif-

ferent, it seemed, from any other at the royal court. Their
Queen might be languishing in the Tower but her subjects ate, drank and laughed as though all were normal.

Presently Meg got up, made her excuses and left the
hall, leaving Bess to finish her fruit. As she sat peeling
an apple Tom Spalding climbed clumsily into Meg's va-
cated seat and reached for a handful of walnuts.
Crushing one in his huge hand, he asked her how she
did.

'Well enough,' she answered.

'You have lost one of your suitors, I observe, and the
other is shorn of his fine friends,' he said.

'Have we not all lost friends?' she said, biting her lip.
How dared he make such a remark with such
complacency?

'Not I. I am glad to have the court free of some of
its high-born rubbish.'

She said icily, 'I hope you do not refer to Her Grace,
my lord.'

He put the nut in his mouth and said heavily, 'No
indeed, Bess. Any fool could see that madam is beyond
reproach, but I admit it gives me pleasure to know that
Rochford is to get his just deserts at last.' Tom had so
often smarted under George's irreverent tongue. 'And I
mislike seeing Henry in such an undignified muddle over
two silly women. I would wish it brought to a speedy
conclusion.'

What a boor the man was. Making him the brunt of
her unhappiness, she said acidly, 'Perhaps you would
wish to try and execute them personally, my lord. You
would wield the axe most enthusiastically, I am sure.'

He looked surprised. ''Tis nought personal, Bess.'

'It is to me. And to those others who love Anne and
admire her friends.'

He considered a moment. 'Still...our loyalty should
be to the King. He looks content enough tonight. Lady
Jane is a likely lass and more amiable than her former
mistress, I'd swear.'

'Amiability being most important in a wife, of course.'

'It is not a quality you are showing tonight, certainly.'
He made a clumsy attempt at wit.

'I am not hopeful of being any man's wife at present.'

He removed a piece of shell from his mouth. 'You
have not promised yourself to young Woodville, then?'

'It is difficult to imagine why you enquire into my
affairs but—no, I have not.'

'Do you look higher, then?'

'I do not look at all. Surprisingly enough, all women
are not constantly busying themselves about the job of
finding husbands.'

He laughed. 'Are they not? If not a husband, then
what? I would be most interested to hear of any other
position you had in mind——'

Bess stood up abruptly and left him in mid-sentence.
Walking along the passages, she looked for a place to
be alone. To think and to find some kind of solace.
Opening a door at random, she found herself in a large
salon, set with easy chairs, its walls lined with bookshelves. A dozen or more candles burned wastefully in
their silver holders, shedding light over the silk-bound
volumes. Since being at court she had not had a book
in her hands and had missed the comfort of losing herself
between the pages. Now she selected one and carried it
to the light. It was in unfamiliar French so she returned
it and took another. She sat down to read. Half an hour
passed as she turned the stiff pages before she heard
footsteps and voices in the passage outside. As they grew
nearer she got quickly to her feet. The door latch rattled
as she went to the far side of the room and slipped
through a narrow door, hoping she could escape into the
corridor. Instead she was now in a small square room
laid out with washing bowl and ewer and other facilities
for toilette, with no window or door. It was unlit and
she stood still, holding the book, her back against the
wall behind the open door. Through the gap between
the door and hinged post she saw the King enter the

library followed by Harry Latimar. She held her breath in the warm darkness; she did not want to be discovered by them skulking in the dark antechamber. Henry was saying, 'He is always so confounded sure that what he says is right. I would disprove him for once...' He went to the bookshelves and ran his hand along the hide-bound covers until he found the one he sought. He took it down and skimmed through the pages. 'I am sure I read somewhere... Call for wine, Harry. I am determined to find the reference.'

Harry opened the door and called to a page, who took his order and set off at a run. When the wine was brought and put upon the table by the King's chair he glanced up. 'Sit down, Harry. I will prove my case if it takes all night.'

Harry sat down opposite and poured wine for them both. For a time there was silence, broken only by the King's muttering to himself as he searched through the book. Bess let out her breath soundlessly and stayed quite still. It was so close in the little room that beads of water sprang out upon her forehead and trickled down her hot face.

After a time Henry said idly, 'You are unusually silent tonight, Latimar. Is the unseasonal weather affecting your tongue?'

'The prevailing atmosphere is oppressive, certainly. But I cannot lay blame on the fine weather.'

'I am not sure I understand you, Harry.'

'And I am sure you do.'

The King closed the book and put it down on the table. 'Then let us say I better prefer not to understand you. You are my good friend and I am loath to tangle with you.'

'Would a good friend remain silent, I wonder?'

There was a brief pause. Henry lifted the flagon of wine and Bess heard the liquid sound of more wine being poured. The King raised his glass to his lips, drained it and lowered it again. 'Say what is on your mind, then. I see naught else will content you.'

Through the gap Bess saw Harry get up. His tall body blocked the light from the candles for a moment then he turned to face the other man. 'I am perhaps the least thoughtful member of those you favour with your close friendship but I don't believe that my careless nature means I love you less. I ask you to believe that it is out of this love that I speak. I ask you to reconsider your actions, to moderate the result of these actions. The dread result.'

Henry moved restlessly in his chair but he spoke gently. ''Tis too late, Harry. There is no turning back from the road I have chosen.'

'There can always be a turning back for a great man— the man I believe you to be. The man I always believed you to be from the day I laid eyes on you twenty years ago.'

'Is it twenty years? Can time be so fleeting? You know when you were a boy and I a young man I used to look at you and think, This boy is like the son I'll have some day. That day will not come while I am chained to Anne.'

'How can that be? She has given you little Elizabeth——'

'Harry, it is over! Must I explain to a man such as you that when passion is dead it is more dead than any other thing? You have cut a swathe through the ladies of my court; I cannot believe that you have not discovered that for yourself.'

Harry said slowly, ''Tis true that I have been...attached to certain ladies, and that those attachments have ended. But I would swear and so I think would they that when it was finished they had suffered no hurt. No harm. Can you declare the same?'

Henry shifted again in his seat. 'We talk of treason, boy—there is no redress for a Queen. For her adultery is treason. And as such demands its own penalty.'

Harry laughed but he was not amused. 'Adultery? Sir, you spoke of my experience with women—then let me offer you the benefit of it. Anne is no adultress.'

Henry blustered, 'I have the names boy. Mark Smeaton——'

'Mark Smeaton.' Harry's soft voice lingered on the name. 'And were you there, sir, when they tortured a confession out of that pathetic boy?'

Henry shouted now, 'There are others. Her own brother among them. They will all confess. All.'

'Never. Not if you waited a hundred years. Hal—come, look the facts in the face. You wish to be rid of your Queen. Very well. But not this way. Not with her lovely neck on the block.'

'You argue so passionately. Should we then add your name to the list of her lovers?'

Bess held her breath. She wished herself a mile away. Wished she need not hear this conversation which put the man she loved in such danger.

There was a longer pause then Harry said, 'Please do. Add Harry Latimar's name to those who love her. It will bring no shame to me, for upon that list are the names of men who would lay down their lives for you as easily and without thought as they breathe.'

'It must be this way, Harry, for she will not be put aside. She will not allow Elizabeth to be put aside.'

Harry sat down again. He put his hands across the table and grasped the King's wrists. In the candle-light the black pupils of his eyes expanded, absorbing the dark blue. 'I find it hard to put words to what I feel. I am not clever when my emotions are seriously engaged but I tell you this. When a strong man does violence to another—and that other is in his power—he does a greater violence to his own self. You spoke of a road a few moments since. Well, that road is the hardest of all to travel, for it leads only to self-disgust.' For a moment his eyes held the King's, then Henry pulled his hands away.

He said angrily, 'If you are not with me on this then you are against me. There can be no middle way. Have a care, Harry, lest you find yourself in the Tower with your friend Rochford.'

Harry lifted the flagon and poured a thin stream of wine into his glass. The King went on, 'It has long been an aggravation to me that that decadent man has your constant loyalty. And I have counted it a weakness in myself that I have let you on so many occasions keep me from punishing his insolence. Now his final contempt for me is apparent in his misconduct with his sister.' Still Harry drank and didn't answer. 'You do not speak for him? During the enquiries you did not speak for him either. Not against—but not for.'

Harry set down his glass carefully and got up. His face was deathly pale and in the dim light his eyes shone. 'I would not speak for George who can most eloquently speak for himself. And I suspect that he sees more clearly than any of us that his King has lost all sense of justice.'

The words fell like stones in the quiet room. Then Henry lifted a hand and swept flagon and goblets from the table. They crashed to the floor and the wine spread red over the rugs. 'We will bear no more discussion of our private affairs. I repeat, if you cannot reconcile yourself to the new order of things you will lose more than your heiress. Now get out of our presence until we can stand the sight of you again.' Harry got up slowly.

Bess watched him leave the room; as he turned at the door to bow she saw the sparkle of tears on his face. The King sat motionless, staring straight ahead of him. His shoulders were bent and his hands, palms upwards, lay loosely upon the table. He looked an old man suddenly and even Bess, antagonistic and scornful, felt a reluctant pang of pity for him. Then he too got up and, kicking back the chair, left the library, slamming the door behind him. She stayed a while in the silence before going through the library and returning the book with shaking hands. Then she opened the door and went quickly along the quiet passages and up to the dormitory.

Only Meg was there. She opened her eyes and smiled. 'You look tired, love. Come to bed now.' Bess bent over and kissed her.

'I will, cousin.'

She undressed and got into the bed beside Meg. Meg reached out and extinguished the candle and darkness reigned. Bess lay on the fine feather mattress and closed her eyes. So Harry had spoken for Anne. Despite his cynicism he had protested at the greatest risk to himself. She was afraid for him, afraid of the result of his championship, but she would not have had him any other way. She had protected the Queen by remaining silent; how much braver was Harry's way? Not merely because of personal danger, but because it had cut him to the heart to criticise the man he loved. She turned over and pressed her face into the soft linen, listening to Meg's gentle breathing. Presently she too slept.

The next morning Harry did not appear at the meals and the hours between dragged unbearably. The King looked thunderous; no one dared to approach him and at the evening meal the conversation buzzed around reports of the confrontation between Henry and his favourite. Bess ate a little and took no part in the speculation and as soon as the meal was complete pressed out of the crush and into the tranquil night. She wandered out into the gardens, scented now with spring flowers, every tree and bush transformed with blossom. The air, though still cool at night, was refreshing after the stale heat inside. Behind her the palace was lit by a thousand stout candles and laughter floated over the May evening. She paused at the entrance to the orchards. It was pitch-dark among the close-growing trees, although a brilliant moon rode overhead.

Thomas Wolsey had laid out the orchards, which covered a considerable amount of ground, and brought a Spanish gardener to Hampton to tend them. Now plum, cherry and peach trees bloomed again in England, their pastel blossoms touching over Bess's head. Around the outer perimeter a high thick hedge kept the destructive deer from straying in from the parkland and the confined area was a maze of interlinking paths. She walked awhile, her mind busy with her thoughts, but after a time she stopped and turned around to go back. She walked for what seemed a long time among the trees and uneasily realised that the sounds from the palace were fainter, the glow of light further away. She felt cold too, the thin silk of her lilac gown no protection from the night breezes. The snapping of a twig underfoot away to her left almost stopped her heart. 'Who is there?' she called through the dark.

A wavering light shone through the screen of branches as Harry said, 'Stay where you are, Bess. I will come to you.'

The light faded, then grew brighter, and a moment later he was before her, a horn lantern swinging from one hand, a fur-lined cloak over his arm.

'Harry,' she said as he laid the cloak around her shoulders, 'you frightened me. How did you know I was here?'

'I followed the scent of your perfume,' he answered. 'This is a curious time for exploring. It is almost midnight.'

'I wanted to be alone awhile.'

'Oh? Shall I leave you, then?'

She took his arm hastily. 'Take me out first. I confess I was lost—all looks the same in the dark.'

'I will take you out, then; it is this way——'

'How can you tell? All the paths look the same.'

'I remember when the orchards were laid out. I was just a boy and my father was Wolsey's good friend. I can walk around the grounds at Hampton blindfold.'

'Poor Wolsey. How he must have hated to give up this paradise.'

Harry laughed bitterly. 'He shouldn't have expected paradise on earth. He played a dangerous game against a more ruthless opponent.'

'How strange—the Queen too spoke of playing a game and said she had gambled and lost.'

'Did she? Well, she is a gallant loser. Wolsey lost his palace and his high position. She has lost far more.'

They were at the entrance now. 'Why did you come looking for me, Harry?'

He pulled the cloak closer about her, and his hands brushed her face. 'I think I shall always be looking for you. Perhaps you will remember that.'

'Why, Harry—you sound as though you are saying goodbye.'

'It will soon be goodbye, will it not? You will go home soon and I . . . I am for France. On the King's command I am to take up duties in the service of the King of France for a time.'

'You are banished, then?'

'Oh, no, not that. Henry is angry that I cannot see his actions in the right light. He thinks a spell away from England will bring me to my senses.'

'He is fond of you——'

'When I was ten and he twenty he was my hero, the older brother I never had. I think he remembers the boy who idolised him. I wish you could have known him then, Bess. He was magnificent and gracious too . . .' His fine eyes softened as he looked back at happier times.

'He is cruel and hard,' said Bess stubbornly.

'Oh, not cruel. Just growing older and disappointed with his life. And becoming more intent on having his way at any cost.'

'So his wife must die, you must go to France, and I——'

'You must go back to the west and marry your good squire and have a little girl with silver-gilt hair and a little boy you might name for the King and . . . for me.'

She turned away. 'I shall do as I please. And I don't please to marry one man while wanting another.'

'Bess,' he said helplessly, 'I am not free to do as I might choose.'

'The contract with Kate Bonney is broken, I hear.'

'Contracts can be renewed,' he said evenly. 'When the King recovers his good temper he will look kindly on me again. He will want to keep such an heiress for one of his friends.'

'Oh, don't tell me any more. There is more to life than bags of gold, Harry.'

She left him and began to hurry towards the palace. He followed her and caught her cloak, but she shook him off. 'No, don't touch me. You have no need to explain, no need to keep my favour. I have no money with which to buy your affections——'

The lantern fell to the ground as he grasped her shoulders. The candle inside it flared and she could see his face was brilliant with anger. 'How dare you say that to me? What do you know of my life? All the love in the world would soon grow stale if we lived in poverty.'

'Why?' She could feel the steel grip of his fingers through the thick cloak. 'My father has lived in poverty for twenty years and he is still caring and loving.'

He took his hands off her. 'I remember your father, Bess,' he said thoughtfully, calm again.

'You do?'

'Henry called him the man of steel. Not, I think now, because he was stronger or braver, but because inside of him he was strong.' He bent to pick up the lantern. 'I am not like that. I am weak and fickle and I like my creature comforts. Good food, fine clothes, jewels...' he fingered the pearl in his ear '...they are important to me. I am shallow, Bess.'

'Would a shallow man have dared to defend the Queen?'

He laughed but his eyes darkened. 'Well, I admire her greatly, you know. She changed us all, ruined some of

us I suppose, but no one can be neutral regarding her.'
He sighed. 'Come, Bess, I must take you back. Your
vigilant cousin will be wondering what we are about.'

She hung back. 'You did not tell me; why did you
come looking for me?'

'Ah, that . . . The Queen has sent a message. She requests her prayerbook to comfort her when . . .' A shadow
crossed the moon, for a moment they were in solid
darkness then it passed. 'And she wishes you to carry it
to her. She asked that most particularly. The King has
consented and I am to escort you.'

The Queen's prayerbook. The little Book of the Hours.
Bess had seen it in her hands a hundred times, her slender
fingers caressing its illuminated pages.

'But . . . why me, I wonder?'

'That I don't know, but it is perhaps her last wish.
We leave tomorrow morning for the Tower.'

'I am proud to be of service,' Bess said resolutely.
'But the Tower—I dread that place.'

'Don't worry, Bess. I won't leave you there. I shall
bring you safely back again.' His face was bland and
there was only mockery in his voice.

'I shall be ready,' she said primly as he opened the
door for her and went inside, leaving the moonlight for
the smoky candle-shine.

Hampton Court was, to Bess, much more sumptuous
than Greenwich. It had been furnished over long years
by a man who loved luxury and obtained pleasure from
the colour and texture of the finest materials. Wolsey
had dispatched his agents throughout the known world
to bring back finely woven carpets and wall hangings,
tables and chairs carved from trees that could never grow
in England, and any exotic ornament they knew would
please their master. Although the palace was enormous
with more than a thousand rooms including two great
banqueting halls, audience chambers, hundreds of rich
bedchambers as well as domestic offices, it yet achieved
a curious intimacy with silk-clad walls and damascene-

carpeted floors. Through the velvet-hung windows no
draught was permitted and a hundred fires flamed in the
fireplaces. There were no cold and bare passages as there
were at Greenwich and even the more modest rooms were
luxuriously appointed. Thomas Wolsey had made it his
own special kingdom and its present master, swift always
to learn, had retained the prize he had snatched in exactly
the same manner.

Bess went now to her chamber and found Meg there
alone. She turned from her embroidery easel but Bess
saw that she had made no progress with the silken
picture. In her hands she held the prayerbook Anne had
sent for.

'You know you must carry this to madam tomorrow?'

'Yes.' Bess looked into her cousin's eyes. 'I hope it
will bring her comfort. Is there more news?'

Meg riffled the little pages of the book. They were
bright with glowing painted pictures, stiff with gold leaf.
'Madam is tried and found guilty. And sentenced to
death,' she said flatly. 'Her brother and the other
gentlemen were executed this day and Her Majesty awaits
the pleasure of the King for the date she dies.'

From somewhere below Bess could hear music, the
plaintive sweet sound of a lute and the husky voice of
Mark Smeaton's successor.

'I can't believe it,' she said finally. But she could, she
did. Her inner sight never made a mistake. She moved
past her cousin to the window and pushed aside the
curtain. The sweet air rose out of the flower-beds below.
Above, Anne's star burned as brightly as it had at
Greenwich.

The next day she presented herself at the jetty. Harry
was there before her and handed her silently into the
royal barge. It was one of the Queen's vessels but Bess
saw that her badge, depicting a falcon rising from a bed
of Tudor roses, had been stripped from its sides and
bows. The oarsmen cast off and she sat beside Harry on

the ornately carved and cushioned seat in the stern thinking that were it not for such a sad reason this journey with him would have delighted her. It was early yet but already warm and she took off her cloak as the sun gained power.

Today Harry was for once at a loss for words as he leaned back, stretching his long legs and staring into the water. Did he know about George and his other comrades? she wondered. He must do, for the court had whispered of nothing else last night and this morning. She wished she could have offered him some words of comfort but his detachment was absolute and she knew she could not shatter that composure. So she watched the quiet water slide by for a while and listened to the regulated splash of the oars dipping in and out.

When they had left Hampton far behind she said tentatively, 'Harry, I am sorry for what I said last night. I had no right.'

He turned his head and looked at her, his eyes narrowed against the strong light.

'It is because I care for you that I was so angry,' she continued. 'Angry to think that you would put money before things worth so much more.'

'I make no excuses for the way I am,' he said mildly.

'And feel no shame for it either, apparently.'

He laughed. 'Be careful, Bess, or you will be apologising all over again tomorrow.'

'You are impossible to be serious with,' she said severely.

'It is hard to sit here on a perfect May morning with you looking so beautiful and talk of serious matters.' He took one of her hands and turned it palm upwards, studying it.

'I am not one of your ladies, to be flattered by fine words,' she said sternly, looking at his bent head.

'No, indeed,' he agreed. 'I hope Richard Woodville is aware of the nature of his bride-to-be. Your birthplaces are close, so presumably he also has a way of saying what he means. Is that not the way you put it to me once?'

She snatched her hand away. 'Why do you persist in talking of Richard as though all were settled between him and me?'

'I recognise determination when I see it. And that young man will never give up.'

She was annoyed but she thought, That is true; Richard is a man to depend upon.

Catching at her thought he said, 'You would have a safe life with him, Bess. Not something to be despised in these times.'

'Perhaps I don't look for safety from a man.'

'Then what do you want, I wonder? What do you want from me? If we had not been...interrupted in the summer-house at Greenwich that night would we be having this conversation now?'

'You have a low opinion of yourself, Harry,' she said quietly.

His face did not change but he narrowed his eyes again. Then he laughed. 'You have a way of turning an argument to my disadvantage, Bess. I simply meant that romance has a way of being diminished when a more practical knowledge of one's lover is acquired.'

She digested this cynical speech in silence for a moment. 'I see—I would have discovered as you have that there is little to choose between one body and another except in matters of finance.'

'It might have been of benefit to you. And to Richard Woodville. You would have found that love, the kind of love you aspire to, cannot compete with security.'

There was silence between them; the barge rocked gently as the oarsmen negotiated one of the many mud islands dotted about the Thames. He asked what she wanted of him; well, she could not answer that without giving too much of herself away. She envied him his ability to protect himself from the emotions which affected her by erecting a charming brittle barrier. Only in a physical confrontation was that barrier dissolved, and she wanted to provoke that confrontation now. On impulse she leaned forward and kissed him.

His mouth opened under hers and, caught off guard, he put a swift arm around her and pulled her close, his head between her and the fast-climbing sun. She felt again the overwhelming yielding sensation and after a moment she freed herself.

'Harry, we are not alone.'

He glanced at the impassive oarsmen, then back at her, puzzled. He was sophisticated, he had been intimate with a great many women, but never before had he experienced such passionate desire mixed with tenderness and loving care for the woman. Combined with the respect and liking he had for her, it made him feel vulnerable. Something in him shied away from this unusual feeling. 'I don't understand you, Bess. You are always mysterious to me.'

She smoothed her hair. What a fool he was; he would weigh the unique emotion they felt for each other against hard cash and find the scales wanting. 'I am sure you will solve the mystery,' she answered at last.

All too soon the swift-flowing current swept them to their destination. They had taken the same route as Anne had two weeks earlier, and, like her, they landed at Court Gate. The Queen of England had been spared the indignity of entering her prison under the sharp wooden teeth of Traitors' Gate.

They were escorted by armed guards to the Queen's chamber and at the door Harry left her to enter alone. Anne was sitting at a small table writing when Bess stepped timidly into the room. It was bare of any furniture save a table and two chairs; on the window-seat lay Anne's lute, its ribbons hanging purple and yellow down to the dusty floor. She turned and rose with her warm smile. The two women touched hands, then Bess reached into her little bag and held out the book. Anne took it and laid it down on the table where it lay like a

tablet of gold between two sheets of black and gilt
enamel. She indicated one of the chairs and Bess sat
down.

'You are in good health, Bess?'

'Yes, madam, but so sorry to see you in such a place.'

Anne's eyes travelled around the bare walls. 'I was
here the night before I was crowned, you know. The
wheel of fortune has turned full circle.'

A faint spear of sunlight found its way through the
narrow windows and rested on the floor between them.
Anne said abruptly, 'I want you to tell me what
you . . . saw that day in Elizabeth's bedchamber.'

Bess started. 'I don't understand you, madam.'

'I think you do. Twice in my presence you saw—or
felt—something. I think the first time it concerned me
and I can guess what it was. The second time it was to
do with my daughter and I beg you to tell me.'

Bess shook her head. She felt very cold and her heart
beat in thick slow strokes. Anne looked down at her
hands. They were ringless now; she wore no ornament
except for a wide band of black velvet about her throat.
She said slowly, 'I see. Well, I have no time to persuade
you. No time, indeed, for anything now. I am already
on borrowed time. Henry, of his kindness, has granted
me this extra day. . .' There was no irony in her voice.
Bess had learned last night that Anne was to have died
the day after her brother but Henry had delayed the execution, some said so that a French swordsman could
make the trip to London in good time to perform his
macabre task.

They could hear heavy footsteps approaching. Bess
rose and went and stood very close to the Queen. Where
Anne's black hair sprang from the pronounced widow's
peak there was a sprinkling of white. 'I saw the Princess
Elizabeth well and happy. Older—much older than you
are today and. . .' she struggled for the right words '. . .she
wore the crown of England and it pleased her well, I
think.'

The door opened with a crash and the Tower guards filled the doorway. Anne brushed past her. 'Thank you for visiting me, Lady Bess.' She picked up the little book. 'And thank you for the ... gift you have given me this day.' Her astonishing eyes caught and held those of the younger girl, then Bess said,

'God keep you, dear madam,' and walked through the open door and heard it slam behind her. Along the dank stone passage leading out into the grim courtyard she walked, then under the dripping archways and out into the sunshine where Harry waited for her. She took his arm and he helped her into the barge.

'You're trembling, Bess.'

She looked to him for comfort but his eyes were empty, his face stony. 'Was it so distressing?' he asked her.

She swallowed. 'I am upset, of course.' She spoke with an effort.

The oarsmen struck out for midstream. Two swans, impossibly white against the dark water, sailed past. Proudly aloof, they ignored the barge and its occupants.

'The Tudor court is no place for the soft-hearted. Yesterday my best and dearest friends were put to death. Should I weep and tremble?' His mouth twisted in sudden pain, but his eyes remained blank. The barge swayed, its bows cresting the water; the road home lay like cloth of silver before them. He said quietly, painfully, 'I spoke just now with one of the Tower guards. He witnessed the executions. George died first and bravely. The guard told me that with admiration in his face.' He looked towards the bank at the jumble of buildings huddling there. 'Many disliked him, you know. He could take the skin off a man's back with his bitter tongue but he was good to me. I have lost count of the times he paid my bills when my creditors were beating at the door. And when I was taken by the sweating sickness and not a servant would come near me George came, sarcastically asking if I would lie abed until they coffined me up. For three days and nights he fed me and changed my linen and held me in his arms when I was raving and would have injured myself. I loved him as I could never have loved a brother but he is dead. Soon all that wit and dark charm will be nothing more than a handful of bones under the cold stone flags of the Tower. He is gone now. They are all gone now and I can feel nothing, can show nothing——' He broke off.

'There is always a place for compassion,' she told him passionately. 'Your attitude is so cold.'

'What I think will not change anything. Their course is run. The rest of us just keep silent and thank God we have escaped.' He fell silent, already regretting the bitter words, the exposure of his hurt.

She said nothing more either. She believed what he said. She had more cause than most to believe in the unalterable course of fate. All the same, she was sure he was not hard and unfeeling. She stole a glance at him, sitting so relaxed beside her, his eyes fixed on the darkling river, one finger straying to the black pearl in the gesture now so familiar to her. He had been part of Henry's court since he was a child; first a page, then a squire, then a knight, and around himself he had drawn a cloak of protection as hard as any metal. Inside that brittle casing was the man she wanted.

The swinging lanterns in the bows and stern were lit when they berthed again at Hampton. As the sun died and darkness followed it had grown damp and chill on the water and Bess hugged her cloak about her. As they left the landing stage a fine rain began to fall, misting her hair and releasing the perfume from the massed bluebells and daffodils lining the garden paths. Harry put a hand beneath her elbow where the overhung path narrowed and a moth blundered out of the darkness and brushed its soft wings against her face. Her heart was sore from her parting with Anne. She would never see her again and knew something vital had gone out of her life forever.

'Don't be sad, little Bess.' Harry put an arm around her shoulders. 'The world goes on, you know; the flowers grow, people die, but more babies are born every minute. A death is no more than a star falling from the heavens.'

Involuntarily she lifted heavy eyes to the sky but Anne's particular star was obscured by the mist. 'And you must be hungry...we have had nothing since breakfast.'

'You go in, Harry. I would walk awhile before the meal. Perhaps I will go to the chapel and offer a prayer.'

'I will accompany you, of course,' he said courteously.

'It is not necessary,' she replied, but he went with her through the cloisters and into the chapel. There was no one else there to disturb the silence. Bess walked between the narrow pews and up to the lace-covered altar. Fat wax candles burned steadily up to the wooden ceiling which was painted midnight blue and dusted with silver stars.

'Do you believe in God, Harry?' she whispered.

He hesitated. 'I believe in fate, Bess. That what must be must be. I have seen no evidence of divine intervention. You no doubt believe in some benevolent God sorting through our affairs and directing events.'

''Tis comforting to believe that, is it not?' she answered evasively.

'Comfort is to be gained from many things. A good meal, a warm fire, a tender woman.'

She said thoughtfully, 'I believe God is in all of us, in the best part of us, that is. If we allow him to be.'

'And if he wishes to share space with the evil contained in most of us?'

'That evil is brought on by circumstances. We are all born good. Or so I think.'

He half turned and looked around the shadowy walls then back at her. 'This is a new mood for you, Bess. I have seen you thoughtful, merry, angry. And loving. But never religious. One could be with you forever and not find you dull.'

His teasing manner took away any pleasure she might have found in his words and she knelt and made her prayer under his ironic eyes and then he took her back through the covered walkways to the palace.

She went wearily to her chamber to tidy herself. She pulled a brush half-heartedly through her hair and changed her muddied slippers for clean. The room was strewn with linen: bed hangings, silk coverlets, pillow covers. She picked up an embroidered cushion cover and saw that the initial 'A' in the intricate design had been painstakingly unpicked and replaced with a 'J' entwined with 'H' and enclosed in a true lovers' knot. Bess frowned then dropped the heavy silk disdainfully. This then was why she and the others had been brought from Greenwich. To obliterate Anne's claim to any part of the most intimate royal articles. Tomorrow she would be required to take part in this task.

Well, be damned if she would. She looked up and caught her reflection in a gilded wall mirror. Her face was as white as one of the bedsheets, eyes brilliant with rage. Then her anger faded. She felt flat and powerless. Oh, I don't understand these people, she thought dismally. Harry would soon no doubt learn to bend his knee to his new mistress. Kate Mortimer, although she would complain of pricked fingers and watering eyes, would nevertheless do the King's bidding and conspire to put Jane Seymour in the place of the woman she had served and professed to love for three or more years. A longing for her home and family swept over her. I will go home, she determined. Meg shall ask permission and Will Soames shall take me back. Back to sane and kindly people.

She went briskly down the stairs and took her place at the table. Meg squeezed her hand encouragingly when she told her what she had decided. 'It is for the best, cousin. Much as I shall miss you, I will soon be gone myself. I shall ask His Grace this very night.'

Later as she watched the dancing Harry bowed before her, inviting her to join the dancers. Scarcely looking at him, she shook her head; she must have done with this foolish longing for what she could not have. He stood a little apart, his eyes moving over the graceful scene, and when Meg rose from her chair with one of the gentlemen he took her place.

'Meg has agreed to ask permission for me to return home tomorrow,' she said abruptly.

'Tomorrow?' He showed no concern but there was a note of uncertainty in his voice. 'We shall all miss you greatly.'

'Indeed?' She noticed that he had not changed his costume; there was a smear of dried mud on one shining sleeve.

'Oh, yes. However, it will soon be dusty and hot at Whitehall, where I must go to prepare for my trip to France. It will please me to picture you standing on your cool Devon seashore listening to the beating waves, bare-armed and maybe barefoot too.' He turned his eyes full upon her.

'I sound quite rustic in your imagined picture, my lord. Perhaps you will soon be adding to it a couple of fat babes clutching at my homespun skirts.'

He sighed. 'What is it about me that makes you want to go to war, I wonder? Such aggressive talk doesn't match that tender mouth.' His eyes lingered on her face.

'I believe it is your…composure which aggravates me. Whatever happens, you remain calm. I long for some sincere reaction from you.'

He met her eyes. 'Then be assured that you have shattered that composure forever, lady. In each waking moment I see your sweet face and in my dreams I know every inch of your beautiful body.' He shifted his position a little to observe the warm colour moving now under the pale skin of her face. He smiled.

'You always go too far, Harry,' she said indistinctly.

He raised his eyebrows. 'I hoped only to part from you in friendliness, Bess. But I see you will still be calling angry abuse from the back of your wagon as you disappear from sight tomorrow.'

She pushed her hair back from her hot forehead. In haste to attend the meal on time she had left her hair loose and it hung over her shoulders almost to her waist now. 'And I see you will never change.'

'Nor you. And I am glad of that. Were you to remain at court I am sure you would even resist shaving some of that gorgeous hair to make it fit under those ridiculous halo caps the other ladies wear.'

'I could be fashionable,' she protested, stung, although she herself thought that the practice of the more fashionable ladies of shaving their hairlines so that the new caps sat more securely quite hideous.

'Your looks are too unusual to conform. Your father too stood out from the crowd. Perhaps it is something from within the de Cheynes.' Again she heard the note of uncertainty in his voice.

'Are we to spend our last evening together discussing court fashions?' she asked.

His eyes rested thoughtfully on Thomasina Beauchamp as she swept by in the dance. She had brought with her from France a solution of white arsenic and lead with which she whitened her skin and now her eyes shone like green stones in her luminous face. Bess had noticed sourly however that she was not so fastidious about the rest of her person. Below the edge of her fashionable gown her skin was quite grey.

'No, indeed. I was only trying to compliment you— to tell you how delightful I find it to be near you.'

She followed the direction of his eyes. 'As delightful no doubt as it was to be near another lady a few short days ago.' Kate had told her that morning with undisguised malice that Thomasina had fallen prey to Latimar's fickle nature and they were no longer a couple.

'That is over now. Besides, most of the time I longed only to drop her in the nearest river and give her a thorough washing,' he replied without changing his polite tone.

Bess laughed despairingly. 'Harry! Really, you are impossible.'

'As you say... I wish I had a parting gift for you to remember me by. But I have nothing in my purse at present. I have been more out of luck than usual at the gaming tables.'

'Perhaps there is some truth in the saying that when you are lucky in love you are unlucky at cards.'

He did not return her smile but something flashed behind his eyes. 'Do you love me, Bess? Truly?'

'Yes, I do. Truly, Harry,' she said deliberately.

He said thoughtfully, 'It is the most precious gift, so precious I scarcely know how to repay you for it.'

'You do not have to provide any payment, Harry. Just do not forget me too soon.'

'Forget you? It breaks my heart to hear you say that.'

'Your heart is not broken yet, Harry.' She held his eyes until his heavy lids dropped and he took her hand and kissed it.

Meg returned and Harry gave up his chair and said goodnight to them both. 'Sir Harry seems somewhat subdued tonight,' Meg commented as the tall figure left the hall.

'It was a difficult day,' Bess murmured. 'I am very tired, cousin.'

'Of course, but Bess—I must tell you that it will be impossible for you to leave tomorrow. The King has forbidden it.'

'Surely His Majesty has more important matters on his mind than my departure.' Bess's scornful eyes followed Henry's progress around the floor in a lively dance.

'I dared not even ask about you. But he has forbidden anyone to leave this court before...the day after tomorrow.'

Bess paled. 'It is for sure tomorrow—Anne's execution?'

Meg twisted her hands together in distress. 'His Grace leaves for Richmond tomorrow at daybreak, the Lady Jane to the riverside home he has prepared for her. When...when it is over they will return to Hampton to await their marriage. Will Soames can take you as you desire, but a day later.' She glanced at her cousin. 'Now, Bess, be calm. It is the way things are; to care too much is to tear yourself apart to no good.'

'Harry said the same in different words.'

'Then perhaps he is learning some sense at last,' Meg said briskly. 'If he also gives up his gambling and woman-chasing then he will lead a safer life.'

Safe. Safe. Everyone at court wanted to be safe. But surely it was the most unsafe place in England, thought Bess, when four gay young men and a blameless woman could be vanquished at the whim of a despot.

'Then if I must stay for another day I must. But I will not work upon the linen,' she declared stubbornly.

'No, sweetheart. It is a sad and desperate task, I do agree. I will take your share and gladly. For it does at least fill the time.'

Bess stayed out of the ladies' chamber until the others were at last abed then crept silently in among the gently snoring girls and tried to find sleep. It was not so easy to come by, however. She thought of Harry, of Richard and of her parents. Soon she would see her mother and father again and she was a little comforted. But what would it be like to be home again? She had lived more fully in the last few months than in the seventeen years before she came to court. She tossed and turned, listening to the breathing in the quiet room, and at last sleep overtook her.

In her dreams Harry stood before her; dressed in a cloak of grey he waited at the foot of her bed and watched her with luminous eyes. She reached out her arms and he dropped his cloak and lay beside her. His body was white, untouched by the sun but hard and muscular. She lay passively until he turned and pressed his mouth to hers, his hands moving demandingly over her breasts, her thighs. Then she clung to him, allowed by the miracle of dreams to be swept away by desire. She awoke breathless in the blackness and lay wide-eyed for a while before sleep came creeping back. This time she dreamed that she was chasing a great ball of light; it floated before her but when she put out eager hands to grasp it for her own it was always just out of reach.

She was awake again at dawn; a beautiful misty dawn. She dressed quietly and slipped from the room. The sun sliding through the fronds of mist found her in Wolsey's knot garden, among the intricate patterns formed of low-growing evergreens with flowers planted close together in the space between which had been a delight to his orderly mind. As yet only the daffodils and blue and white grape hyacinths bloomed, but green buds had appeared on the rose bushes. Next month they would be a riot of sweet-scented colour. And she would not be here to see it. She stood quite still and listened to the cooing of the white doves as they fluttered and jostled for position on their cotes. She found a little bark seat and sat down, an odd lethargy sweeping over her. After a while she heard a commotion and knew that the King must be leaving. Harry would go with him; perhaps even at this moment he was searching for her to say that final goodbye. If she hurried now to the great gatehouse she could see him for the last time. Instead she sat in the sunshine, the dainty birds at her feet.

She was still there at noon when she heard the faint thunder of cannon borne on the wind sweeping down from the city. Without knowing how, she knew she was hearing the signal that the royal murder was over, and she rose and walked slowly back to the palace. As she passed under the gloomy stone arches leading to the cloisters a figure detached itself from the shadows and touched her arm. She stopped and looked up into Tom Spalding's dark face. She nodded and prepared to hurry by but he put out an arm, barring her way.

'Excuse me, sir, I have duties to perform.' She avoided looking at him, but felt the usual distaste for his nearness.

'Ah, yes. I have heard that you leave the court tomorrow, Lady Bess.'

'As you say. I must therefore pack my belongings and make my adieus.'

He fixed his eyes on her averted face. 'You are dismissed from court, my lady?'

'No, sir, I choose to return home at this time. Now please allow me to pass.'

'You are in such haste to return to your farmyard, lady?'

'I look forward to being reunited with my family— and to the cleaner air in the west,' she said coldly.

He flushed, her words recalling his humiliation at Harry Latimar's hands in January. 'You mislike the air at Hampton?'

'I find it somewhat tainted lately, sir.'

He smiled cynically. 'I imagine you refer to matters which affect us ordinary subjects not at all, Bess. I wish now to discuss a matter which does affect us most deeply.'

A soft breeze blew up through the corridor of pillared arches and teased at her hair. She brushed back the silver strands impatiently. 'I can think of no matter which could possibly concern us jointly, Lord Spalding.'

While she inspired tenderness in Harry Latimar she brought only Tom Spalding's aggressive nature to the surface. He longed to take her by her slender shoulders and shake the disdainful expression from her face. Controlling himself, he put a placating hand gently on her shoulder. Even so, she paled.

'How dare you touch me? Allow me to pass at once or I shall summon help——'

'And who will come, I wonder? Your gallant protector is at this moment with the King, no doubt ingratiating himself with his new mistress to be. He is done with the old, and with you. Now you will do me the courtesy of listening to what I have to say.' His grip tightened.

She stopped struggling and closed her eyes. 'Say what you have to say, then, Lord Spalding.'

He cleared his throat, her sudden stillness disconcerting him. 'Your father is far from court, Bess, and the Lady Margaret scarcely the proper person to...advise me. So I must apply directly to you.'

'For what, my lord?' she asked, her eyes still closed.

'Bess,' he said awkwardly, 'I am asking you to be my wife.'

Her eyes flew open—she stared at him. Certainly she did not lack proposals of marriage, she thought ironically, although never from the right man. But this proposal must be the strangest of all. He could not be in earnest. 'You are joking, of course, sir.'

He released her and stepped back a little. 'It is no joke, Bess. You must know how I feel regarding you. I have made it plain enough in the last months.'

'What has been plain is your refusal to concede that I find you quite loathsome,' she said. The lack of expression in her voice made the statement more insulting than if she had cried it aloud. Furious anger leaped into his face.

'You dare to say that to me? The penniless daughter of a crippled useless man, the cast-off of a rake. You should thank God for an honest proposal from one of your own rank. Obviously you prefer the attentions of an oafish country squire or a notorious scoundrel——'

'Strange words to the woman you would make your wife,' she said coolly.

'I would marry you because I cannot have you any other way——' he said, goaded into bluntness.

'You will not have me any way at all.' She raised her voice.

There was a silence. Then Bess heard the rustle of silk and, turning, saw Kate Mortimer coming through the cloisters. Kate paused, taking in the explosive situation at a glance. She said, 'Dear Lady Bess, I have looked high and low for you.' She curtsied mockingly at Tom. 'You must excuse us, sir; this lady's cousin has sent me to bring her in haste to supervise her packing.' She slipped an arm around Bess's waist and steered her firmly past the glowering man and along the path. Inside the safety of the palace walls she looked at Bess, amused. 'You do not leave us until tomorrow, Bess; I believe there may be time for you to gather even more proposals of marriage do you exert yourself a little.'

Bess shuddered. 'That horrible man. What made him think...? I do not like him within six feet of me and he wishes to marry me.'

'There is perhaps something to be said for your maidenly approach to gentlemen, sweetheart,' Kate mused. 'It seems to inflame them to offer you lifelong security. I am inclined to think I have been mismanaging my own affairs a little. I believe even Tom Spalding's brutish charm may be preferable to the old dotard I must shortly become a wife to. Should I try my luck with your reject, think you?'

'Do not even think of it. Harry—Harry said to me once that he would not even trust his horse to Lord Spalding.' She flushed as she said his name and Kate glanced at her. Harry had indeed looked for Bess that morning to bid her farewell, and only an express command from the King had prevented him from staying at Hampton until she was found. But what use to tell her friend that? She had known Latimar for many years now and thought Bess no match for that gentleman's penchant for rich living.

She said cheerfully, 'Well, perhaps you are right. I shall have to see what diversion may be available beyond my husband's failing sight.'

Bess laughed. 'Dear Kate. I shall miss you very much, you know.'

'And I you. But should I wish to find you again I shall simply follow the trail of discarded suitors from here to the Tamar River.'

CHAPTER SIX

THE next day she was on her way home. Will Soames
stole a look at her as he urged the horse on; a younger
and stronger horse than old Grey. Meg had insisted on
this and on making the new wagon as comfortable as
possible for her cousin. Putting in soft cushions and a
fur laprobe in case the fine weather should turn chill
again and tucking a vast wicker basket of provisions
under the seat, she sternly instructed Will on the care of
his young charge. That morning, despite Bess's protests,
she had herself packed the white silk dress and the amber
velvet in her cousin's shabby trunk and lovingly helped
her to dress in the lilac silk, over which she placed her
best dark purple cloak lined with coney. Letting Meg
perform these kindnesses, Bess had not had the heart to
tell her that a farm was no place for silk and velvet. She
felt that fussing over her departure made Meg forget for
a moment the previous days' events. Meg too had
changed from the assured young woman of a few months
ago; without realising it she now saw so many things
through her cousin's forthright eyes and her life seemed
less worthwhile to her. She had already decided privately
that when she returned to her mother's estates she would
press for more help for the sick and the poor, and had
even made tentative plans to use some of her private
fortune for almshouses and maybe even a hospital for
sick children. She kissed Bess goodbye with tears in her
eyes and made her promise to write when she could.

Now they were on the road and Will was aware of the
change in the timid girl he had brought so reluctantly
south in January. Her manner was still pleasant but she
was in command of herself and of him. The purse of
gold Meg had entrusted him with and Bess's obviously

rich clothes ensured them good treatment wherever they went but she behaved as though she were in a dream, hardly seeming to take in her surroundings and his efforts on her behalf. Now that she did not notice him he wanted very much to please her. He had seen her now and then at Greenwich and when she had left for Hampton he had contrived some reason to take him there too. He hardly knew why. Except that in an odd way he was proud of her; a dainty prideful maid who had attracted a measure of attention in exalted company. From a distance he had kept his rheumy eyes on her and guessed now that her distracted state had something to do with one of the young gallants he had seen buzzing about her. He also considered her to be indirectly responsible for an amazing piece of luck which had befallen him. He had been in the thick of a drama such as he would never see again in his lifetime: the downfall and consequent beheading of a Queen of England. As a pedlar this would be a valuable source of custom to him, for he and his like carried the news around the country as well as their wares. With a little embellishment on his part the story would serve him well. While some farmer's wife was agog to hear how he had been a witness to all manner of exciting events he would insinuate himself into her kitchen and would probably not leave it again without a sale. He did not concern himself with the rights and wrongs of the case—that was not the business of folk such as him; what was one woman more or less in the scheme of things? But he did thank Bess for placing him in the right place at the right time. So the journey passed uneventfully, even pleasantly, as Bess's home drew slowly nearer.

They rumbled through the village at twilight and Bess, breathing in the pure country air, felt suddenly warmly expectant. A few more miles and she would be there. She must put behind her the highly coloured life she had just left and try to forget it had ever been. True darkness was falling as the eager horse drew them up the slope and there before them lay the sturdy farmhouse. She could smell salt on the wind as they clattered into the yard and she could see a faint light flickering from within the house as she climbed stiffly down from the wagon and beat gently on the door. It opened at once and her mother peered out. 'Mother!'

'Bess! Oh, Bess.' She was enfolded in her mother's arms, smelled again the scents of baking and lavender and part of the sad weight depressing her heart dissolved. They clung together a moment. 'But, Bess, we didn't expect you. Is anything amiss?'

'No, Mother. It was time to come home and so here I am.'

Her father came then and took her into his arms. 'Bess! Dear child, I am glad you're home.'

'And so finely dressed.' Her mother ran the palms of her hands over the smooth silk. But her father looked anxiously into his daughter's eyes.

Bess smiled quickly at him. 'Oh, I am glad to be here. But I'm so tired . . .'

'Come straight to bed, child, and I will heat milk and honey,' Joan said, bustling away to cover the emotion which had threatened to overcome her at the unexpected sight of her beloved child.

Will Soames, who had been watching the scene in silence, raised his cap to Robert and urged the horse out of the yard.

Bess let herself be put to bed and, drinking her cup of milk, tried to answer her mother's questions. She had come home of her own free will, Cousin Margaret had sent her good wishes and a warm invitation for Bess to join her again at any time she chose in the future, and no, there was no mishap or trouble involving Bess. Joan busied herself unpacking Bess's trunk, exclaiming over the new dresses, keeping up a constant flow of questions until Robert de Cheyne came to the doorway and said mildly, 'Come, Joan. Bess is home now. Tomorrow will be soon enough for all her news.' He urged his wife gently out and the door closed softly behind them, leaving Bess thankfully to the darkness.

As her eyes grew accustomed to the dark the room took shape; everything was at once strange and yet so familiar. The little oak chest one of her uncles had made for her fourteenth birthday stood beneath the embroidered text of the Lord's Prayer which she had most painfully stitched throughout her ninth year. If she stretched out her hand she would feel the garland of flowers that Uncle Bob had carved into its lid. Over her rough wooden chair her mother had reverently laid the white silk dress. It glimmered palely in the moonlight like a ghost to remind her of Harry's words that night at Greenwich. Her room was in one corner of the farmhouse where the roof sloped sharply downwards and she could only stand upright in half of it, but her friends thought her lucky to have such a place all to herself while they shared their sleeping hours with brothers and sisters. Now she wished for company. It had been such a long time since she had been completely alone, and her thoughts were not helping her to the rest she craved. She gazed up at the whitewashed ceiling, seeing first Meg's round face with its sweet, anxious expression, now Richard Woodville's fair features twisted in hurt and anger as it had been the morning he had said goodbye to her. Then Anne Boleyn's face rose before her, her black eyes vibrant. Tom Spalding's face with its malevolent glare flashed into view and she turned her head restlessly to escape it. But Harry's image eluded her, although she tried to conjure it. She looked towards the curtains blowing at the tiny unglazed window and remembered that her mother had made them from one of her old dresses, pink flowers on a blue background. She fell asleep at last, thinking of how pleased she had been the day she had helped to hang them, back in the time when such things had pleased her and she did not hanker after quicksilver and stardust.

* * *

She woke to the cock crowing and the noisy squabbling of hens scratching for their food. She washed and dressed, pulling on the brown woollen dress she had last worn to go to court and brushed her hair, flattening it determinedly beneath a linen cap. Then she rolled up her sleeves to the elbow. She had no mirror to see how she looked but could guess that her reflection would not please her. Her mother was already in the milking shed but Robert had waited to breakfast with her.

He stood up when she came into the room which served as kitchen and dining-room for the family. He kissed her fondly.

'I waited because I want to talk to you, Bess.' He took his seat again and watched her cut a piece of bread and spread it thinly with butter. 'There is ham too, if you would like it,' he said, enjoying the sight of his pretty daughter after her absence.

'This is all I need, thank you, Father.' She noticed seemingly for the first time how handsome he was, how fine his eyes and well-shaped his mouth. Despite his lopsided body he was an attractive man.

'We had a visitor last week—a young man called Richard Woodville.'

She stopped eating, startled. 'Richard? Here?'

'He delayed his journey back from Greenwich to call here. He asked me for my permission to come back when you were at home. You knew of this, I think?'

She looked down at her plate. 'Oh, yes, Father, but——'

'He was quite candid with us, Bess. He told us that you had refused him—although he would not say why.'

In the yard she could hear her mother collecting the milk pails.

'Your mother was very taken with him. She thought him a very…suitable young man,' her father said gently.

'Yes, Father. He is that.'

'But not for you?' She looked up and saw her father's blue eyes studying her gravely. 'Is there perhaps someone else you have grown to care for?'

Bess hesitated. She would have liked to tell him all about Harry, for she was sure that he would understand. Harry was the kind of young man Robert de Cheyne had spent his youth with; perhaps he would even remember the boy from his days at Henry's court. In her mind's eye she saw Harry riding the most untamed horse from the palace, red hair blown back in the crisp wind, eyes blazing with elation; Harry dancing with the Queen, holding her attention with that odd mixture of deference and arrogance he showed towards the most powerful. Harry playing every game as though his life depended on it, but when—rarely—bested, always turning it to graceful defeat with a shrug of his shoulders.

Eventually she said, 'It is different at court, Father. At home here if a boy and girl like each other and the parents do not object it is arranged and all goes ahead. At court it seems to be the other way about. The parents do the choosing.'

He showed no surprise at the turn the conversation had taken but said mildly, 'Well, of course, there is more involved between the great families. They like their fortunes to be held together.'

'Oh, money...' She rose from the table and walked impatiently around the room.

'It is a useful commodity.'

'You and Mother have never had much and ... well, look at you.'

'Yes, look at us.'

'You're happy, though,' Bess insisted.

There was a silence. The day was growing warmer, pools of sunlight lay on the flagged kitchen floor.

'Oh, yes, of course,' Robert said at last. 'But when I saw you arrive yesterday, so beautiful in lilac silk...I wished I had not been so hasty. So angry and bitter after my accident that I was content to cast off all old friendships and be forgotten. To make my life here away from so much that is important and vital.'

'But you are not forgotten,' Bess protested. 'Why, Father, the King...' She told him quickly what Henry had said of him.

His eyes lit up and an expression she had never seen before drifted over his face. Then the more familiar resigned look settled again and he said, 'He said that? Well, I suspect he and I are both much changed. Certainly the man I knew would never have discarded his beloved wife for a pretty face.'

And he has done worse now, much worse, thought Bess. For Robert spoke of Queen Catherine, and Anne was that pretty face. She had not mentioned the events which had preceded her departure from court; the news would come soon enough, no doubt spreading at this moment from Will Soames's lips. She finished her bread and butter. 'I must help Mother. I have not forgotten how much there is to do here.'

He caught her arm as she passed him. 'Don't forget Richard Woodville either, Bess. He is a fine boy and will be a fine man. I would be happy to welcome him as your husband.'

After a few days at home Bess felt she had never been away. She was so busy that she scarcely had time to think and only at night could she think of Harry Latimar, and then she thought of nothing else. After that first night his image came back with shattering clarity; his arrogant head, the clear dark eyes and brilliant ironic smile. She saw clearly the tall slender body and white hands and recalled the words of every conversation they had ever had. In the mornings she went about her work with determination and energy but the expression in her heavy eyes worried her mother.

Joan had begun a campaign to persuade her daughter to take Richard's suit seriously and brought his name constantly into conversation. She chose to believe that

Bess's abstraction was caused by her having been a part of the terrible events which Will Soames had so dramatically described to her. She was disappointed that Bess would not speak about it; indeed the only time Bess ever took part in a conversation about the Queen was during Sunday lunch at Uncle Bob's. All the family were there and Bob was presiding over a huge piece of his own beef. Carving knife in hand, he swiftly sent the plates from hand to hand. Discussion turned to one of their near neighbours, unhappily married and miserable.

'Were he a king he could dispatch the old crone with a sharp sword,' sniggered Bob's eldest son Ned.

'He'd be hard put to it to have anyone believe she had been up to mischief with half a dozen men,' returned his wife.

Bess looked down at her plate, at the thin slices of savoury meat, the mounded vegetables.

'Come now, Katie,' said Joan, 'we want no such talk at a Christian table. Besides, Will said few believed such wicked tales.'

'There's no smoke without fire, Aunt Joanie, and her being one of the devil's own she belong in the fire where no doubt she's gone for all eternity——' She broke off as Bess pushed back her chair and stood up.

'How dare you speak so?' she cried. 'What do you know of her, to so slander her?'

'Bess,' protested her mother, 'sit down, child.'

'I'll not sit down with anyone who blackens her name.'

'Then go somewhere else, miss,' Katie said sharply. 'Don't come to my home and give me your orders.'

Bess went to the door and wrenched it open. She ran through the yard and round into the stable and leaned against one of the stalls. Her father followed her and stood silently while she struggled to recover herself. She turned to him. 'She was not what they said, Father.'

The horses moved nervously among the straw, upset by the tremor in her voice. Robert put his arms around her and patted her back. 'I had not realised you knew her very intimately, Bess.'

Bess pressed her face into his shoulder. 'I knew her,' she said, her voice muffled. 'And those men who died declaring her innocent of the lies told about her.'

'Poor child. Tell me—'twill make you feel easier.'

She wished she could tell him but how tell the story without mention of Harry who was so much a part of it? If she once spoke his name all would come out, all the longing and misery and to what purpose? It would only make him unhappy and would solve nothing.

She sighed. 'I cannot, Father. I was wrong to talk that way to Ned and Katie. I will come in now and apologise.'

Her father pushed back her disordered hair and smiled. 'Very well. But should you wish to speak of it in the future I should like to listen.'

She had gone back and made her apologies and forced down the cooled food and they had not raised the subject again in her hearing. But it had made her mother even more determined to pursue the match with Richard. Bess had been in troubled waters obviously and now Joan was eager to bring her safely to harbour with a good, kind husband.

A brief time after she showed Bess a letter brought by Will Soames from Richard's mother. It was a polite and casual missive introducing herself as the mother of her daughter's friend and enquiring kindly after Bess's health now she was again at home. It was accompanied by the gift of a splendid fruit cake, crammed with dried fruit and costly spices and almost too rich to stay in one piece. Joan had been impressed by both letter and cake and inclined to believe that Richard considered Bess's refusal to marry him anything but final.

Bess privately cursed Will Soames; on the road again in his trade as pedlar he had taken his wagon over the Tamar into Cornwall, stopping off at the Woodville estate to gossip about Bess de Cheyne being home again. She dreaded Richard coming with a high heart to talk her into marrying him. She imagined that he thought that now she was living simply on the farm again her desire for Harry Latimar would have faded. He had insisted that she was dazzled by him and it was true, but she was dazzled by what he was, not by what he had. If his spirit lived in the body of one of the village boys she would have settled as happily into a thatched cottage as into one of the largest palaces in England. So she resisted her mother's efforts and after a while Joan left her puzzling daughter in peace to do her work and keep her own counsel as the early summer days spun out and the evenings lengthened.

But if Joan had laid down the cause for a time Richard had not, and one sultry day as they were sitting down for the midday meal a small boy on a large horse clattered importantly into the yard and jumped nimbly down. In his none too clean hands he held a sealed letter for Bess's father. 'I'm to wait for the answer, sir,' he announced stolidly, his eyes sliding past Robert to where Bess stood in the doorway, around which wild roses were just unfurling their ragged petals.

Robert frowned over the parchment. He could read well enough, unusual for a knight in those times, and had taught Bess too when she was very young. Now he saw that the letter contained a warm invitation from John and Emma Woodville for the de Cheyne family to visit them at the week's end. The Woodville estate was just beyond the Tamar River, half a day's journey away. They would stay the night there and return home upon the Sunday.

Robert looked thoughtfully at his daughter and his wife bubbled with excitement. 'It is for Bess to say, Joan. Our going might imply that she is willing to consider their son's offer of marriage.'

Bess leaned against the stout post supporting the door lintel. It was very warm; she felt drowsy and unequal to the task of putting out the eager light in her mother's eyes. When had Joan last been more than a mile from

her home, put on her best dress, eaten a meal she had
not prepared, or helped to prepare, herself? Besides,
sooner or later she knew she must tell Richard to his
face that his case was hopeless. She would rather meet
him on his own ground for this. 'We will go if you agree,
Father. Richard is my friend and I would like to see him
again.'

The boy was dispatched with the message that the de
Cheynes would leave at daybreak on the coming Saturday
and hoped to reach Woodville Manor by midday. Joan
was beside herself with happiness but she only said,
'Thank goodness I have finished sewing your new dress,
Bess. You will wear that for the journey and have your
pretty mauve silk for the evening.'

Inspired by the gowns Bess had brought back with
her, Joan had used some of her small savings and pur-
chased a length of material to make up what she considered a suitable costume for her daughter. It was a
rose-pink linen, modestly high in the neck and trimmed
on the sleeves with lace from one of Robert's long-
discarded shirts. It suited Bess and her mother was satisfied that Mistress Woodville would find no fault with
the way her pretty, well-mannered girl was turned out.
She herself would wear the only dress she had apart from
her workclothes: black wool and too warm for the
weather, but as long as Bess was suitably clad she was
content. Robert would wear a buff costume, very old-
fashioned in cut but of beautiful quality and immacu-
late as it had been carefully hung away and protected
from moths for the long years since he had left court.

All in all they looked a handsome family as they set
out in a wagon borrowed from Uncle Bob. Her mother
had left minute instructions with two of her nephews,
who had been delegated to do the farm chores in their
absence, and then put her home out of her mind and
prepared to enjoy her unexpected holiday. She had high
hopes of the outcome of the trip, which would solve a
problem which had been occupying her mind for many

a long year. Years ago she had privately sorted through
the likely candidates for marriage with Bess and had
come to the conclusion that none of the local young men
would do. Since her daughter had come home from court
that fact had become even more apparent. Bess was the
same amenable girl but yet subtly changed. It was hard
to decide in what particular way but little things drew
her mother's eye; her turn of phrase was different, the
way she walked with unconscious pride and held her
head, but most of all it was the way in which she saw
life now. The light-hearted child was gone and in its place
a thoughtful woman. Richard Woodville was the answer
to a prayer, and if Joan had her way he would be her
son-in-law within the year.

They arrived as the Woodville stables' clock struck
twelve and, crossing the wide expanse of green before
the manor, a sense of inevitability swept over Bess, for
it was the house that she had seen with her inner eye
that day by the river when Richard had bid her farewell.

He had been watching for them and hurried out at
once to greet them. He swung Bess down from the wagon
and she could not deny the pleasure it gave her to see
him again. He held her a moment before setting her down
and looking eagerly into her face. 'Bess. Dear Bess,' he
said, swallowing hard. She smiled up at him and he
turned to welcome her parents and escort them all into
the house. His mother and father also welcomed them
warmly and Joan's sharp eyes noticed that, while
Richard's mother was at first wary of the girl her son
had fallen so suddenly and absolutely in love with, within
an hour she was enchanted with her.

The introductions and pleasantries over, they all relaxed around a table covered with snowy starched linen
and laid with highly polished pewter plates. An atmosphere of solid comfort was evident everywhere at
Woodville Manor; the furnishings were not opulent or
pretentious but they were the best of their kind; the food
was well cooked, competently served and plentiful, and

the cider they drank sweet and potent. Every member
of the household, from the little maid who unpacked
the de Cheyne trunk to the master himself, was well fed
and pink-cheeked with health. Joan found time, while
enjoying these comforts, to reassess Richard, and found
him as suitable as the day he had stopped, caked with
mud and tired after his flight from the capital, to make
their acquaintance those weeks ago. Handsome, yes, and
solid and courteous, but most of all kind. Like all
mothers of gentle daughters she did so want the man
Bess married to be kind, and he impressed her as being
so. That he was desperately in love with Bess was obvious in the way he looked at her. Joan, earthy as all
her country sisters were, detected no lust in those looks,
no unnecessary touching of her daughter, and was satisfied that the young man had fallen deeply in love with
Bess for all the best reasons. She settled down to let all
take its course.

   After the leisurely meal they were taken upstairs to
rest in the rooms allotted to them. Joan and Robert had
been given a large and elegant room at the front of the
manor and she stretched out on the bed after removing
her warm dress while Robert accepted his host's invitation to be shown the estate. Bess was shown to a smaller
room at the rear of the house and, had she never seen
Greenwich or Hampton, would have considered it luxurious. As it was she barely noticed the pretty room, but
looked out of the window at the countryside and enjoyed what she saw. The manor had been built by John
Woodville's father, Thomas, when he had made his
money and, loving the land so much, he had tried to
ensure that it could be seen from his home by every angle
possible. Hundreds of windows, all glazed in the new
way and criss-crossed with lead, enabled the watcher in
the house to see the rolling meadows and rich brown
earth from the back and the smooth shining waters of
the Tamar and flourishing gardens from the front. Bess
tidied herself and came down to find Richard waiting

for her at the foot of the stairs, his eyes warm with affection.

'Would you care to let me show you around my home, Bess?' he asked her shyly. Although she was so plainly dressed and not shining in fine borrowed clothes and jewels as at court, he found her less approachable somehow. She was more reserved and he missed the candid way with which she had talked to him during their time together at Greenwich. He had watched her descending the stairs with her quick light tread, her hair about her shoulders, and a sharp pang of longing had taken hold of him. He would make her promise to marry him this very day, he decided. The uncertainty was disturbing his days and making his nights a torment. Perhaps the new guarded expression in her eyes was merely a defence against the knowledge that she was being looked over by his strong-minded mother. She slipped a hand in his and a flush spread over his fair face; the touch of his hand on hers had no effect on her, however.

He showed her the house with pride. Each room was a testament to Emma's good housekeeping. Like many of the houses of that time it had one great hall for everyday living, the walls hung with tapestries, a vast fireplace at both ends now laid with apple logs, and kitchens adjoining. Also on the ground floor was a small parlour where the lady of the house could sit and sew or play her music on the elegant spinet. A gallery upstairs led off into two great bedchambers and a number of small guest-rooms.

After Bess had admired the manor Richard took her out into the spectacular day. Equal order reigned in the grounds. The flower gardens directly before the house were carefully tended with not a weed to spoil them and rioted now with summer colour. They lingered in the rose garden a little, the air almost tangible with the heavy scent.

'You look well, Bess, but thinner, I think,' he said, surveying her.

She smiled. 'I was growing fat and lazy at court, Richard. It is good for me to have some real work to do again.'

'But 'tis hard work on a small farm, I know. Here you would do just as much or as little as you chose. Helping my mother with her herb garden, and with the preserves in season. Light and dainty work suitable for my...wife.'

Bright sunlight slanting over the house behind him lit his fair head, leaving his face in shadow. She walked a little way ahead and turned to face him. He lifted a hand.

'Say nothing yet, Bess. 'Tis too soon I know, but...'

The warmth of the sun combined with the perfume from the massed flowers made her light-headed; languor spread through her. Why not accept Richard's proposal now? Why not please her mother and his? What was there in the future to compare with marriage to this strong handsome boy? But still she could not actually say the words that would commit her and after a moment he said, 'Yes, 'tis too soon. Come, let us continue the tour.'

As they took the path around the house he wondered again about her relationship with Latimar. Wondered at the attraction of such a man for Bess. He set his teeth as the picture locked in his memory forever of them together in the summer-house rose before him. He saw again Latimar's white hands on her, the shape of his mouth, the mouth that had just kissed hers before they had sprung apart—— He pulled himself up. There was nothing to be gained from thinking of that, but how he hated the man and wished he had gone to the block with his friends.

They visited the stables last, where she joined her father in admiration of the sensitive satin-coated creatures. John Woodville had been disconcerted by Robert de Cheyne's obvious breeding at first, but the other man's charm and pleasure in all he was shown disarmed him. He had been more than sceptical of Richard's choice of a girl without means, but now he felt his son had chosen well. The Woodvilles would be lucky indeed to capture this lovely daughter of a knight, so pleasing to the eye and modest in her ways.

At eight o'clock they sat down to dine. Emma had planned carefully and produced a meal which did her credit, and she was justly complacent as each course was enjoyed. Joan complimented her lavishly on every dish, particularly the syllabub made with her own hands. Bess was radiant in her silk dress, Richard possessively proud by her side, and the two sets of parents began to think pleasurably of a late summer wedding. Bess herself began to feel more and more confused; before she had come here she had been so sure of her feelings, so determined in what she would say to Richard to cut the tie and have done with the whole business. But now she found herself seduced by the easy beauty of this place, by Richard— no longer the awkward country boy out of his depth in a palace but a good-looking prospective master of a handsome estate.

When the meal drew to a close and the sky outside darkened Richard asked her father if he could take Bess for a walk in the gardens. Approaching the apple orchards he stopped and touched her gently. 'Bess.'

She turned reluctantly. A bright moon had risen overhead and the wind from the Tamar shook the last blossoms from the trees already laden with the hard young fruit. He put out a tender hand and laid it on her hair where the moonlight cast its pale sheen.

'Bess, you know why I asked you here. When we spoke at Greenwich you were…unsettled. It was unfair to press you then. But now you have been home a while and, well, my feelings haven't changed. If anything they have grown more powerful. I want you for my wife, Bess.'

Among the apple trees one of the stable cats moved like a ghost, a silver-grey beneath the moon. She could not speak for remembering another man in another orchard.

'Oh, Bess, be kind to me; we could be so happy,' Richard pleaded.

She hesitated. What was the use of remembering? Always longing for what she could not have. Harry was probably even now on a ship bound for France. In his cynical philosophy she was a dream which could never compete with the reality of his life. Was she to spend the rest of her life wanting him? Richard was offering her a future; she could grasp it with both hands and make him happy and herself fulfilled.

Richard sensed her indecision and took her face in both hands and kissed her, hungrily, desperately. His kiss made up her mind more definitely than any of his pleading words could have done, for she felt nothing. No leaping of the senses, no desire, only a passive feeling of waiting for it to end. It was no use—she could not pretend. Now or in any time to come.

As he had felt her hesitation he now knew that her resolve spoken that day at Greenwich had hardened into determination. For a moment he was stunned, then a flood of anger engulfed him. What did she want, then? He had laid out for her inspection his home, his family, himself. And if she had demanded the sun itself he would have burned his hands trying to get it down for her. He could have struck her and enjoyed it. Just as quickly his anger died and he stepped back. 'We'd best go in now,' he said, his voice muffled.

The cat followed them over the lawns and pressed its sleek body to Bess's skirts before streaking ahead of them and disappearing into the shadows. With difficulty she said, 'There will be someone else for you, Richard. I know there will.'

He said. 'I shan't marry now, Bess.'

She could not answer him. She would never be able to make him believe her. But she knew that the woman she had seen, the mother of his child, coming out of

Woodville Manor on a summer's afternoon in the future, was not herself. It was some other woman whom he would turn to once he had forgotten her.

The house was quiet when they went in and he lit one of the candles fixed into brass holders standing ready on the table in the hall and put it into her hands without looking at her. She went up the stairs, cupping her fingers around the shivering flame, and in her room undressed and climbed into bed. On a table by the window a little earthenware dish of dried lavender and rosemary perfumed the air. She blew out the candle, closed her eyes and tried to sleep.

After a long wakeful night she was very tired. She dressed herself in the pink cotton at the open window which showed her it was another perfect day. Emma had planted her herb garden at the back of the house to protect it from the river winds and she could smell the spicy mixture from where she stood. As she lingered there, reluctant to go down and face the others, Richard rode out from the stables on a dappled grey horse. He reined in below her and looked up. As she leaned out he raised his hand briefly and then the horse leaped forward and dust spurted from beneath the mare's hoofs. In a few seconds horse and rider had disappeared into the ring of trees surrounding the lawn.

At breakfast it was obvious that Richard had told his parents what had passed between he and Bess the night before. His mother's angry flush and his father's bewildered and truculent manner confirmed this. Richard's two brothers had died in their infant years; he was now their only son and the joy of their life. Now he was desperately unhappy and they were furious with the cause. Joan de Cheyne was anxious and preoccupied. What could have gone wrong? she wondered, looking to her husband for help. Bess thanked God for her father; he kept up a casual stream of easy small talk and immediately after the meal gathered his women together and handed them into the wagon, bidding a courteous farewell to his host and hostess.

Joan allowed the house to disappear in the distance then let out her pent-up breath and launched a tirade at her daughter, demanding to know what had happened. On being told that Bess had refused Richard, finally and irrevocably, she was first struck dumb and then voluble again in her abuse. Bess, tired and distraught, burst into tears.

'You might well cry, miss,' her mother said furiously. 'As good a man as I have ever seen discarded like a piece of rubbish . . . and for what, I would like to know——?'

'Be quiet, Joan,' Robert said, his eyes on the dark ribbon of water they were about to cross.

'I will not be quiet.' Joan was more angry than Bess had ever seen her. 'That beautiful house and all that land—all to be his one day. Those kind folk who would have made her so welcome——'

Bess put her hands to her face and sobbed harder. 'That will do, Joan,' Robert said sharply. 'Stop crying, Bess. You disgrace me by behaving so on a public road. If you will not have the young man you will not, but I'll be damned if you will make a spectacle of yourself.'

The two women fell silent. The sun dried the tears on Bess's face and her mother loosened the neck of her dress and rubbed her damp palms on the skirt. It was a miserable journey home.

In the dark farmhouse Robert said goodnight to Bess and escaped to bed; two journeys in the jolting wagon had aggravated his condition and he wanted nothing more than to stretch his painful limbs in comfort. He had demanded no explanation of Bess and would not. Although saddened by her decision, for he liked Richard and his family, she after all had to live with the boy if they married and he was not the type of man to force his pretty daughter into anything she found distasteful. He doubted whether he could in any case. He knew that the general view of Bess was that she was gentle and malleable but he sensed that underneath that soft exterior lay a strength of character which could not be coerced. He put out his light and closed his eyes.

Bess undressed and got into bed but did not extinguish her candle. A short while later the expected visit from her mother came. Joan came in, drew the chair to the bed and sat down. She had undressed and wore a loose blue cotton wrap and her hair, released from its binding, hung over her shoulders. She was still a very pretty woman, thought Bess, waiting in trepidation for the onslaught. But Joan did not appear angry. For a moment she said nothing then she reached out and took her daughter's hand.

'I have not come to berate you, Bess, but I would like to understand why you have refused the young man. Tell me what it is that displeases you. It is perhaps something that can be talked about and resolved.'

'I do not love him, Mother,' said Bess quietly.

'Love . . .' Joan linked her fingers with those she held. 'Love will come, child. You have known him such a short time—surely if you allow yourself time it will come.'

'It has come already for Richard and I cannot, try as I might, return it.'

Joan let go her hand and stood up. She took a turn around the room. 'You have grown up so much lately, Bess, that I feel I may be quite frank with you. We—your father and I—talked with the Woodvilles during our visit and made it plain to them that we would not be able to provide any sort of dowry for you. In return they made it clear to us that no dowry was expected. Richard wanted you just as you were. Can you see what an unusual situation that is? They could have a dozen girls for their son, all bringing with them large settlements, but they were content for him to take you quite penniless. Bess, it would be impossible for such a chance to come again. Please reconsider. At least say you will think it over for a time.' She sat down again.

It was a long speech for her mother to make, usually a woman who said what was necessary in a few words. It also occurred to Bess that although Joan's West Country accent was pronounced her vocabulary and the phrasing she used were unusual too for a farmer's wife. 'Tis father, she decided, who has set her a little apart from her neighbours, and it was his subtle influence that had enabled Bess herself to slip so easily into the life at court.

'Would you have married Father if you had not loved him?'

Joan looked disconcerted for a moment then she said slowly, 'No—no I would not. But had I never met him and had been courted by one of the farmers hereabouts I would have married most gladly. Never having known such feeling, I would not have missed it——' She stopped, aware that this statement did not strengthen her case, then went hurriedly on, 'And had something prevented your father and me from marrying, then I would still have counted it better to be a wife and mother than a maid all my life,' she finished briskly.

Bess turned her blue eyes on her mother in an assessing glance. 'Then we are different, Mother,' she said with finality.

Joan thought she had done well to keep her temper and to try to reason gently with her; now that cool look annoyed her greatly. She got up. 'I see you are a foolish girl, Bess. You obviously do not want my advice and I won't wear myself out trying to make you see how childish and stubborn you are. I think maybe Richard is to have a lucky escape.'

With this parting shot she went quickly from the room and pulled the door shut loudly behind her. Bess pulled the covers up under her chin and her eyes filled with tears. Perhaps she is right, perhaps I am stubborn and childish, for I have ruined Richard's life. I have made my mother unhappy and all for a handful of dreams. Because a man pleases my eyes, touched me so that my heart races, has an expression in his dark eyes that I cannot forget.

July came and every flower in the land seemed to scent the warm evenings; the hedgerows were bursting with wild roses and honeysuckle and everywhere Bess turned there seemed to be lovers hand in hand. As the month progressed it became unbearably hot. The sun rose relentlessly each morning and died in crimson each night, not a cloud passed over the burning sky and the barnyard smells invaded the farmhouse. Bess did her work as usual, but always conscious of her mother's resentment. As far as Joan was concerned her daughter was in disgrace and it made her irritable and quick to lose her temper. Bess tried to please her, tried to be willing and pleasant, but the atmosphere of disapproval and the hot and sleepless nights caused her spirits to sink even lower. She lost weight and the hollows in her cheeks deepened.

Late one afternoon, when she had finished her chores and her mother had grudgingly allowed her some freedom, a longing for the cool seashore came over Bess and she ran over the meadows and on to the cliffs. Below her the sea stretched smooth as glass under the sky and the wind lifted her hair from her hot face. She ran down the overgrown path and, slipping off her shoes, trod over white sand until the water could wash over her bare feet. She knew that Joan would have even more to complain of at this lack of modesty but oh, how lovely it was to feel the chill sea lapping around her ankles. She tied up her skirts and flung her arms wide; her hair escaped from its cap so she took off the linen strip and let the long silver strands stream in the breeze. She danced in the water, turning this way and that, until a figure on horseback riding slowly along the cliffs brought her to her senses.

She walked out of the waves and hastily dried her legs on her petticoat. She looked about for her cap and tried to rebraid her hair. The rider remained motionless for a while, dark against the bright sky, watching her. Then he turned and began to descend the path, his horse picking its way daintily among the clumps of grass and sea thrift. Who was it? Richard, come for a final attempt to win her? Surely not. She shaded her eyes with one hand but the sun was full on the figure's back as he came riding down the stretch of sand towards her and she could not see his face. So she stood quite still and Harry Latimar was upon her before she could realise it.

'Well, Bess, you are just as I imagined you, I see.'

She looked up at him sitting easily in the saddle as his horse moved under him, its liquid eyes on the rolling surf. He slipped lightly down from the saddle. 'You look as if you had seen a ghost. I am merely flesh and bone, I assure you.'

Still she couldn't speak, couldn't move. 'Bess,' he said laughing and taking her hands, 'speak to me.'

At his touch she came to life. 'Harry...I can't believe you are here. I thought you in France. Why have you come?'

A wave, rushing up the shore, rippled over one leather riding boot. He looked down at it ruefully. 'It is permitted to visit an old friend, surely? Have I called at an inconvenient time?' His clear eyes strayed over her dishevelled hair and downwards to her bare feet.

'My shoes...I left them somewhere,' she said vaguely.

'I believe I passed them on the cliff path,' he said politely.

'I must go home. I must find my cap.' He *would* come now and find her barefoot, her hair loose and tangled.

'Must you hasten away? 'Tis a beautiful place, your Devon seashore.' His eyes roved over the glinting sea before returning to her face.

'Did you call at the farmhouse? Did someone tell you I was here?'

'Why, no. I just had a fancy to explore the countryside and was quite amazed to recognise you practising a new dance step upon the sand.' He walked a little way along the shore and scooped up the scrap of linen. He put it into her hands.

'Shall we walk a little?' He held out a hand and looped the reins over one arm.

She took his hand and they moved slowly down the beach. In the shadow of the overhanging cliff he took off his jerkin and laid it on a rock.

'Be seated, Bess. I am anxious to hear all your news.' Commanding his horse to stand, he looked enquiringly at her. She sat down.

'News? I have no news, Harry.'

Underneath his leather jerkin he had on a loose shirt of some thin soft material. She averted her eyes from his exposed white throat.

'Indeed? On my journey here I chanced upon a pedlar named, I believe, Soames. He was full of a tale that you and your family had visited the Woodvilles to arrange your marriage to their son.'

'It came to naught.'

'Ah. A disappointment for you?'

'No. It was my choice.'

He stirred the sand with the toe of one boot. 'So you are still heart-free, Bess?'

'So it would seem.'

He bent to pick up a starfish, dried out by the sun. As he did so she saw he had a half-healed wound just above his heart. She said in alarm, 'You have been injured? Was there some accident in the lists?'

He straightened up, examining the crumbling fish. 'No, 'tis a legacy of a disagreeable interview with Lord Spalding.'

'With Tom Spalding? But . . . he attacked you?'

'I fear it was the other way about. He merely defended himself. To no great avail, however.'

'You did not . . . ?'

'Kill him? No. At least he is still breathing.'

'But what was your argument about?'

'Oh...he spoke slightingly of a lady of my acquaintance. I could not let it pass.'

'Was the lady myself?'

He looked down directly into her eyes. 'It was.'

'And you defended me,' she said gently. 'As you defended Anne.'

'Not quite in the same way. But I am afraid the habit is growing upon me.'

'You have changed, Harry. You are growing more...caring.'

'Indeed.' He lifted his black eyes to the sky, now filled with crying gulls. 'I scarcely know myself.'

'Well, I thank you. I dislike Lord Spalding and cannot grieve for his injuries.'

He laughed. 'No. But—tell me—what of Richard Woodville? A different prospect altogether. I thought him someone to respect. To love.'

'I do respect him. But I do not love him. At least not in the way he would wish and would have the right to expect if we were to marry.' She stood up and shook the sand out of her skirts.

'Nevertheless he loved you. As did Tom Spalding, however unwelcome that might have been.' He tossed away the fish, crumbled now to dust. 'I have come to regard love with more respect lately; I'm sure I do not know why. Lying on my sick bed recovering from Tom's unlucky thrust, it occurred to me that I had given my love to so few people. One is dead, one is so changed—— Well, no doubt I was morbidly feverish.'

When she said nothing he asked abruptly, 'Did you refuse Woodville because of me?' He was very close to her; his sleeve brushed her bare arm but he did not touch her.

'No. Because of myself.' There was a pause. The tide was washing in now, covering a little more of the sand each minute.

'Does your wound cause you pain?'

'A little... It is nothing.'

She put out one hand and touched the scar with the tips of her fingers, feeling the hard ridge of puckered skin above the tender flesh of his breast. He shivered slightly under her hand. 'You could have been killed,' she said faintly.

He took her hand in both of his. 'Not so. I am lucky, Bess.'

'I think I must go back now, Harry.'

'Of course. I shall escort you home.'

'Thank you. My father will be pleased to see you.'

'I am looking forward to meeting him again.'

He whistled to his horse and helped her over the shingle to the foot of the cliff slope. He lifted her on to the animal and walked beside her. Halfway up he retrieved her shoes and fitted them carefully back on her feet before springing lightly up behind her. A variety of emotions took hold of her as he put one arm around her waist and flicked at the reins.

As they rode her hair blew back into his face and he took the shining mass and laid it over one shoulder. 'You would come and find me so unkempt,' she said resentfully above the pounding of hoofs.

'You are just as I expected,' he returned teasingly, his breath warm on her neck.

Her mother and father were in the yard as they rode in. Harry lifted her down and removed his cap as Bess breathlessly introduced him. Robert de Cheyne looked the younger man over delightedly. 'Harry Latimar. My boy, I remember you very well.'

'And I you, sir. I am happy to see you again.'

Bess watched them clasp hands. Two of a kind, she thought; there was about them both something which drew the eye. They went inside and Joan put ale and little spiced cakes on the scrubbed table. She tried to catch her daughter's eye but Bess drew out a chair and sat down, her eyes fixed on Harry.

'You're a long way from home, boy,' Robert said. 'Are you on the King's business?'

'No, sir. It is my own personal business I am about. I had a whim to visit Devon—I have never been west before—and to renew acquaintance with a friend.'

'You intend to stay long?' Joan asked.

'A few days, I believe. I thought to find lodgings in the village. Can you advise me?'

'You will stay with us, of course,' Robert said. 'It is only cramped accommodation we can offer you but there is a bed—and you are most welcome.'

'Oh, any bed will suit me, sir,' Harry said, raising innocent eyes to Joan.

She said, 'You will wish to see to your horse and re-fresh yourself after your journey. Robert——'

Robert rose and said easily, 'I will show you where, Harry.'

They left the kitchen together and Joan looked at her daughter, her lips prim. 'Each month seems to bring a new young man to our door, Bess. I shall shortly begin to wonder how you spent your time at court.'

'He is merely a friend, Mother,' Bess murmured. 'Shall I help you with the supper now?'

'I think it would be better if you went to your room and attempted to tidy yourself. I dislike seeing my daughter looking like a gypsy.'

Bess smiled, sensing the thaw at last, and Joan smiled in return but when Bess had gone her thoughts were anxious. Richard had impressed her at once with his sin-cerity and she had felt him not so very different from the young men she knew. A little more educated, ob-viously wealthy, but underneath he was a farmer and so familiar to her. But Sir Harry was quite a different animal. Even a week's hard riding and the plain clothes he wore could not disguise what he was. It showed in his arrogant bearing, the set of his shoulders, the mani-cured hands and a dozen other ways. She turned her attention to preparing the meal with a sigh. She was inevitably reminded of the day she had first laid eyes on her husband; had Bess been struck by the same lightning bolt? But Robert had been, without mincing words, damaged goods; this man must surely be able to pay court to any lady he chose. For what reason, she wondered, had he sought out little Bess de Cheyne?

Bess changed into her pink dress and vigorously brushed her tangled hair. She caught it back with a ribbon and sat down on the bed to put on her slippers. She could not take it in that Harry was here. Why? Her mind darted here and there looking for an explanation.

'Bess.' Her mother's subdued voice through the door. 'Come out now and have supper.'

She joined them at the table and Joan served the simple meal: a hearty mutton broth with sweet hunks of that morning's bread. Bess looked hopefully at her father to see if he could solve the mystery but his eyes were on his steaming bowl. He said grace in his beautiful voice, then asked Harry how he had left the King. Was he in good health? Harry responded with the news that there had been another royal wedding at the end of May and the supper-table conversation revolved around this.

Outside in the yard a dog barked and above in the darkening sky the birds were calling to each other. The sun was sinking inch by inch, leaving a fiery glow which promised another radiant day to come. Some of Joan's excellent cheese completed the repast and she and Bess rose to clear away the dishes.

'We shall sit in the parlour awhile,' Joan said when the plates were stacked for washing.

Poor Mother, thought Bess; entertaining a visitor was going to be a strain for her when she obviously longed for her bed after a long day.

They trooped into the seldom-used parlour. Joan plumped up cushions and stirred the shallow bowls of pot pourri with one finger. It was a source of pride to her that she had an arrangement with the only farm in the area big enough to sacrifice land for a flower garden and rich enough to buy costly spices for the making of the fragrant stuff. Her knowledge of healing remedies, handed down by her mother, was well known, and she supplied these to the Shapley farm in return for two sweet-smelling bags delivered twice a year. She walked around the sparsely furnished room, straightening the tables and chairs, and when she was satisfied all was in order she sat next to Bess on the settle. It was a little worn in places but brightened by embroidered linen squares sewn over the threadbare places. Harry dropped into a chair opposite the window, the last of the sun resting on his glossy hair. Robert began painfully to lower himself into a straight wooden chair with solid arms. Once he had got his limbs mobile to cope with the day's work he could manage very well in walking and working around the farm, but by this time of night he was stiff and uncomfortable. Harry watched him without offering any help and when Robert was settled he began to talk. He recounted some amusing anecdotes about the people he thought Robert might remember, Bess put in a sentence or two and Joan asked a question now and then. It was all very pleasant and easy.

When the sun had sunk and twilight invaded the room Joan rose, drew the curtains together and lit candles. Harry said, 'I remember you used to enjoy a game of cards, sir.'

'I did occasionally. Do you play, Harry?'

Bess laughed inwardly. Did Latimar play cards? Did he breathe?

'In truth I believe it was your father who first taught me the rudiments,' Robert remembered. 'But I could not compete with him or my other wealthy friends. I had no gold to lose and one cannot of course risk what one does not have.'

'No, indeed,' murmured Harry, catching Bess's eye across the darkening room. He lowered his first. 'I had it in my mind to play a little now to finish a pleasant evening.'

'Then I will leave you,' Joan said shyly. 'I have never played and would spoil the fun.'

'Oh, please stay, my Lady,' Harry protested. 'Bess plays, I know, and we could make a foursome.'

Joan blushed at the unfamiliar use of her title but remained as Harry jumped up to place a table handy so Robert need only lean forward a little to lay his cards, and moved chairs up for Bess and her mother. He took a pack of cards from his jerkin and Bess saw with a little jolt that it was George Boleyn's own deck, bearing his crest in silver and black on the plain side. Harry held the cards in one hand and fanned out the painted squares with his thumb. He explained the rules of the simple play to Joan. 'We will play for points, shall we? Whoever has the most points when play ends is the winner.'

'And what is the prize?' asked Bess.

'We need no prize, Bess,' he said reprovingly. 'To win will be sufficient reward.'

He dealt the cards around the table. Bess noticed her father give him a thoughtful glance as the white hands handled the cards with expertise. Bess found charcoal and paper; she would keep the score. Joan played nervously at first but soon she began to enjoy herself and to laugh at her mistakes in response to Harry's charm. Bess had seen him charm a great many people since she had known him. It was not done in any condescending way—he just had a talent for bringing out the best in his fellows. She hadn't seen her mother look so free of care for years and her father—her father had discovered a comrade that night as he and Harry exchanged remarks across the table and laughed together.

It was late when Bess totted up the score and found that Harry had won. He looked delighted. 'What a shame there was no money involved,' she said.

He raised his eyebrows but said nothing in reply.

'And now it is time we found our beds,' said Joan. She gave Harry one of the candles to light him to his room and Bess the other. 'Tomorrow we are invited to Christopher Shapley's to celebrate his daughter's wedding.' She hesitated then went on, 'You will be welcome too, Harry, should you care to join us.'

'That is most kind. I look forward to it eagerly.' He turned to Robert, who was still seated. 'Are you ready to retire, sir? Then may I help you? It has been a long day for you—I blame myself for keeping you up with my town-bred ways.' He slipped his hands under the older man's arms and pulled him gently upright.

'Thank you, my boy. You are stronger than you look.' It was a measure of how their relationship had progressed throughout the evening, for her father normally hated anyone to assist him in any way.

Bess's room was filled with moonlight and bright as day. She set down her candle and thriftily pinched out the flame between thumb and forefinger. For a moment she stood undecided then she left the room and walked quietly through the kitchen to the little room beyond. Harry's door was open, his candle still burning. The room he had been given, the only spare one in the farmhouse, had originally been planned as a store-room. It was meagrely furnished with a truckle-bed and a rag rug upon the floor. There was no window, only a large square slab cut through the wall, a piece of muslin nailed tightly over it to keep out flying insects. An upturned box served as a night table at the head of the bed.

Harry was sitting on the uncomfortable-looking bed, the pack of cards in his hand. He looked up. 'Bess! Is anything amiss?'

She closed the door behind her. He said, 'I don't think your mother will like you to be here.'

'My mother will know I have just come to talk with you, Harry.'

'Ah. Well, I have only the bed to offer you to sit upon.'

She sat down beside him. He returned to his contemplation of the cards. 'You miss him,' she said simply.

A month ago she knew he would have shrugged his shoulders, put away his memento and changed the subject. Now he said, 'I do. Not in any morbid way, you understand. Just sometimes when I see some unusual sight I think, Now that would have vastly amused George. And maybe when I am in conversation and there is malice spoken I think, If George were here he would send the speaker away with his ears ringing from one of his swift rejoinders in a way I never could. I took these cards from his rooms. Stole them rather, since I asked no one's permission. I did ask for permission to have Anne's hound Urian for my own. And wished I had not, for Henry chose to remember the tales of the beast being an evil spirit and had it speedily put down. However...' his dark eyes sought Bess's '...what brings you here?'

'It is what brings you here I wish to know.'

'May I not visit a friend? We are friends, are we not?'

'Harry, we are scarcely that. There is between us more—and less—than friendship.'

'If you continue to look at me like that there will be a great deal more, Bess,' he said gravely.

She jumped up. 'Talking with you is like trying to catch water in a sieve. I ask straightforward questions; can I not have straightforward answers?'

He lifted his long legs from the floor and stretched out on the bed, propped by the two hay-stuffed pillows Joan had found him. 'I do not know the answers. I don't know why I came here.' His voice was suddenly flat and she saw that he looked almost ill. His face was drained of any colour and around his eyes there were shadows of fatigue.

She put a hand on the doorknob. 'Well, I must not keep you from your rest. I thought to say that you do not have to come with us tomorrow. I think it will be nothing in your line—a very simple affair——'

'But I am looking forward to it very much. Do you not wish me to come?'

'Of course I do, but——'

'Are you ashamed of me, Bess? Do you not wish to present me to your friends? Your other friends. I promise

I will behave in exemplary fashion.' He was laughing at
her now, the moment of depression passed.

'I am sure you will. Very well. Now you must sleep;
is there anything I can get for you?'

'Thank you, I have everything I need. For the
moment.'

'Then goodnight, Harry.' She opened the door.

'Goodnight, sweet Bess.'

CHAPTER SEVEN

SUSAN SHAPLEY'S wedding day dawned bright and sun-filled. It had rained gently during the night but the air was not cleansed of its humidity; the promise of a heavy storm was still there. Bess was at work early in the little dairy; it was her favourite occupation on the farm, especially during warm weather, as the stone building with its scrubbed flagged floor and thick walls was cool. After evening milking her mother would put the rich milk into shallow bowls covered in muslin and overnight the cream would rise to the surface, ready to be skimmed off and made into butter in the cumbersome churn. As the nearest farm to the village the de Cheynes had a small but welcome trade in butter and cheeses and Bess took pride in the skill, which earned a few pennies for her ribbons and hose. She had reached the stage of forming the yellow butter into square slabs with the deft use of wooden bats when Joan came in with a mug of ale and perched on the stool while Bess wrapped the neat squares in muslin and packed them ready for delivery later that day.

'I have pressed your pink dress for this afternoon,' she said as Bess picked up her mug and drank thirstily. 'I think it will be suitable.'

Bess wondered suddenly what Harry would wear. Did he have his saddlebags stuffed with his gorgeous court apparel? Would he appear among the modest company this afternoon glittering in silver tissue? She smiled.

'You are happy today, Bess,' Joan observed. Bess glanced at her; it was unusual to see Joan sitting at her ease at this time of day. She had probably come to question her about Harry. It was unlike her to have waited this long. But Joan only chatted awhile and then

211

left Bess to scour the milk pans and other utensils. When she had cleaned the dairy she took the butter into the farmhouse larder and found her mother putting a jug of ale, two pewter mugs and a napkin of honey cakes into a wicker basket.

'Carry these out to your father; he is mending the fences out in the far meadow. Harry is with him and there is plenty for both.'

The hot July sun had been shining for several hours but underfoot it was deliciously damp and cool against her bare ankles as Bess walked over the fields. She felt light and happy today—the future was uncertain but right at this moment knowing Harry was under the same western sun and not far away on French shores filled her with joy. She skirted the cornfields, admiring the tall stems, each ear ripening to maturity. It would be a fine harvest this year, and with the small flock of sheep and healthy cattle they owned all doing well the de Cheynes would meet the coming winter in fair fettle.

She found the two men working on the gate of the stock enclosure. As she approached she thought with amusement that Harry Latimar had never expected to soil his white hands propping up a gate-post. They greeted her with pleasure as she poured the ale, handed the little cakes. Harry's skin would never tan the dark colour of her father and his fellow farmers but his face showed a faint flush, as did the throat and V of pale skin above his white shirt. As they emptied their mugs she refilled them with the last of the foaming beer and then sat a little apart on the dry grass. It was so quiet that she could hear the muted thunder of waves on the nearby shore above the buzzing of insects and rustling of small creatures in the fields.

'Hold the post steady, Harry, while I nail the new wood to it.' The sharp retort of the hammer cut into the peace of the morning.

'You enjoy this life, sir?' Harry asked.

Her father considered a moment. 'Lately I find I do. There is satisfaction in taking from the earth the result of what you have sown and having to rely on your own hard work for your daily food. It was not always so for me. At first I was a poor workman and the mistakes I made many, but now... yes, I enjoy it well enough.'

'It is a hard life, though.'

'It is. But there are compensations in living close to the land. There is a reality about the changing seasons, the constant renewal of life, which is not apparent when living in a town or city. The people too are of different stuff. There is no time to waste on the trivialities of life. Do you think you would like to be a farmer, Harry?'

Harry brushed the woodchaff from his hands. 'I think I am not that persevering. You are twice the man I will ever be.'

Robert laughed. 'When you were a page and caught in some piece of devilment you would always claim how weak you were, how lacking in strength to resist the temptation of sin. It saved you many a clouting, I recall. Who could beat a child so ready to admit his frailty? I suspect you use that same ploy now to avoid commiting yourself to anything serious in life.'

Harry laughed too, but not in amusement. 'You see too much, my lord. It is a peculiarity of the de Cheynes.' He glanced at Bess but her eyes were intent upon the wind rippling through the yellow corn.

''Twas not meant as a criticism, my boy,' Robert said gently, packing away his tools.

Bess repacked the basket and got to her feet and they went back to the farmhouse to prepare for the festivities that afternoon.

The Shapley farm was five miles down the valley. It was a large and prosperous place compared to the neighbouring holdings but, like Robert and Joan, Christopher and Martha Shapley had only one child, their daughter Susan, whose marriage was celebrated today. Chris was a large red-faced man with curling black hair, which had been inherited by Susan, who looked her best today in primrose silk with a wreath of white and yellow daisies in her curls.

Everyone welcomed the de Cheynes warmly; Robert was not quite one of them but no one could disallow his courage in fighting his handicap for twenty years and at last turning his farm into a moderate success. Joan had always been popular from a child and her kindly response to any sickness and freely given medicines to help cure it was greatly appreciated. Bess had featured in many of the local boys' waking dreams and there was lively interest from them in the tall young man on the aristocratic black horse who was accompanying the de Cheyne wagon. He introduced himself, omitting his title, and they appraised him under cover of their jovial handshakes. Susan came over, blushing, to be congratulated and Bess gave her the bride-gift she had made. Knowing that most of the gifts would be purely practical—pots and pans for the newly-weds' kitchen, or linen for beds and table—she had unpicked the ruffle from her lilac silk gown and sewn it into a lace collar. Harry, with the air of having considered long and hard over the bride's present, produced a necklet of fragile silver flowers studded with sea coral. By country standards it was a costly piece, but so exactly right that Susan must wear it there and then and present her pink cheek for Harry to kiss. Bess's mind flew back to a scene she had witnessed at court when he had staked his horse against a string of emeralds in a dice game, won, and had immediately wound them around Thomasina's throat and kissed her with exactly the same pleasure in having given a pretty woman something she wanted.

Trestle-tables had been put up under the shady oak trees before the house and were groaning with food: succulent hams and sirloins of beef, pork white within and crisp without, baby carrots and peas and freshly baked bread and cheeses ranged along one side, fruit cakes, tarts and fruit pies along the other. Martha Shapley had been planning this day for a long time and, looking around at her neighbours enjoying her good fare, was almost too excited to eat herself. She cast an anxious look at the sky; the sun was filmed now in fine clouds, and the air held the unmistakable threat of rain before dark. She didn't look at her husband, who had suggested having the feast in the barn to avoid a sudden storm. She wanted the barn for dancing later and had found time to supervise the hanging of gay lanterns in the rafters, and raising a platform for the hired musicians. The celebrations would go on well into the evening and the large and airy barn was perfect for a large group to dance. If only the rain would hold off until after the meal.

Bess sat next to Susan's cousin Jack. At first he was too tongue-tied to speak to her, but the plentiful ale, more potent than he was used to, soon made him talk-ative. 'It must be near two years since I seen you, Bess. We heard some time back you'd gone to London on a visit. Some said you'd not come home again.'

'Well, I have come home,' said Bess, glancing up the table. Harry of course had found the prettiest girl present to sit with, and Mary Banks tossed her curls in delight under his barrage of charm.

'You home for good, then?' Jack was single-minded.

'It would seem so, Jack,' she said as Mary popped a piece of wedding cake into Harry's mouth and blushed at her forwardness.

'I always liked you, Bess. A lot.' Jack pressed the hand beside him meaningfully.

Harry turned his head and gave them a swift calcu-lating look.

She said with a smile, 'No, you didn't, Jack. You used to call me a stuck-up piece and put spiders down my neck whenever we chanced to meet.'

Jack laughed heartily. 'Well, perhaps I did. And you maybe still are but it suits you. I'm doing well now, Bess—I got a good rich farm and a bit of money behind me. I shall be settling down with a likely girl any day now.'

Oh, dear, she preferred the spiders to this. If Kate Mortimer were here she would be claiming that Bess de Cheyne could not be with a man five minutes without bringing him to the brink of a proposal. She smiled again and slid her hand away.

When everyone was pleasantly full they sat around the tables drinking and talking until the first warning drops of rain began to fall in large warm splashes. Everybody got up hurriedly and ran laughing to the house, carrying as much as they could of the remainder of the feast. Then they made a dash through the downpour to the barn. Breathlessly shaking water off their hair and clothes, they looked expectantly to the trio on the dais who struck up a lively tune. Jack seized Bess and swept her into the crowd.

The steps, danced since babyhood, came back to her immediately and she gave herself up to the rhythm. Jack, although heavily built, was sure-footed enough and very masterful. He held her tightly and spun her dizzyingly. Over his shoulder Bess saw Mary shyly demonstrating the steps to Harry, who wore an expression of extreme concentration on his handsome face. She danced the next and the next with Jack, then pleaded thirst and persuaded him over to the jugs of ale and cool lemonade standing in the corner of the barn. Sipping her drink, she saw a dark glass bottle being passed around among the young men and Jack grabbed it and added some to her lemonade.

'This will give you strength for the evening to come,' he declared, ignoring her protests. She had had nothing but weak ale and milk since leaving court and although she didn't like the raw taste of it it made her pleasantly light-headed.

Harry materialised at her elbow. 'May I have this dance, Bess?'

Jack looked mutinous. 'She've promised it to me.'

Bess said gently, 'Harry is my father's guest, Jack. I think I must dance with him.'

'You are using your considerable experience in dealing with ardent swains to good advantage, I see,' Harry said, leading her out on the floor.

'I hope you are not using your rather different experience today, Harry.'

He looked puzzled. 'What can you mean?'

'I mean Mary Banks is quite besotted with you already.'

He swung her round then drew her close again. 'How gratifying. She is most charming.'

'And very innocent and young. You will turn her head; she is just a country girl.'

'I believe you used to so describe yourself. I have not turned your head with my attentions yet.'

'Your attentions are so variable. First hot, then cool— my head has no time to become adjusted. Since coming to Devon you have been quite aloof.'

'Do you expect me to attempt to ravish you under your father's roof?' he said in the devastating way he had of producing big guns against her little arrows. She flushed.

'Why must you always be so outrageous?'

'I beg your pardon, I am sure I did not raise the subject.'

'What subject? I meant only that you profess affection for me and when I turn my back you are cozening some other lady,' she said severely.

'I believe there is a delightful country expression which answers you: that is the pot calling the kettle black. Scarcely have I ever left your side before a queue has formed. Richard Woodville, Tom Spalding and now your bucolic young farmer Jack.'

His words were as usual light-heartedly spoken but there was an undertone to them which made her say quickly, 'I was but being pleasant to him. It is that kind of occasion and I am still free, as you pointed out when you arrived. And happy to be home again. Surprisingly so.'

'I am not surprised. I could easily be seduced by this lovely place, and by the people here.' His deliberate use of a provocative word made her even more aware of his hands on her.

He moved his hands from her waist and slid them gently up her back. She missed a step. 'You have been drinking brandiwine, Bess. It has an odd effect on those unaccustomed to it,' he remarked. The music came to an end and she saw Jack shouldering his way through the couples. Harry gave her up without comment and the lines formed for an old country measure. She saw her mother led out by Chris Shapley and smiled across at her, thinking how pretty she was even in her old black dress, with her eyes shining and her face aglow.

The evening flew by. Bess refused any more to drink from the dark bottle but presently felt a headache pricking behind her eyes. She took advantage of Jack's helping himself to more to drink to slip outside for air. The rain had ceased and the moon was up. She leaned on a rail in the cool air and watched the purple clouds banked in the west. It was an unsettled evening but her head cleared as she shivered a little in the fitful breeze blowing over Chris Shapley's fruitful acres.

'Bess—I been looking for you.' Jack came stumbling over the ground towards her.

She sighed. He had been drinking for some hours and was no longer steady on his feet.

'I am ready to go back in now, Jack. I am refreshed by the clear air——'

'Juss a minnit.' He towered over her. 'No hurry, I don't mind a while alone with you. You're a lovely lass, Bess.'

'Thank you, Jack. But we must go back to the dancing now. My mother will be looking for me.'

'Can dance out here, can't we? More private, like.' He put his arms clumsily about her.

Harry came out of the shadow of the barn. 'Lady Bess, do you wish me to escort you back to the dance?'

'No, she don't,' said Jack angrily.

'I think perhaps she does,' returned Harry gently.

Bess started towards him and Jack shot out a hand and took her by the wrist. She pulled instinctively away and the mark of his fingers showed up darkly in the moonlight on the delicate skin of her arm. Jack renewed his grip. Harry's eyes narrowed. 'Take your hand from the Lady Bess or I will take your head from your shoulders,' he said quietly.

Jack shouted with laughter. 'You daft beggar. You'll do no such thing.' He ran bleary eyes over Harry's slender figure.

Bess released herself again and Harry sprang forward and pounced on the other man. As he did so Bess realised that she had never seen him truly angry before. The insolent anger he had shown on a few occasions at court paled beside this controlled fury. Out of the corner of her eye she saw a number of men come out of the barn and stand silently watching; her father and Chris Shapley were among them. Thunder rolled menacingly from the storm clouds as Harry systematically used his fists on the other man. Jack was a stone heavier and fit and strong from an outdoor life but he was no match for such destructive strength. He sagged at the knees.

Robert de Cheyne said, 'Enough, Latimar.' He barely raised his voice but there was a note in it Bess had not heard before. Harry heard it too and stepped back. Jack slipped from his grasp to the ground.

There was a dangerous pause, then Harry passed a hand over his hair and went to Chris Shapley. Behind them the party in the barn had become hilarious, the music swelled and a burst of applause shook the building.

Harry said, 'I must apologise, sir, for taking part in such a brawl on your property and on such a day.'

Chris considered him a moment, then he said mildly, 'Jack was never able to hold his drink.' It was a

handsome speech from a man very fond of his kin and
known to dislike outsiders.

'Fetch your horse, Harry. Bess—go in and tell your
mother we are leaving,' Robert said briefly.

Jack's brothers hauled him to his feet. Bess went back
to the barn and found her mother. The de Cheynes said
their goodbyes to Chris and Martha and climbed into
the wagon. Harry sprang into the saddle, wincing slightly.
He pressed a hand to his breast. On the ride home Joan
chattered happily, unaware of any tension. Bess and her
father were silent and Harry rode a few feet behind them,
also silent under the lowering sky. Outside the farmhouse Joan went in ahead of them, declaring herself too
tired to do anything but go straight to bed. The other
three looked at each other.

'I am more sorry than I can say, sir,' Harry said at
last.

Robert began to unharness the horse. 'There is no great
harm done, I think. Jack will awake with a few bruises
and his pride a little dented. But I never knew you had
such a temper, my boy.'

'No more did I. I am deeply ashamed.' Harry backed
his horse and led it away towards the stable.

'Father—it was not his fault. Jack was being
most . . . objectionable.'

'A man must govern his temper. And he had not the
right.'

'You're angry.'

'I dislike any arrangement where those taking part are
ill matched.'

'Jack is far the bigger man,' she protested.

'I am not speaking of Jack.'

'You mean Harry and me,' she said after a moment.
'But Father, you like him, I know you do.'

'Yes, I like him. He is very likeable . . . but he is also
wild, Bess. Beneath that smooth surface there is a confused man. A man uncertain which path to take and
one, maybe, who will never make up his mind. Such

people are dangerous to those around them. I do not wish you to be hurt while Harry Latimar finds his way.'

'He would never hurt me,' she said stubbornly.

Robert finished unbuckling the harness. 'I know him, Bess. And once I knew many like him. He was made to sail along the pleasant waters of life. Such men add much to their surroundings; they are charming and gay and the world would be a less exciting place without them. But I believe some event, or events, has knocked Harry off course and now he is forced to find resources within himself that I am not sure he possesses.' He smiled. 'You really know very little about men, despite the fact you attract them so readily. However—perhaps I am tilting at shadows. He has not declared his intentions regarding you to me. Nor, I think, has he spoken anything definite to you.'

'He has not spoken of marriage, no.'

Robert let this ambiguous statement pass. 'Well, we must sleep now. 'Tis past midnight. Take your mother's medicine box and go to Harry,' he added. 'I think the boy sustained some hurt in his confrontation. I am for my bed...'

She found him lying on his bed. He protested when she laid the little box on the floor and opened it purposefully. 'It is nothing, Bess.'

'Then let me see.' She lifted his shirt. There was a bruise forming above the wound and where the skin had begun to heal a little blood escaped.

'It will heal again,' he said, sitting up and moving defensively back against the wall.

'We must not risk infection.' She poured a little alcohol on a wad of cloth. 'It will hurt.' He pulled his shirt together hastily.

She laughed. 'Which would you prefer, my lord? A little pain now or a lot later?'

'None at all,' he said sulkily.

'Now be a brave boy. 'Twill soon be over.' She pressed the cloth firmly on to his flesh.

'All women are cruel,' he murmured. As she leaned
over him he could smell the perfume which was peculiar
to Bess: a mixture of rosewater and her own body scent.

'There—it has stopped bleeding. I believe all will be
well.' She smeared a little balm over it. Before she could
straighten up he took a handful of her hair and pulled
her gently towards him. She sat down on the bed and
looked down at him. He wound the hair around his
fingers. 'Bess—are you angry with me for disgracing you,
after all?'

'There was no disgrace. Jack was handling a lady
roughly and you but stepped in to prevent him——'

'Before that, when he was but dancing with you, I
badly wished to do him physical harm. I did not know
I was capable of such jealousy. It is most disquieting. I
have never before cared what my women did, or with
whom.' He released her hair and she put back the cloth
and pot of balm and closed the box. 'In truth, I can
scarcely understand any of my actions of late.'

The candle, reduced now to a stub, flamed briefly then
the wick sank into the melted wax and went out. For a
moment the room seemed in total darkness then the
broad shaft of moonlight slanting in through the square
opening enabled them to see each other, though dimly.

'Bess,' he said softly, 'lie with me tonight. Not here—
but out under the moon where there will be just us two.'
He could just make out the shape of her face surrounded by the halo of her hair. 'Once you wanted me.
You said one night was better than nothing at all. You
said that to me.'

She shook her head without speaking.

'Why not, sweetheart? What has changed to make you
refuse me?'

'You have changed, Harry. You wish to have me tonight so that in the morning you can say to yourself,
There, she is but a woman like any other. The rest of
what I feel is only moon-dust.' She turned her head so
that the light fell full upon her face. 'You have come to

a crossroads in your life, Harry. Much has happened in the last few weeks and I am part of your confusion. But nothing will be solved without your making up your mind what you truly want.'

He said, 'You know, tonight as I rode home I was thinking. Just six short months ago I was happy. I had everything a man could want: enough money to enjoy myself, fine clothes, jewels, any woman I wanted and the love of my King and the company of my friends. Now my friends are gone and I can never return in full measure that love of Henry's; often now I see him as you described him... And the only woman who now interests me must torment me.'

''Tis torment for me also, Harry,' she said with an effort.

'Then why not, love? Shall we not go now and find some special place to make our bed?'

Why not, indeed? Because at Greenwich she had gone to the summer-house without doubts. Now she felt nothing but doubt and loved him too much to offer any less than the whole of her. She thought, Richard loved me for my nature and personality alone, with no thought of physical pleasure; Tom Spalding thought only of that. I want a man in whom both loves are equal.

Harry watched her struggle in silence. He had no shame in asking her to go out into the night with him. What Bess decided she would decide of her own free will and would not be swayed by what he said. It occurred to him that he respected her with the regard he had only as yet given to a man. He wondered again at the fascination she held for him; even the way she drew her brows together in concentration as she thought was of the minutest interest to him. How bewitching she would be in the moment of surrender—he could not begin to imagine how she would look, what she would say or do. She was a woman in a million.

Now she said decisively, 'I cannot, Harry. Not for any lack of love but because it does not feel right to me.'

He was surprised by his lack of disappointment; rather he felt like a man playing a game against an opponent whom he admired so greatly he could not bear to defeat. He could not resist a mocking thrust. 'Then you must go to your chaste bed and leave me to mine. You at least can be content in your iron resistance of temptation.'

'You cannot provoke me, Harry. I am beginning to know you better now.'

Had she read his thoughts? He got off the bed and opened the door for her. 'I should light you to your room, I know. But I fear my candle is no more, and also that once there we should find some fresh bone of contention to gnaw. I must rest for I am convinced that even the Sabbath in this busy place will be arduous.'

'No such thing, Harry. Tomorrow we will merely go to church to contemplate our many sins. Our pastor is most conscientious and lectures us quite sternly. You should have ample time to review yours.'

He bowed and let her pass, feeling that as usual she had had the last word.

Sunday was an easier day on the farm, broken as it was by the trip to the village church, but even so the usual morning chores had still to be done. Stirring at last, Bess was guiltily aware from the amount of brilliant sunshine flooding her room that she had slept very late and left the work to her mother. She poured water from the rose-patterned jug and washed hurriedly, brushed her hair and left it loose upon her shoulders. She took her Sunday dress from the chest, shook out the creases and put it on, buttoning it in haste.

Joan was just serving breakfast as she came into the kitchen, apologising for lying abed so late. She smiled at her daughter, thinking as usual how sweet she looked in the demure white stuff with its tracery of silk embroidery about the neck and cuffs. Harry got up and courteously helped Bess to her seat. Joan put a platter of bacon and eggs on the table and poured milk into the mugs. The clock on the dresser struck eight, its bronze casing burnished in the sunlight.

Joan sighed. 'I did so enjoy myself yesterday. 'Twas splendid to dance again.'

'You were the prettiest lady in the room,' said Robert. 'Had I been able I would have snatched you from Chris Shapley's arms. He was an old admirer of yours, I believe.'

Joan blushed becomingly. 'You know very well that I never glanced his way again once I had laid eyes on you, my love.'

The two younger people at the table watched this lover-like exchange in silence. Bess glanced at Harry. He wore a smooth grey costume she remembered from court but no jewellery. She noticed for the first time that the black pearl was missing from his ear and wondered if he thought it too flamboyant for wearing in such modest surroundings. He looked oddly bereft without it, as he still practised the trick of touching his lobe with one long finger.

Robert helped himself to the crisply frizzled bacon. 'We are to go to my brother-in-law for the midday meal after church service. He has a little mare I had thought to buy for Bess. She is to celebrate her eighteenth birthday in three days' time. I would welcome your opinion of the animal, Harry. I would be sure she is gentle enough.'

Harry drained his beaker of milk with apparent enjoyment. 'I shall be glad to see the creature, sir. We should not wish Bess to be endangered by too sprightly an animal.' His play on words reminded Bess of her escape on Sprite from Tom Spalding on the day of the picnic.

She said repressively, 'I am a better horsewoman nowadays. I had a slight mishap on a too spirited horse at Greenwich, Father,' she explained. 'Harry saved me from injury.'

''Twas of no account. I could not let anyone run away with Bess,' said Harry as Joan turned to him in concern.

'You rode much at court, Bess?' her father asked.

A shadow crossed Bess's face. She recalled the pretty mare Anne had given her, the rides in the sharp winter air with Meg and her other friends. She remembered how that same mare had featured in her interview with Cromwell in the dark days after Anne's arrest. She remembered her satisfaction at having foiled the man contriving the Queen's downfall—all to no purpose, for the worst had happened nevertheless. The sunlit kitchen darkened and she felt again the grief for Anne, and her brother George. She swallowed painfully.

Harry said gently, 'She rides most elegantly, sir. As she does all other things.'

The little village church had been stripped of its treasure by the King's men, as had every other. But it retained still a quiet dignity and Bess took her place in the pew next to Harry, her mood one of gratitude for a little peace and time to think. Sensing her sadness, he would have liked to take her hand and hold it for comfort. His own grief had moved a stage further into anger now and it was one of the reasons why he had sought this time away from Henry's court. He knew his temper was uncertain and did not trust himself to participate in the celebrations following the new marriage without allowing the anger and resentment to show. He contented himself with letting his shoulder touch hers now.

The service was conducted by Father Lucas with dispatch, for he knew his flock would appreciate a little free time on their day of rest, and the congregation rose to sing. Bess shared a book of hymns with Harry and raised her sweet voice in musical praise, conscious of how close he was. She studied his hands as they turned the pages, noting the extraordinary length of the fingers, squared at the tips, the pronounced half-moons and their whiteness. Uncle Bob's family from his ancient father right down to his three-month-old baby grandson were present, as were the Shapley clan. Jack Shapley sang hoarsely through swollen lips, his eyes fixed broodingly at Harry Latimar's elegant grey back.

After the hymn Father Lucas delivered a gentle sermon along the lines of loving one's neighbour as oneself and then the worshippers, perspiring freely in their stiff Sunday best, were free to go out into the dazzling day.

The de Cheynes exchanged greetings with their friends outside the lych gate beyond the churchyard. Jack Shapley came down the wide church steps flanked by his brothers; as he came closer Harry drew a little apart from the de Cheynes and turned to face him. Those men who had been interested spectators the previous night prepared to enjoy another dramatic result of this meeting. Jack advanced steadily and stopped before Harry, who said politely, 'Good day, sir.'

Blushing furiously, Jack returned his greeting, then said, 'Seems to me I made a damn fool of mysel' yesternight.'

Harry gave him a coldly appraising look. 'Perhaps we were both taken by midsummer madness,' he suggested.

Jack shifted his eyes to Bess. 'You bested me and I don't have no hard feelings t'wards you. And I hope you nor Bess do t'wards me.'

Bess shook her head. 'Then,' said Harry amiably, 'let us forget it.'

Jack stuck out his hand and Harry gripped it. The scene dissolved and everyone moved away to their horses and wagons, disappointed or relieved according to their natures.

'What was that about?' asked Joan curiously.

'Jack was a little over-friendly with Bess at the dance; Harry took him to task,' Robert said.

'And thoroughly, by the looks of those bruises.' Bess could detect a note of satisfaction in her mother's voice.

'Not all would have apologised for making free with me,' she said pointedly as Harry handed her up into the wagon and got in beside her.

'Not all would have considered it necessary,' he agreed. The subtle reverberations from last night's scene in his room lay between them.

Bob's wife set a good table and the savoury smells filled the enormous kitchen as they sat down to eat. Bob's eldest son Ned sat beside Bess; they had been fast friends since childhood and she wished she could like his wife a little better. But Kate Beechwood, thin, red-haired, sharp-tongued without being amusing, had made it clear from the start that she both envied and despised her cousin-in-law. Envied because any woman would envy all that shining beauty and despised because of what she considered Bess's prissy ways. Kate cast sharp eyes on Harry, whom she was seated next to. He was well set-up, she had to admit, and handsome if you admired those pale overthin looks, but as pernickety in his ways as Bess, wiping his lips before drinking and passing around the plates and salt and water jug as though they were all crippled.

'We heard about the goings on with the King and Queen,' she said challengingly.

He turned courteously to her. 'Indeed.'

'She was a friend of yourn, someone said. And His Majesty, too.'

'That is so.'

'Well, she've gone now. And some say good riddance.'

Across the table Bess tensed.

'Do they indeed?' he queried politely.

'They do. And what do you say?' Kate said.

'I say I miss her greatly and grieve for her daily,' he said, turning dark eyes on her.

Robert said smoothly from the head of the table, 'Your little one is thriving, Kate; he is a fine boy.'

Kate dropped her eyes to her plate. 'He is doing well enough.'

The conversation turned to babies; both Bob's daughters expected to add to the family within a few weeks. Bess watched Harry; there was nothing in his face to show the exchange had upset him, but he ate nothing further and made no attempt to engage any of the Beechwoods in conversation.

After the meal the women went to sit in the parlour. Kate lifted her little son from his sleep and, unbuttoning her dress, gave him his lunch. Bess went out to the grassy paddock in which Bob ran his horses. He usually kept only work animals and a handsome saddle horse for himself, for none of his womenfolk rode. Pearl, the little grey mare Robert wanted for Bess, had been a rare bargain he had come across at a Cornish auction. She was a delicately sturdy grey with splashes of charcoal on her hindquarters and chest.

'She's beautiful, Father,' breathed Bess as Ned brought her to the gate on a leading rein.

'And gentle too,' Ned said. 'She've been well treated and ridden only by a lady, I would swear.'

Bess put her foot on the lowest bar of the gate and stepped up. She leaned forward and ran her hand over the silken mane. Above her lightning forked across the sky, but as the blue light engulfed her she saw only a stronger light and the paddock grew dim. Suspended as always within time she saw in clear-cut detail scudding white clouds, green turf, slender hands gripping the reins, sensed panic and despair and then nothing but the sparkle of green water as she spiralled down. A moment later, as if looking down from the brink of a precipice, she saw the twisted figures of horse and rider among the sharp tan rocks.

She toppled forward and would have fallen had not Ned reached out a swift hand and steadied her. 'Nay Bess,' he half laughed, 'do not throw yourself at the animal's feet.'

Uncle Bob, a pleased smile on his face, said to Robert, 'Shall Bess try her now?'

'No,' said Bess sharply.

'We would not buy her without a trial, surely, daughter?'

'I do not want her,' said Bess.

The smile faded from Bob's lips. 'Come now, girl——'

Robert interrupted. 'She looks a likely little mare, Bess. Do you not fancy her?'

''Twould be a spoiled miss indeed who would not fancy such a gift,' Bob said angrily. He was not disappointed not to make the sale, but he had been asking only a modest sum of his brother-in-law and resented his generosity being so flatly rejected.

Robert was disappointed too; this was the first time he had ever had the wherewithal to purchase something truly fine for his beloved child and he was hurt that she should so summarily dismiss it. He only said however, ''Tis for Bess to say, Bob.' He put an arm about the other man. 'Come, let me sample again your excellent ale and we will discuss the fickle nature of women.' Bob allowed himself to be persuaded back to his farmhouse, not at all mollified, and Bess could hear him grumbling about the ingratitude of children and about parents who made rods for their own backs by soft treatment.

Ned led the little mare away as another flash of lightning rent the sky, followed by a crack of thunder. The pretty animal danced sideways on her rein.

Harry, who had watched the scene without speaking, stepped forward and lifted Bess gently from the gate. As he set her down something in her face disturbed him. He put his arm through hers and they walked along the path surrounding the paddock until they came to the ancient oak in whose shade Bob had raised his farmhouse thirty years before. He let her go and leaned back against the wide trunk. 'What is wrong?'

'Nothing is wrong.'

He studied her intently for a moment. 'Come, Bess— tell me what is troubling you.'

'There is nothing, Harry.'

'I think there is. Can you not trust me?' he asked gently.

''Tis not a matter of trust.'

'Then what?'

She ran her hand up and down the rough bark. He caught it and held it. 'Don't, darling—you will injure yourself.'

The sincere concern in his voice, the unusual tenderness not often present in his manner disarmed her. 'Sometimes I see—I think I see—that which presently comes to pass. A...picture of events which have not happened yet but which will,' she said abruptly.

He showed no surprise, no involuntary recoil from her. 'And this was one of those times?'

'Yes. I saw Pearl in a wild gallop. I saw her and her rider fall over a clifftop to their deaths.'

'I see.' He was still holding her hand; he drew it to his breast.

'I am quite sure you don't, Harry,' she said with a catch in her voice.

'How often do you experience such visions?' He might have been asking how often she had headaches, ate apples.

'In a year—maybe half a dozen times.'

'And always what you see is proved true?'

'Always. And there is never anything I can do to change it.'

'You believe that had you owned Pearl you would have met such a fate as you describe?'

'Oh, no. 'Tis never for myself I see. Only for others— that is what makes it so hard to bear.'

'This foresight—it is always of a gloomy nature?'

'No...often 'tis something pleasant. But either way I would wish it gone from me.'

'Who else knows of this?'

'Only my mother, and I have allowed her to believe the...gift died with childhood. She was most uneasy when she found out about it.'

He raised her hand and his lips absent-mindedly caressed her fingers.

'And that is what it is, surely? A gift. Strange and wonderful.'

'You do not think me a witch, then, Harry? You are not afraid of this power of mine?'

His eyes wandered over her upturned face. He said slowly, 'Perhaps I am a little afraid of the power you have over me, Bess, but it is not to do with what you have just told me.'

She withdrew her hand.

'Have you never been tempted to share any episode with those involved?'

She hesitated then said quietly, 'At court I told Her Majesty something about her daughter. It was of comfort to her, I think. But that is the only time I have spoken.'

He didn't ask her what it was, and she went on, 'It is a secret thing, you understand. Not something... not a part of me to share with others.'

'I would never wish to share any part of you with others, Bess.'

Rain began to patter in the leaves above; the greenery was so thick that it could not penetrate but fell straight down outside their sheltering-place translucent in the sun still shining from the west.

'We will not be struck by lightning, do you think?' said Bess apprehensively.

'I think that part of the storm is over; it will just rain now for a while.'

"'Tis bad for the standing corn, a heavy rain.'

'But 'twill clear the air at last.'

As they discussed the weather and the crops Bess could hardly believe she had told him something she had kept to herself, lived with often painfully all her life. But she could not regret it—the relief of finally unburdening herself was immense. And she felt sure that no one else would have accepted it in quite the way he did. He had an objective mind capable of absorbing this new and startling facet of her without its disturbing his image of her. She stole a look at him. He was different since coming to Devon and yet the same. Certainly she was seeing a kinder man than had been visible at Greenwich or Hampton. Richard Woodville had been wrong when he said Latimar was not kind. His kindness was apparent in easy casual ways; in his treatment of his host, never pitying but cheerfully helpful, recognising always the older man's indomitable spirit. Half-teasing towards Joan, he showed her a great deal of respect, not at all at odds with the fact that she worked almost continually at very menial tasks.

'Harry—how much longer will you stay with us?'

'Am I unwelcome so soon?'

Must he always answer a question with another question? 'Of course not. But I wondered, that is all. 'Tis unusual for the King to part with you for such a long time, surely?'

He didn't reply. 'You are still good friends?' she persisted.

'I have his permission for leave of absence,' was all he would say. His hair in the green light cast by the pale leaves was a curious coppery colour. 'To set your mind at rest, however, I will say that I shall think of returning to court after I have helped your father with the harvest.'

'You will help with the harvest?' she said, surprised.

'Why not? I am told that any extra assistance is welcome. Do you doubt my ability to wield a scythe, Bess?'

'Do not take me up so. I meant only that 'tis hard and gruelling work. Those here are accustomed to such backbreaking labour.'

'And I of course find any task other than lifting a pair of dice too arduous to contemplate.'

'I simply find it hard to imagine you in such a role.'

'Then you must come out into the fields to witness this curious sight.'

She laughed. 'I will indeed, and be there when the sun goes down to apply soothing balm to your aching muscles.'

'All will be worthwhile for me, then. I think the rain is lighter now. We should return to the house.'

She sighed. 'And I must make some excuse for refusing my father's birthday gift.'

A substantial tea was set out in the kitchen and the others were waiting for them before making a start. Bess found no excuses were necessary and suspected her father had asked them not to mention the incident with Pearl. They enjoyed the splendidly risen scones and apple jam spread liberally with clotted cream, talking only of the forthcoming harvest: the gathering in of the results of their labour throughout the year. Aware of the long days ahead, the de Cheynes made their farewells before early evening. Rain was still present in the wind but the sky had cleared and a low sun lengthened their shadows in the lanes.

The following day they were up at first light. The dull thundery weather preceding harvest week was replaced by bright though cooler days welcomed by the reapers in the fields.

The de Cheyne harvest was a small undertaking compared with the surrounding farms and had been done other years with the help of two of Bob's prolific family, with Bess and her mother working as hard as they in the cutting and tying up of the sheaves. Robert could not, even with the greatest will in the world, convince his body that it could swing a scythe in the bending, swooping movement necessary, and had always to content himself with the binding only. This year, with an extra pair of hands in Harry, two of Bob's youngest grandsons had been delegated to help the de Cheynes and they were in high spirits to be out of sight of their stern grandfather. They were Simon and Ralph Beechwood, a lively pair of twelve-year-old twins, the twins in fact that Bess had foreseen while sewing their baby clothes. They were tall and strong and set to work with cheerful grins. They were great admirers of Bess and were curious to see how her dandified city-bred young gallant would manage a man's work in the cornfields; they were prepared for a few laughs at his expense. Disappointingly, after a slow start, Harry proved no different from their older brothers. He had a natural ability with any physical activity and soon attained the gracefully efficient rhythm necessary as though he had been bred to it.

Bess worked alongside him. Joan had protested this year at her daughter's taking part in the hard work and Bess wondered if she thought she would lose grace before their aristocratic visitor. She gave in at last but tied the ribbons of a shady straw hat under Bess's chin in an effort to prevent the sun staining her face. Actually Harry had frowned slightly when Bess had accompanied them to the fields but had made no comment. After a few minutes in which she had demonstrated the handling of the scythe he had drawn off the leather riding gloves he wore to protect his hands and offered them to her. To please him she took them; they were as soft and supple as skin and she experienced a thrill as she put them on. 'You will have blisters by dusk, Harry.'

'I look forward to the treatment I know you have in mind for them,' he said blandly.

She bent again to her task and he watched her a moment. She wore a shabby print dress, the sleeves turned up to her elbows and sturdy thick-soled shoes over her bare feet, but this rustic apparel took nothing away from her beauty, he thought. Her face under the drab straw hat was as pure and lovely as it had been beneath the pearl and silk cap at Greenwich.

At noon they paused for the picnic lunch brought out to them by Joan.

'We progress very well,' Robert said as they ate and drank, savouring the spicy pasties and cooled ale. 'We will make a farmer of you yet, my boy.'

Harry examined the welts already forming on his hands. 'Indeed. But I fear my lute will remain untouched for some weeks to come.'

'You play?'

'A little. I have—had a friend who was most accomplished on the instrument.' His eyes took on an inward-looking expression. George Boleyn had, like his sister, performed beautifully on his lute and written the lyrics too for a number of popular songs at court.

'It is a pleasant talent,' Robert said. 'I do not possess it myself; 'twould perhaps be wasted in any case in my present life.'

'Uncle Jack will play his fiddle at the harvest feast,' volunteered Simon. ''Twill be a marry romp, wi' dancing and fun the night long.'

Merry indeed, thought Bess with a sudden sinking of heart, but after it Harry will be leaving here.

They worked until the light faded and the two Beechwood boys jumped up astride their old pony and disappeared into the gloom. Joan had prepared a rich rabbit stew with wild mushrooms and they ate enormously despite their exhaustion.

After the meal Harry presented his hands for Joan's inspection. 'A disagreeable result of having spent an idle life previously,' he said regretfully as she tutted over them and rubbed goosegrease in. She looked after her own and Bess's hands as best she could but they were inevitably coarsened by the chores they did, and Robert's were as hard as horn. For some reason this man's hands brought home to her the gulf between him and Bess, and the anxieties about his intentions towards her child rose again to the surface. For as far as she knew Harry had not spoken for Bess, and Robert had told her that he would be leaving after the harvest was finished. She herself would be almost glad when that moment came, but what Bess felt she could not discover. She sighed, thinking that at the outset of the year she had sent away a daughter as open as the day and received back a secretive, withdrawn woman.

The hard work continued until the fields were flat and divested of their golden treasure and the sheaves were bound and laid out ready to be loaded on to a wagon and stored. Harry and Bess continued to work side by side but little conversation passed between them. On the final day of work as the sun was setting only the last of the corn still stood. This Simon and Ralph bound together and Bess instructed Harry that no one would cut the last stalks as therein was believed to dwell the Corn Spirit. She and the boys picked up their sickles and threw them at the bound stalks until they tumbled down. 'This way neither one of us is directly responsible for cutting the Corn Spirit down,' she said seriously. Harry raised his eyebrows.

Robert was thanking the Beechwood twins and giving them each a coin—not in payment, for they were only helping their family and no payment was due, but in appreciation of their efforts.

Bess continued, 'When all the corn is gathered in I will make the Corn Dolly from the last sheaf—a little female figure of corn. It will hang in mother's kitchen as a good omen for next year's harvest.' She laughed suddenly. 'We are a superstitious breed in Devon. But I like it, for it has always been so and some things should not change.'

His dark eyes were on her face; he seemed scarcely to take in what she said. After a moment he said, 'At Hampton, when you told me you were leaving the court, you said that I would never change. Do you still think that?'

She thought a little. 'What people really are they remain, I think. So it must be that you were always as you are now.'

'Which is?'

   She laughed again, but differently. He was asking more
than his words declared. 'I hardly know, Harry.'

   Perhaps she would have said more and he would have
told her what was in his mind to prompt his question,
but Robert called to them to go in for the evening meal
and there was no chance to hold further conversation
that night.

CHAPTER EIGHT

THE day of the Harvest Feast, to be held as usual in Uncle Bob's great barn, coincided with Bess's eighteenth birthday and she came in to breakfast to receive warm greetings.

She accepted her mother's gift—a daintily sewn and embroidered lawn pillow edged with lace and stuffed with dried sweet-smelling herbs—with pleasure. Knowing how little free time Joan had, she was aware that she had sat up late at nights to make it. When they had eaten Robert rose and went out; Joan and Harry took Bess out into the yard and made her close her eyes and wait a little. When they allowed her to open them it was to see Robert leading up a small cream-coloured mare. He had learned she was for sale in a village near the Cornish border and Harry had ridden over last night when Bess was abed to inspect her and bring her back if she proved suitable. Now he took her hand and placed it on the mare's neck, looking encouragingly down into her eyes. She smiled at him.

'Do you like her, Bess? We took a chance in buying her unseen by you,' Robert said anxiously. 'But I had set my heart upon a mount for you.'

Bess put her arms around the mare, pressing her face into the rough mane, then in an equally swift gesture around her father's neck. 'I love her, Father. Thank you, thank you.'

Harry put her up astride the animal; she was not so elegant as Pearl but gentle enough and pretty with her cloudy cream markings. He had given her no gift that morning, only kissed her hand and wished her a happy day. His riding out last night, four hours there and back, after a hard day, was surely gift enough, she thought, taking her present through her paces around the yard.

'You look most splendid, Bess,' her father said. 'And Bob has got over not selling me the grey. He has made twice the price he was asking of me in accepting an offer from John Larch. Little Rose Larch will be delighted with her, not being given to the sudden likes and dislikes of my daughter.' He smiled, proud of her riding so gracefully around the dusty yard, her head up, her back straight.

Bess faltered and drew the mare up. Harry crossed the yard and lifted her down. 'I will take the mare into the stable and unsaddle her, sir,' he called over his shoulder to Robert.

Robert and Joan went to continue their work, well pleased to have made their daughter so happy. Harry ran his hand over the horse's taut flank, his eyes on Bess. After a moment he said, 'If, under cover of darkness, I were to take Pearl, ride her across the border and let her free——'

'You would be hanged for horse-stealing, she would be returned to Rose and all would be as I saw it just the same,' she interrupted dully. 'It is as though written and cannot be changed.'

'Then do not look like that, sweet,' he said gently. 'You are an observer, nothing more. No blame can attach to you.'

'I know that. But do you suppose it makes it less hard to bear? It is cruelly hard to see things concerning my neighbours, but I fear—I dread that I shall one day see some dire sight involving those I love.'

He could not answer her, could not comfort her, and had only to watch her walk away into the house.

Later that day Joan washed Bess's hair in a tin bath in the yard. She rinsed it with vinegar to enhance the shine and rubbed it partly dry. Then she laid the heavy hair over Bess's shoulders and told her to sit in the sun to allow it to dry. After the unremitting work of the last days Bess found it hard to sit idly and presently she walked down to the gate and sat up on the top bar where she could look out over the meadows. In the distance she could just make out the figures of Harry and Robert. They were engaged in the eternal work of repairing the boundary fences. As she watched they completed their task and stood leaning on their mended railing, talking. Her father would miss Harry greatly, she thought. He had said nothing to her about riding away tomorrow but surely he could delay no more? Henry had decreed that he should go to France, and go he must.

Her hair was drying now, though still dark with water where it grew thickest around her head. From the lane came the rumble of wagons and the sound of shouts and laughter. She turned her head; Uncle Bob's farm wagons swayed by, decorated with boughs of oak and ash entwined with flowers, the horses drawing them also garlanded, red ribbons tied into their harnesses. A dozen or more men and girls rode atop in triumph on the corn and waved at Bess as they went by. She waved back and slipped down from the gate. It was growing late and she must wash herself and press her dress for the evening's gaiety.

She would have dearly liked to wear her lilac silk for the feast, but regretfully decided it was too grand. So she ironed her white Sunday dress and at six-thirty sprinkled rose essence on her hair and wrists and joined the others in the kitchen. She had put up her hair and threaded white ribbons through the silver curls but already several heavy strands had escaped and framed her face.

Her mother and father were arrayed in their best and Harry wore the dull metallic grey costume she remembered from court. He still wore no jewellery but his belt was embellished with beaten silver, his hair brushed to a sheen.

'You are beautiful, Bess,' he murmured as he handed her into the wagon.

'You are, too.' She smiled at him.

'A restrained beauty, I hope. I would not wish to appear before the kind of men who can work as I have worked these last days each day of their lives as a dandy.' He spoke seriously.

'You care what they think of you?'

'Indeed I do.' He mounted his horse and led the way out.

That arrogant Latimar should care for his standing before country farmers would have been incomprehensible to his former grand friends; they would believe he had sunk low indeed. But Bess considered it showed he was growing in stature. Her father flicked the reins and they moved off.

The celebration was in full swing when they arrived. Harry need not have worried about their opinion of him; the Beechwood twins had testified that Latimar could hold his own with the best of them in hard manual work and they greeted him with enthusiasm. Mary Banks advanced shyly to renew her acquaintance and invite him to join her in the dance.

Bess sat down with her mother and looked around her with affection. She had attended these affairs since she was a toddler who would, before the evening was done, fall asleep in Joan's lap, and had always enjoyed them immensely. Tonight, however, her spirits were at a low ebb and the reason for that lay in the knowledge that tomorrow—or the day after—Harry would be gone. Almost angrily she drank several glasses of cider and at last her depression lifted a little. Through a welcome haze she saw Harry dancing closely with Mary; let him dance, she thought—she would also.

The evening wore on; a magnificent supper was put on. Beef and cream pastry pies, roast geese from Bob's own farmyard, mutton and apple pies and a great stew served in trenchers of bread were followed by plum pudding and baked apples, all washed down with vast quantities of cider and ale. Bess danced every dance and sang the traditional harvest songs with apparent joy. The Mell or Harvest Supper was considered the crowning of the farming year and as such must be participated in with the greatest fervour. But Harry did not approach her throughout the long evening and she was reminded of how he had withdrawn himself from her at court. He is gone from me already, she thought.

When the sky was black and lit with the round harvest moon Robert came to her side. 'I will take your mother home now, Bess. It has been an exhausting time and I will welcome my rest. Harry will escort you home when you are ready.' She looked at him. 'He has my complete trust,' Robert assured her.

Some hours later Harry presented himself to her and asked if she was ready to leave. She couldn't deny she was tired and allowed him to take her hand as they made the rounds to thank Bob and his family. Outside under the cold stars he lifted her on to his horse and sprang up behind her.

'You have enjoyed yourself tonight, Bess?' he asked her.

'I have. And have no need to return the question, since 'twas obvious to all how much you relished your evening.'

He tightened his grip about her as they rode over the stony ground beyond the Beechwood acres. 'You are put out in some way?' he queried.

'I would have enjoyed myself a little more had you bothered to take me around the floor,' she said sulkily.

'I thought you content to dance with your old friends.'

'Did you, Harry? Did you?'

'You are angry,' he discovered in surprise.

The wind was rough now; it whipped at her hair and she turned her face against his breast to speak. ''Tis our last evening, is it not? I wanted to dance with you, Harry.' He made no reply, but she felt his breathing quicken.

In the lanes the trees on either side had joined their
branches overhead and it was so dark they could scarcely
make out the winding road. He pulled gently on the rein
to slow his horse and they paused at the crossroads. To
their left was the lane to the farmhouse, to their right
the cliff road. He swung the horse right. 'We ride abroad
at this late hour?' she asked.

'I thought to visit the seashore for one last time.' He
urged the great black horse to a gallop.

On the clifftop he reined in again and they took the
downward path to the shore slowly, carefully. The water
lay before them, black and turbulent. Although so dark
in the country lanes it was yet still light at the sea's edge.
He dismounted and lifted her on to the sand. His horse
stood uneasily, as debris on the beach was tumbled by
the wind off the sea. It was not cold, sheltered as they
were by the cliff.

She said with difficulty, 'You leave tomorrow, Harry?
To rejoin the King before leaving soon for France?'

'I do. But in his graciousness he has rescinded the
command that I go to France. In other words he
has . . . forgiven me my bitter outburst at Hampton. You
have heard of this, I believe.'

'I was present, Harry,' she said quietly, 'for I was in
the antechamber of the library that night you begged for
the Queen's life.'

He was not surprised by her disclosure; almost it
seemed to him inevitable. 'So you heard all. Oh, Bess,
it was an awful conversation. While he spoke slightingly
of George and casually of ridding himself of Anne—my
friends—I thought at any moment I would strike him.
And yet through it all, I still loved him. That fact made
me feel . . . less sure of all I thought important. That I
could still care so much for a man like that——'

'It is an old loyalty, Harry,' she suggested. 'Forged
before ever you knew George or his sister.'

'Of course. But what happened that night changed me
all the same.'

'For the better,' she declared. ''Tis no bad thing to see one's heroes in a clear light. It does not make you less that you still love him. Rather it makes you more.'

'You would think well of me no matter what the circumstances,' he said wryly. 'So you agree I should go back?'

'I do. You belong there, Harry. You are too much a part of the bold pattern of the court to be content in any other place. And Henry will need you. I think in the future he will need all his friends.' There. She had spoken the truth as she saw it, though it broke her heart to send him away.

There was a long silence, then he turned to her. 'And you, Bess? Where is your place, where do you belong? You fit most comfortably into any company. You have been confidante to the highest in the land and yet you are also one of the good plain folk we have just left this night.'

'I cannot answer that. For I do not know myself.'

He moved closer to her and lifted a strand of hair from her face. 'I think you do. I think you know very well your place is with me.'

'With you, Harry?'

'Bess—do you think I would, or could, ride away without you tomorrow? Do not look at me in that manner, sweetheart. For it is an honourable proposal you receive at last from Latimar. I have asked your father this day for leave to ask you if you would marry me.' He loosed the curl and it sprang back against her cheek.

'You wish to marry me?'

'You are taken aback? But surely a proposal of marriage is no novelty for you?' Even at this moment he could not keep the amusement from his voice. 'I am in earnest, sweetheart, and to prove it I have brought you a betrothal ring.' He reached into his shirt and brought out a little velvet pouch. He tipped the contents into her hand.

She held the ring up to the moonlight: it was one of the new-fashioned double rings, a ruby cut in the shape of a crude heart and a large diamond, the two linked by bands of pale Italian gold.

She said thoughtfully, 'You brought this with you from court? It was in your mind to ask me but you have been here all these days and said nothing.'

'A man does not give up his freedom lightly,' he said reprovingly.

Still holding the heavy ring in her palm, she turned and let the wind cool her face, run its careless fingers through her hair. She turned the jewel in her hands; even her unsophisticated eyes could see it represented a great deal of money. 'It is beautiful. It must have cost you a fortune.'

'Not a fortune. I exchanged it for something I no longer cared for.' His fingers casually touched his ear.

Distracted from her thoughts, she exclaimed, 'Oh, Harry! Your fabulous pearl, your good-luck piece. You swore you would never part with it.' No one knew where the black pearl had come from; it had passed through the hands of foreign sailors and merchants before he had acquired it in a legendary card game which had lasted three days and nights. George Boleyn, who had coveted it greatly, had told her that Latimar would gamble his gold, his horse, the very clothes on his back but never his black pearl.

'A good-luck piece is of no account unless it brings you what you want most. And I want you, Bess.'

The diamond caught the cold light from the stars; the ruby was subdued, awaiting a brighter light to bring it alive. 'What of Kate Bonney? Would the King not relent?'

'I did not ask him to so do. I asked instead for leave to come here and ask for you.'

'And what did His Majesty say to that?'

'He said I was a damned fool and deserved to be a pauper all my days.' He laughed suddenly, exultantly.

'All my life I have chased gold, Bess. I have been prepared to gamble all I possessed for more gold. After you left I realised that the most reckless gambler at court was afraid to risk some pieces of metal for the greatest prize of all. You are that prize—that most desirable prize.'

'But Harry—all you said; you convinced me—almost—that love was not enough——'

'But I did not convince myself. I want to marry you. To have you for my own. I have from the first; I just had my desires a little mixed.' His teeth flashed white and she saw his ironic smile. He scanned her face. 'Why are you still hesitant?'

'Perhaps because I hear no mention of love from you, Harry. All else has passed between us but never that word.'

'Oh, sweetheart, would you wrench from me a declaration of love at this late date? Have I not shown it enough, often enough?'

'Tell me why you did not ask me that first day, the day you arrived.'

He sighed. 'I foresee years ahead of explaining myself to you, darling. When I do it so badly... Very well. When I came here I came in arrogance to make little Bess de Cheyne my wife. I felt—and I know I will incur your displeasure in saying it—that she should be grateful for the honour. But as always when in your company I began to question myself. And it came to me to wonder not if Bess was good enough for Latimar but, on the contrary, was Latimar good enough for Bess?' He laughed wryly. ''Twas a most unpleasant notion, I assure you. And always within me there was this strange resentment that finally a woman had caused me all the heartache and despair that I had so long escaped. I swear for a time I both loved and hated you. To that dilemma of emotions add my confusion and grief in the aftermath of the dreadful time at court and you will understand I was...uncertain.'

She considered all this in silence for a moment. The wind had died now; a curious lull occurred for a time. 'And what finally resolved you?'

''Twas the afternoon you told me of your gift. I had a strange experience of my own; oh, no wondrous vision but a revelation all the same. i saw the years lying before me if you were not by my side, and they were empty. Empty, Bess. Whatever we make of our small portion of time together, I know it will be the best of what there is.'

'The best of what there is,' she repeated thoughtfully. 'It will be that only if you will not shut me out from who you really are, Harry. I will not wander the boundaries of your life, keeping house, bearing your children, turning a smiling face whenever you choose to seek my company. I will be part of that best.'

'You are frightening me, Bess. Shall I have no soul of my own?'

'Then be frightened. For ours will be that kind of partnership or nothing at all.'

He glanced at her, at her clear-cut profile, her straight shoulders. This was the real Bess now; a thrill ran down his spine as the waves threw themselves against the sand at her feet.

'Women, it seems, are never satisfied. You took me to task once for wanting you without honour. Now—when I come humbly with a ring in my hand—you do not know your place after all.'

She laughed. The gay sound was flung back by the renewed wind gusting up the shore. 'Not so, Harry. I know my place is with you.'

'On your terms only?'

'On mutually agreed terms.'

'When you came to court you were an innocent child, gentle and womanly. You are altered,' he said sadly.

'I am not altered, Harry. 'Tis you who are altered. The process began gradually; you hardly noticed it but it was at work in you. 'Twas why you could not stand by without protest when injustice reigned at court, why you fought Jack Shapley, why you helped my father with the harvest. You have lost your immunity to those around you, sweetheart.'

He looked out to sea; the horizon was obscured by clouds but beneath them ran a fine straight line of light. 'This process—I am better or worse because of it?'

'Oh, better. Better. For now you have opened your eyes and see clearly.'

'You make it sound like victory,' he murmured. ''Tis a painful state if that is what it is.'

'It is. And wanting to marry me is part of it all. You love me; now tell me I am right.'

'You are right.'

'Oh, but that is not enough.'

He groaned. But the last weight had lifted from his heart; she understood him. His fears, his dark thoughts. He need never face the dark night again, for she would share it with him. He had been right—she was a woman in a million and he was one step away from keeping her forever. 'Is there any more to say than that I love you?' he asked simply.

'You have not said it yet.'

'I have said it in several different ways tonight.'

'But I wish to hear the words spoken so I may put them away to take out when I can no longer make you say them.'

She teased him now, but she was no match for him he knew. If he chose he could take her now. It was a lonely shore and she would not resist him, for Bess de Cheyne had thought about it and decided finally she was his. Instead he did it her way; he sketched a graceful bow and took her hand. 'I love you, my sweet Bess. You are my lady and will be for evermore.'

He took her in his arms and immediately there was for her the familiar feeling. No golden ball of light this time, no picture: just a sensation of great happiness. Not contentment or security—more vital than that: a feeling of being exquisitely alive. He felt her tense and drew back. 'Is there some other point you wish to wrangle about? Shall we spend several more hours discussing it before you accept me? Or will you pick up the hand you are dealt and play?' He smiled, but a strong emotion flashed in his dark eyes.

He would probably break her heart a thousand times: he would surely gamble away any money they had, and he would always sail too close to the wind of Henry's fitful patronage; there would be nothing safe about a life with Harry Latimar. But how could safety compare with how he made her feel, by being near her, by holding her in his arms? And she was strong; she was her father's daughter. Harry would not have it all his way.

She slid the ring upon her finger decisively and put her arms around him. He pulled her close. After a long moment he took his mouth from hers. 'I see my lady likes to gamble too,' he said.

'And occasionally to win,' she answered.

A WOMAN OF LITTLE IMPORTANCE

Sheila Walsh

Left with the sole care of her sister's children, Charity Wingate knows she must apply to the children's grandfather, the Duke of Orme. The Duke's only surviving son, Lord Alistair, tries to persuade Charity against this, for the Duke is a vengeful bitter man.

But with no help from her own family, Charity has no choice – only to find the Duke's actions even more punitive than she feared. Lord Alistair, reluctantly drawn in, is struck by Charity's loving care for the children and, recalling his own barren childhood, is prompted to help . . .

Experience the thrill of 2 Masquerade Historical Romances Absolutely Free!

*Experience the passions of bygone days
in 2 gripping Masquerade Romances - absolutely free!
Enjoy these tales of tempestuous love from
the illustrious past.
Then, if you wish, look forward to a regular supply of
Masquerade, delivered to your door!
Turn the page for details of 2 extra FREE gifts,
and how to apply.*

An irresistible offer for you

Here at Reader Service we would love you to become a regular reader of Masquerade. And to welcome you, we'd like you to have two books, a cuddly teddy and a MYSTERY GIFT - ABSOLUTELY FREE and without obligation.

Then, every two months you could look forward to receiving 4 more brand-new Masquerade Romances for just £1.99 each, delivered to your door, postage and packing is free. Plus our free newsletter featuring competitions, author news, special offers offering some great prizes, and lots more!

This invitation comes with no strings attached. You can cancel or suspend your subscription at any time, and still keep your free books and gifts.

Its so easy. Send no money now. Simply fill in the coupon below at once and post it to - Reader Service, FREEPOST, PO Box 236, Croydon, Surrey CR9 9EL.

- - - - - - - - NO STAMP REQUIRED - - - - - →

Yes! Please rush me my 2 Free Masquerade Romances and 2 Free Gifts! Please also reserve me a Reader Service Subscription. If I decide to subscribe, I can look forward to receiving 4 brand new Masquerade Romances every two months for just £7.96, delivered direct to my door. Post and packing is free, and there's a free Newsletter. If I choose not to subscribe I shall write to you within 10 days - I can keep the books and gifts whatever I decide. I can cancel or suspend my subscription at any time. I am over 18.

EP05M

Mrs/Miss/Ms/Mr _____

Address _____

_____

_____ Postcode _____

Signature _____

The right is reserved to refuse an application and change the terms of this offer. Offer expires December 31st 1991. Readers in Southern Africa please write to P.O. Box 2125, Randburg, South Africa. Other Overseas and Eire, send for details. You may be mailed with other offers from Mills & Boon and other reputable companies as a result of this application. If you would prefer not to share in this opportunity, please tick box. ☐

mps
MAILING
PREFERENCE
SERVICE